PRAISE FOR

DYING TO LIVE

LIFE SENTENCE

"This is existential horror fiction pushed to the limit: terrifying, disturbing, with some surprising moments of humor, and a deep, abiding humanity that extends from his living characters back to his zombies. *Life Sentence* unfolds like a grand tragic opera, and in the end emerges as a poignant and powerful meditation on love, sacrifice, and mortality... one that also just happens to scare the bejeezus out of you."

—Bram Stoker Award Winner Gary A. Braunbeck, author of *Mr. Hands* and *Coffin County*

"A thinking man's zombie novel. Paffenroth has looked beyond the initial bloodshed to what happens after the end of the world. He explores deep philosophical issues while never letting the horror fan go hungry for gore."

—David Wellington, author of *Monster Island*

"*Dying to Live: Life Sentence* is a thought-provoking study of the human condition. Paffenroth showcases his literary talent and maturity in this sequel that pulls off the impossible: it surpasses the original. Terrifying and uplifting, tragic and heartwarming, *Life Sentence* is more than just another zombie book. It's a true work of art."

—Michael McBride, author of *Bloodletting* and the *God's End* trilogy

"There is an unabashed humanity here reminiscent of the best of John Irving. There are action scenes here that James Rollins and Clive Cussler would be proud to call their own. And there is an insistent intelligence here that is uniquely Kim Paffenroth. He is on a roll. Join him for the ride of your life!"

—Joe McKinney, author of *Dead City* and *Quarantined*

DYING TO LIVE
LIFE SENTENCE

by Kim Paffenroth

Permuted Press
The formula has been changed...
Shifted... Altered... *Twisted.*
www.permutedpress.com

Dedicated with much love and gratitude to some of the teachers who graciously put up with me and my earlier attempts at fiction writing: Marion Finch, Louise Holladay, Ruth Meeker, Lois Sharp, and Marylou Williams

A **Permuted Press** book
published by arrangement with the author

ISBN-10: 1-934861-11-1
ISBN-13: 978-1-934861-11-0
Library of Congress Control Number: 2008932538

Cover art by Bob Freeman.
Edited by D.L. Snell.

10 9 8 7 6 5 4 3 2 1

When we are born, we cry that we are come
To this great stage of fools.
—Shakespeare, *King Lear*, IV.6.179-80

Call no man happy until he is dead.
—Solon, ancient Athenian law-giver

Chapter 1

It's funny, the things you remember, and even funnier, the things you think you remember but aren't sure. So many times, I'll ask my parents or someone else about something I think I remember—a place we went, a summer night by the river, a neighbor's dog or cat—only I can't *quite* remember who the people were or exactly how old I was at the time, or some other detail. I give every piece of information I can—the clothes we were wearing, what the weather was, or the smells (I always remember the smells vividly and perfectly, I think)—but they shake their heads and say they're sorry, they don't remember. It's not that they simply can't recall the lost detail I'm searching for—the whole scene doesn't exist for them, even the parts I've described.

Sometimes they'll laugh and say it's just a funny trick our minds play on us, and they don't just mean that it's funny in the sense of odd or strange, but really that it's funny, that it makes you laugh. I know they mean well, but I don't think it's funny in that way, because I see how much our memories make us who we are, make us different from one another, make us miserable or happy. They're funny in a way that makes me angry sometimes, because I can't help the things I remember, and I certainly can't help the things I've forgotten or the things I never knew. I didn't get to pick what goes in which category, and neither did anyone else, unless they've willfully lied to themselves, which seems to me a terrible and dehumanizing act. I'll never think this haphazard kind of memory is fair—let alone the laughing kind of funny—because it's not, and because it's hurt so many people I know.

The older people, they remember the world the way it used to be, and the memory usually hurts them. It's where they belong, really, and this is all some bad second half to their existence, an exile in a strange and terrible place that they shuffle through, mostly for the sake of the younger people like me, I think. And even though their obvious pain makes us want to hold them and love them and take the hurt away, we can't, because it's not ours to bear, or even understand. Never mind all the hundreds or thousands of people they saw torn into screaming, bleeding meat—a memory the youngest of us have been spared—it's their memories from *before* all the horrors that really separate them from us. We don't know what a "real" root beer float tastes like, or what makes a "real" Fourth of July or a "real" Christmas so different from the ones we have now, or any of the thousand other things they recollect while shaking their heads wistfully, while we just look at them and blink and wish we could love them enough to make them forget. But they don't, and we can't. And I don't think memories that anguish and separate people like that are very funny at all.

My mom and dad—Sarah and Jack are their names—they have those memories, like all the older people—like Jonah and Tanya, whom I called "uncle" and "aunt" when I was much younger, and then "Mr. Caine" and "Ms. Wright" when I got a little older. I don't like to say Mom and Dad aren't my "real" parents, though that's how some people say it. Their love has always been completely real to me, as real and overwhelming as hunger or thirst or death itself, and I don't ever want to say anything to take away from that. They're not my biological parents is what I mean; both of my biological parents died long before anything I can remember. I've been told that my mom died when I was born, and my dad was murdered by very evil men when I was just a baby. I've been told about my dad many times, about how kind and brave he was.

I have a single picture of my parents. They look so young in it, in their twenties, about the age that I am now, as I write this. They look alive and happy and free in that picture, but all those feelings are trapped in the past, even for the ones who were "lucky" enough to keep on living after the dead rose and the world they knew died. My parents and the others look at a picture like that and they see a door they'd climb through if they could; I see a window on a world I never knew, a world that has as little reality or relevance to me as a fossil or a diorama in the museum where we used to live when I was little, when the dead still controlled most of the area.

For the people my age or younger, like Tanya's daughter, Vera, or my brother, Roger (as with my parents, I try not to preface his relationship with "step-," as I've known and loved him as a sibling my whole life, and he certainly grated and annoyed me as a child just like a "real" brother would), this is the only world we've known. We have a good life, I think. The people I love are in this world, this "real" world, and wishing for something else or something better seems disloyal to them. Perhaps even worse, it seems ungrateful. Being ungrateful is selfish and childish, and we all have tried hard to learn not to be like that. In fact, growing up and putting away childish things is a big part of the story I am telling now, the story of the things that happened that summer when I was twelve years old.

Once Milton started to herd the living dead away from us, when I was still a baby, our lives got much safer. Even today, no one knows how he had the power to repel the dead with his presence, but some would call it a miracle for our survival; anyone being appropriately grateful, I think, would at least call it a blessing or a gift.

The first people in our community had all been living in the old museum by the river, walled in and safe, but unable to move about and always worrying that the dead might break in and make us all eternally hungry and awake and mindless. Over the years, as we took more land back from the dead, we met other survivors. They had all found some secure, defensible place, like we had with the museum. Some were in an observatory at the top of a mountain, some had occupied a monastery deep in the woods, and some were on an island in a big lake. A handful of people had lived in some barricaded buildings in a nearby town, hopping from roof to roof across bridges they had built, as I am told my biological father did when I was first born.

They found another group in a huge building full of all kinds of things; the older people said it was called a "mall," and they laughed because they had found people there. They tried to explain why it was funny, because some old movies had people hiding in a mall when there were zombies outside. I still didn't get the joke, but people have often told me I don't have much of a sense of humor. Sometimes they say it ruefully, because they say I used to laugh a lot when I was a baby.

Each of these new groups became a part of our community, though we had few formal rules. My dad explained to me that when they had lived in the museum, he and Milton had more or less led the group, and they'd had many more rules. But with so much land cleared of the hungry dead, plenty of room and farmland was available for the few hundred people we had managed to bring together. With people more spread out and not jammed on top of one another, the rules of an armed camp under siege were relaxed, and there seemed much less need for a formal government. The concept of government—and the even more alien ideas of a state or nation—was one I had come across in old books, but I had a lot of trouble understanding exactly what it meant. And except for a tiny bit of reflected glow from the fireworks and celebration of "freedom" that we still have on the Fourth of July, I've always gotten the impression that government isn't something from the former world that the older people miss very much.

But if the older folks were stuck in the old world, while we younger people were completely a part of the new, I think it was hardest of all on those just a little older than myself, just old enough to remember that the dead once lay still, old enough to remember their parents and others being torn apart in fountains and pools of their own blood, or dying slow deaths from the infection or starvation. When I looked at my slightly older peers, I saw the kind of ghosts that were the strongest and most bitter, the kind that didn't live in your mind or even your heart, but in your bones. I could be happy, or at least content with the new world; my parents could be regretful or resigned to it. But for the people in between, for the people whose childhood had been interrupted by the rising of the dead, the effect seemed much more lasting, deep, and alienating.

A few people were in this age group, the generation between me and my parents, people like Will, who was a young man when the story I'm now telling took place. They had called him Popcorn when he was a boy, because they had rescued him from an abandoned movie theater, and there was this food they called popcorn that was traditionally served at movies. He was raised by Mr. Caine and Ms. Wright, and he subsequently announced that his name was Will—never William or Bill or Billy, just Will. It was a matter of some speculation whether he had christened himself this, or whether he had suddenly remembered his name from before, or even if he had known it all along and kept it secret till it suited him to reveal it.

People Will's age seemed like they could only be angry and disappointed in this new world. Their anger could either be directed towards the dead, or towards whatever concept they retained of God or the devil—it didn't seem to matter, or even to be separate in their minds—while their disappointment was most keenly and consistently directed at the living. They remembered each and every smile and kiss and embrace from the time before, and they remembered every scream and gasp from when death shattered that dream and robbed them of every hope and love they had ever had. And they never forgave, it seemed—not the dead, not the living, and most especially, not themselves. Both the older and the younger tried to love their pain away, but this seemed to be even less successful than it was with my parents' generation. My parents had lost the future as they had hoped or expected it would be, so they clung sadly to the past. People like Will saw both the future and the past as empty, meaningless, and painful—a broken promise from a cruel stepmother, a betrayed vow from a wanton and faithless lover—and they often lived just in the present, taking risks, snatching at small pleasures, seldom speaking or getting close to others. Or so it seemed to me then.

It was not surprising that Will began to accompany Milton into the wilderness to help round up the dead, though he hardly seemed to get the kind of satisfaction from this job that Milton did, and of course it was much more dangerous for him, since he didn't have Milton's immunity to the ever-hungry corpses. For Milton it was a service both to the community and to the zombies, or as he called them, "our dead brothers and sisters." For Will, it was an escape from the living, to be among a group for which he had no more affection, but which were, in a way, much better company for him, for they were quiet, unquestioning, uncomprehending, and most of all—so long as one could avoid their hideous and voracious jaws—utterly undemanding. Perhaps it was for the best, though I still wonder if it was either necessary or good for Will to spend so much time among the living dead.

The other thing that makes memories not so funny in the humorous way is that sometimes people hide their memories from you, even if those memories involve you directly. I've found this with my mom and dad. I've always—as far back as I can remember—noticed that my dad looks at me differently than my mom does. With her, the love is not only unrestrained, it's exuberant and inquisitive and joyful. With him, though his gaze was always as unconditional and even passionate as hers, there was something about it that was not exactly held back or guarded, but something that expected and even wanted me to be cold and guarded and in control—around everyone, but towards him most of all. My mom would do anything to protect me; my dad would trust me to protect him or anyone else. I'd say it was a father-daughter thing, except that Jonah has always looked at me the same way as my dad does, so I'm almost positive they know something about me or my biological dad that no one else does.

It's almost like they have treated me or expected me to be like Milton, with a special power or insight, but I know I don't have that. I've seen the dead, and they look at me just like they look at everyone else, with uncaring and uncontrollable desire, and I get just as queasy and scared around them as anyone else. I sometimes wished I could just ask my dad or Jonah what they were thinking when they looked at me that way, but I always knew I wouldn't, I wasn't sure they would tell me anyway, and I was pretty sure that I didn't want to know.

And that leads me to a memory I was thinking of again this morning, for about the millionth time. It led me to think more about memories and how they work and why they matter and why I might want to write down those from my twelfth year before they flit away or mutate or whatever it was that happened to this other, older memory. This memory—which I think is my earliest recollection of anything in my life—is that I'm playing freeze tag with a bunch of other little kids, all of us about four years old. We are playing in a large field. It's hot and sunny, but in a nice way— not uncomfortable, but just perfect and invigorating. Bugs—not the kind that bother you, like flies and mosquitoes, but moths and butterflies and dragonflies and even an occasional bee—zip and bounce over the grass, which is pretty tall compared to us little kids, above our waists. There is a line of trees edging the field. I am frozen, waiting for someone to tag me and unfreeze me. I look back over my shoulder, and I see the adults farther away, under a big tree out in the field. They have the tailgate down on a pickup truck and they're getting food out for everyone. My dad turns toward me, and I see his face, see it change from the expectant and happy look he usually has with me to fright. He shouts something, but I can't make it out. He runs to the front of the truck and fumbles under the seat, then he runs toward me. I see he has a gun in his hand, a big pistol. Now he's shouting and waving, but I still can't understand what he wants.

That's when I hear something else, like a dry whisper, incoherent but so insistent. It's almost like the wind through the city streets, filling up the dead places between the empty buildings. But this is closer, quieter. And most of all, I know as soon as I hear it that this sound is personal, intimate, meant only for me. I turn and the dead man whispering his inhuman desire for me is right on top of me. He's naked, dry, scabbed, scarred, and withered. He grabs my bicep at the same moment I start to scream and try to pull away. His mouth opens as he leans down—grey, mostly toothless, the tongue wriggling obscenely. I twist myself around and turn from him, screaming more loudly and shrilly, but there's no getting my arm free. I hear the shot and the dead man's nose and eyes disappear, a ragged hole in his face. The mouth is still there, but now it's silent and the tongue isn't moving. The dead man turns slightly and collapses next to me, but the hand is still clamped on my arm. I thrash about, not looking, not thinking, just screaming and writhing, and now the hand's grip finally loosens slightly and its long, blackened nails are dragging down my arm, scratching me. I throw my head back and howl with a mixture of rage and revulsion and relief as my whole tiny body springs back and away, landing at my dad's feet.

This is one of those things that I think I remember, but I'm not sure. I think if I asked my dad, I could find out whether this memory was real, but I don't want to. I don't ask. I never have. I think I remember a moment of perfect, carefree joy, and I think I remember a moment of sudden and extreme terror. I want to hold on to both—to the possibility of both, not the certainty. To be certain of the horror that afternoon would be too much for me to bear, I know it would be; it would expand and grow till it blocked out everything good and beautiful I've ever had. To be certain and convinced that such a horrible scene never happened would be a lie and would further shut me off from those like my parents and Will who know they've seen such things, many times over, and much worse. To be certain of the joy would be to fall back into the ingratitude I mentioned before, to take for granted or pretend I deserved such bliss—then, now, or ever. To know for certain it had never happened would again be too much for me to bear. So I hold the both of them in this perfectly balanced, perfectly uncertain memory, one that I've never shared with anyone until now.

As I say, it's funny the things you remember, and funnier still the things you think you remember. And funniest of all? To be— not just to *have*, mind you, but to actually *be*—such a willing, willful collection of memories, sometimes choosing and sometimes refusing to choose from among all the things you think you remember. But that is what I am, and I suspect it's what you are too, if you'd admit it. My name is Zoey—survivor and heir of a dead world. And these are my memories of one tiny part of my life.

Chapter 2

This is my journal. My name is Wade Truman, though I didn't know that for a long time. There are a lot of things I don't know so well, even now. I do know how to type, for some reason, but I don't seem to know as many words as I think I should. I try to learn new ones, but it's hard for me to study. I lose concentration or something happens to distract me. All my memories start a few years ago, yet I'm sure I existed before that, because when my memories start, I already knew lots of things, just not perfectly, and all the different ideas and memories—if that's what they are— don't necessarily connect. So it seems like I've remembered all sorts of complicated things and words, but forgotten some very basic and necessary things, like how to walk right. And how to talk.

I remember the first time I tried to talk. It is, in fact, almost my first memory, right from when I first awoke, lying on my back on the pavement. The concrete felt hard and warm on my back. But inside I felt cold. I had no idea where I was. I heard sirens and gunfire in the distance, and closer to me, this low moaning punctuated with growls and wails. I sat up. I could see blood all over

9

me and all around me, and there were people around me, and they were all bloody too. They held their red, dripping hands up to their mouths and they slurped and chewed as they eyed me and growled.

I looked down and saw that I was torn open in the middle, and a lot of my insides were gone. It didn't hurt, though, not exactly, which surprised me, though I wasn't sure what pain felt like. I was just surprised I didn't feel much of anything, even though something was obviously wrong with my body and pieces of it were missing. All I felt was a little cold and stiff. And that was when I first tried to talk.

At first my mouth just moved noiselessly, and I thought maybe the part of me that could make speech was missing too. I felt my throat and that seemed intact, but no air was coming out to make the sounds, so I concentrated on breathing in and exhaling. I tried to say something like, "I've been hurt," but nothing came out right. It didn't sound like words, but all harsh and wrong—just raspy, wheezing sounds. It sounded a lot like the moaning I heard all around me.

Even though I couldn't understand what the moaning meant, I was speaking the same as everyone around me, and that made me feel better, though I was disappointed that I couldn't communicate with anyone. I still feel bad about that, like I'm missing something much more important than my intestines or my liver, whose absence I really haven't noticed over the years.

I now live in this group of buildings with the other people like me. They can't talk either. I must have known how to type very well before, since I can still do it, even though I don't remember how to speak. The typing came easily, even if it still seems slow and none of the other people here know how to read it. I suppose I must have known lots of ideas and problems and questions before, because even though I don't breathe or sleep or talk, I can still think of a lot of things, and I wanted to write some of them down since I can't say them out loud anymore, and I thought other people might be interested in them.

The older man, the one who makes me feel uneasy and scared, he put us here not too long ago. The other people who can't talk must also feel scared and uneasy around him because, like me, they walk slowly away whenever he gets near. At the time, I didn't know why he put us here, as we were fine where we were, I thought. Maybe it was to punish us, as I heard later that he was going to put us in a prison. He can talk. He spoke to us loudly, but with kind-sounding words, so I didn't mind going where he wanted, if it made him happy and he thought it was best for us.

The older man led us out of the city after he found us there. He had two dogs to help move us in the direction he wanted. It was funny, but as we walked, I wondered why I hadn't thought of it on my own, to leave the city where I had been at first, and I couldn't really tell why. It just hadn't occurred to me.

I made a note that I've tried to remember since then, not to sit around doing nothing, though sometimes it's so difficult, and the urge is almost overwhelming, just to sit down and forget all the things that need to be done. But giving in to that urge just doesn't seem right, because I remember as we walked away from the city that it felt so good to see different things, all the fields and trees and flowers and other things. There is a whole world out here, and we should feel good about it. "Good" isn't the right word. "Grateful"—we should feel grateful for it, I think.

We walked out of the city, about twenty of us, and a younger man joined the older man. The young man didn't make us feel uneasy or scared the way the older man did, just by his presence, though as soon as I heard him, I felt a little scared; he seemed harsher and angrier than the older man.

As he talked with the older man, a lot of people in my group tried to get close to him, to attack him. They felt threatened by him, I think, and so did I. They also felt hungry, I'm sure, because I know I did, but I didn't want to attack him—partly because the kinder, older man seemed to be his friend, and also because I remembered back when I was first in the city, years before the man took us out, I had been with some other people who couldn't talk and they were all battering on a door to a big building. The door gave way and we all rushed in. There was screaming, and blood everywhere.

I felt hungry, so hungry. It gnawed and tore at me, the hunger. I had been hungry for as long as I could remember, since waking up days before. So when I saw someone on the floor, with other people tearing her apart, I took some. I even punched and clawed at others to get them out of the way so I could tear off a bloody piece of the woman. I just wanted the hunger to go away, but it was a cruel joke on us as much as on her.

When I ate some, it burned my mouth, literally. My mouth had been so dry and cold, and now it felt like it was being scalded with burning liquid, and like I was drowning in the slippery, greasy wetness of her blood, all at the same time. It was the most awful thing I've ever felt. I clutched my throat and shook my head from side to side and tried to swallow, and I was sure it was going to kill me, the burning and drowning sensations were so intense, first in my mouth, but then even worse in my throat, like throwing up backwards, even though later I realized I wasn't sure what throwing up felt like; I just remember it was very unpleasant and it burned. But what was worse was that once I swallowed, it seemed to make me even hungrier. My stomach—or whatever was left of it—had been a dull, pained pressure in my middle, but almost as soon as I swallowed, it gave a wrench, and its insistent demand filled me completely, as if my limbs and head could feel hunger as well—as if every part of me were writhing, twisting, screaming in need.

From somewhere I suddenly remembered that drinking salt water was like that, and many people lost at sea died when they drank the sea water, because the more they drank, the thirstier they got, until it killed them. Isn't that funny, that I should suddenly remember that? And from where? I had just awakened a few days before, and I knew I hadn't heard that particular fact anywhere since waking up. I still am not sure. But I knew from then on not to eat, because it just made things worse.

So I didn't want to attack the younger man and I didn't press forward with the others. But I could hear the two of them talking, even as I hung back.

"Do you want me to help herd this bunch to the prison, Milton?" the younger man said.

I didn't like that at all, because I knew what the word "prison" meant. The other people didn't react to this description of where we were going, they just kept grasping at the younger man. But I hung my head, for I remembered what I'd done back in the city to the woman I'd partially eaten. I felt like I deserved going to prison, though I was surprised it had taken them so long to catch us. I didn't think all the people with me had been there when we had eaten the woman and the others, but maybe they had eaten other people or done other bad things, and we were all being punished together.

The people with me didn't seem to understand what was being said, they just milled around as the man called Milton kept them back. "Stay behind me, Will," he said to the young man. "We'll take some of them to the prison, but it's getting too full. I'd like to take some to that fenced-in place we found a while ago."

The younger man called Will said, "That can't hold many."

"No, but Jack says it's not close to anything important, and he's marked it on the map so people don't stumble on it by accident. And it'll help ease the overcrowding. Don't worry, Will, we'll find other places. We have to.

"I've been watching them. They fight each other sometimes, and some of the bigger and more violent and aggressive ones hurt the smaller. They even hurt the women and children among them. It's wrong. They don't eat them, of course, and that makes it even worse, like they're just doing it out of cruelty or rage, and I had always hoped they wouldn't be capable of that, at least. Sometimes they hurt them to the point where they can't move, and then you or I have to put them out of their misery. That's not right. I'd like to put the less aggressive ones somewhere else."

Will shrugged. "All right."

And so we marched on. It took us a couple days. At night some of the people would wander away, and Milton would bring them back in the morning. But they couldn't get far in the dark, and mostly we sat down at night and didn't move. Will would climb a tree or something else, like a billboard or an electrical tower, in order to sleep and to keep away from us.

By the time we got to our destination, the men and the dogs had separated us into two groups of about ten each. I hoped, given Milton's description, that my group wasn't going into the prison. Some of the other people had already hit and growled at me when we were walking before. We got to a gate in a huge fence that ran for what seemed like miles around a big building. I guessed this was the prison. The area behind the fence seemed to hold thousands of people like me who couldn't talk. They pressed up against the fence, or milled about, or sat on the ground. The man called Milton unlocked the gate and the other group of ten filed through. Milton relocked the gate, and he turned to our group and led us away.

We walked again, across a highway with many empty cars and trucks on it, across fields, and we eventually came to another high fence. Milton unlocked the gate in this fence, let us enter, and locked it behind us. At first we tried to push against the fence, but that didn't make much sense to me after a short while. It was nicer here than at the prison, as it wasn't crowded. But I still didn't like being locked in. I wondered if it was just a nicer prison, since I hadn't attacked and eaten as many people as some of the others.

Mostly, I just wanted something to do, so I went looking around the little buildings inside the fence. The buildings were low and narrow, and they had these doors that slid up, like a garage door, only there were lots of doors down each long side of each little building. When we first got here, the big sign above the buildings read "MINI STORAGE," but it blew down in a storm after that. The sliding doors were all locked. I think I lost track of which ones I'd tried and which I hadn't, but I'm pretty sure after a couple days that I'd tried every door. I had hoped there was something inside the buildings, even though I didn't know what to expect or what I really wanted. I just knew I wanted something to do besides sit there with the others, and I had hoped the doors into the buildings would provide something.

And I remember very distinctly, on that day when I knew I was stuck there and none of the doors would open, that it was raining. I sat under the little overhang by one of the sliding doors. Though I don't exactly mind being wet, I vaguely remember that it's something I'm not supposed to like. "Vaguely remember"? I usually think that's the only kind of remembering I do now, but I suddenly had a very vivid memory of something called crying, and it was what I wanted to do then. But I knew as soon as I thought of it that it was even more lost to me than speech was, so I just sighed and sat there as it got dark and cold and the rain kept on through the night.

The next day the sun rose on a beautiful, clear, warm morning. I got up and started trying the doors again, in case I had missed one, but mostly just to have something to do. I heard a sound behind me, and I turned to see that it was the younger man, Will. He was watching me. I pulled on the door handle as I looked at him, trying to make him understand I wanted to open it.

He shook his head and smiled grimly. "Nobody in there to eat, fella, just somebody's old stuff. Sit down and relax."

I shook my head as I looked at him. The others inside with me went to the fence near him and pressed against it, so he had to run to one side of them to see me again. "Did you shake your head at me?" he shouted, before running back to the other side of the little crowd as it shuffled over and blocked his view of me again. "Do you understand what I'm saying?"

I pulled on the door and in my mind I said, "Why, yes, I do, and could you please open this door?" but all that came out was a pained roar, so then I nodded instead.

He looked very surprised, and he stepped back and sat away from the fence until Milton joined him. I could hear them talking again. I envied them, that they could talk so easily to one another, make themselves understood by another person, rather than being trapped, alone, in their own minds. "I think one of them understands what I say!" Will said.

Milton stepped towards the fence, and the others on my side of the barrier shuffled away from him. Milton looked surprised, though pleased in a way. "Really? Which one?"

Will pointed to me. "That one, the guy wearing the suit with his guts all ripped out, sitting by the door to one of the storage units. I just was playing with him, and I said there wasn't anyone in there to eat, he should leave the door alone, and he shook his head, like he understood. Then I asked him if he understood, and he nodded!"

Milton now looked at me. "And just as importantly, Will, it sounds like he didn't want to open the door just to find someone to eat! This was another thing I dared hope for—that if we got the less aggressive ones alone, they might be able to remember more and think more clearly."

Milton smiled at me, and I knew he was even kinder than I had thought before. I tried to smile back, but judging by how they both grimaced, I thought it was probably another one of the things I had forgotten to do the right way.

Chapter 3

Most days that spring I spent a lot of time with my dad. As a twelve-year-old, it was my time to take my first vows of service to our community. Milton, Mr. Caine, my mom, and all the adults would teach me, give me advice, help me adjust to new expectations and new responsibilities. But, of course, the bulk of the responsibility for my training fell on my dad. He relished it, I know, as he would in a couple years when he had to train my younger brother, Roger. My dad has always loved teaching and helping people, and the fact that we were family made it all the sweeter to him. It helped that most of the training was "guy stuff," as he put it, and he was proficient in those kinds of activities. He'd laugh and say that even in the "regular" world—his world, the old world—he probably would've tried to make his daughter into a "tomboy" (another of his archaic phrases), but now the community expected him to do so. It was as if that made it okay and he didn't need to feel bad about it.

And of course he wasn't the only one who enjoyed it. We both did. We were together and in the outdoors and having fun—hunting, fishing, tracking. If most of the time the world could seem desolate and abandoned and lonely, at least for part of that spring we could feel like there was the right number of people in it—namely, two—safe, alive, and devoted to one another. On those days I didn't mind how my dad looked at me differently; that gaze drew out something strong, harsh, and unforgiving from deep inside me. I didn't feel his expectation like a burden or an imposition, but like how I think he's always meant it—as the deepest expression of his love, as his admiration and hope for me. And like every girl, whatever her situation and whatever her dad's expectations, all I wanted to do was please him—again, even if I didn't fully understand or appreciate it at the time.

But it was hard on my mom, seeing me gravitate to my dad so much. She also taught me a lot of the things that needed to be done for us to survive—sewing, weaving, gardening, gathering fruits and nuts and herbs in the summer, then canning, drying, and smoking all the food we'd need for winter. She was one of the few people with any medical training, and it had to double for both people and animals, so as the numbers of both people and live-stock grew, she'd take me around to help with all the various births. I'd seen more than my share of human and animal babies born by the time I was twelve, and many more since. Like every-one, my mom had adjusted to this new life and had found strengths and skills she never knew she had.

Life was harder on her than it was on my dad. It was hard on people like Mr. Caine and Milton, too. Mr. Caine had been a professor and Milton had been a scientist, and now they lived in a world where those skill sets weren't in demand, and they'd had to retool in middle age.

But for Mr. Caine or my dad or many of the other people, even the older people, life without the things they'd been used to had some small benefits, even though everyone was always quick to add that they weren't worth the awful price in blood. Our world was far more dangerous and uncomfortable, but it was also more free, less hectic, in many ways less anxious or burdensome than the one they'd lived in. Mr. Caine and my dad and others would sometimes laugh at a lot of obsolete things I had very little under-standing of—student loans, credit cards, mortgages, car pay-ments—all of which, apparently, had made their former lives often unpleasant, and which had magically disappeared twelve years ago. In fact, I am told they had all disappeared the day before I was born.

My mom seemed to have less vivid or numerous memories of the bad parts of the old world, and less appreciation for any of the good points of the new. She's always loved me and my dad and my brother—I'm not saying she doesn't, or that it's any less than we feel—but more of her had shut down the day her world died, and she'd always have more regrets than other people. She held on to old customs more than most people. She wore her hair long, for example, while most everyone else kept their hair short, just for comfort and convenience and hygiene. She kept me in frilly, girly clothes way longer than most moms did, if they even bothered to do so at all when their girls were very young. And once the city around the museum was cleared and we went looking for a home, I know she picked the one she did because it had a piano in it, even though she came up with other reasons.

A few people knew how to play more practical instruments, like guitars—instruments that you could carry around easily, and fix and tune on your own. A piano was probably not the best choice for an instrument with a future in our world, but Mom remembered how to play, and she wanted one. Roger and I both learned how to play, along with some other kids whose parents made them come over for lessons, and maybe now there will be pianos and piano-players in the next generation. But all her gestures, as beautiful and true as they were, always had that touch of the poignant, the nostalgic, the sunset rather than the sunrise.

Learning to play the piano had some other collateral benefits for me. The other kids started calling me "Piano Girl," which may not sound like much of a nickname, but I was so relieved to get it after spending my first years being called "Zombie Girl." I don't think a five-year-old girl ever got in as many fights as I did.

I was always kind of tall and gawky, and my black hair and pale skin didn't help, but worst of all I was adopted, and the identity of my biological parents was a matter of dark, morbid, sinister speculation. After I would have a fight with other kids, Mom and Dad would talk to the other kids' parents, of course, but it didn't make any difference. They might take a day off, but then they'd be back at it, saying my real mom was a zombie and my real dad was crazy, and I'd start punching kids till they beat me down, then I'd come home and say I'd fallen and refuse to identify who did it.

Given what I've heard and read since, it looks like some things didn't change so much between the old world and the new, but unfortunately, it seemed to be some of the ugly parts that stayed the same. So by teaching me piano, my mom indirectly helped me to get picked on less, and Dad helped more directly by teaching me how to fight, no matter how often he protested in front of my mom that I was supposed to "just walk away." When I was ten, I got taller and bigger than most of the other kids my age, especially the boys, so Piano Girl was getting along a lot better and more peacefully than Zombie Girl had.

Teaching me to fight led naturally into training me for my first vows to the community. I remember one day shortly before my vows—which were scheduled, as was tradition, to take place on the summer solstice. Dad and I went out to the big field to practice. It was an oddly beautiful place for the kind of practicing we had been doing there since I was little, and which we'd increased now with my vows approaching. It was an idyllic place, with butterflies flitting about and the steady drone of grasshoppers. It was much like the field where I thought I remembered being attacked, though it wasn't the same one. The grass was only just above my knees now. This one had no woods nearby, at least not big ones, but just scraggly little trees scattered in clumps. One big hickory tree stood in the middle of the field; in the fall, we would gather its nuts, and among the smaller trees there were lots of blackberry bushes that we'd pick later in the summer. Neither of the field's offerings was in season that day, however, and it was not a day for such peaceful pursuits.

We found our spot with the grass still matted down and brass casings all over the ground. It was about thirty yards from the big hickory, from which my dad had hung an old, cast iron frying pan years ago. We faced the big tree as we got our stuff out. There was a light breeze and it wouldn't be too hot today, though it had warmed up enough for me to take off the coarse woolen jacket made by my mom. About thirty yards to our right was an old wooden fence, and my dad and I had set four coffee cans on top of it as we'd walked into the field. The same distance to our left was the rusted hulk of a tractor. My dad took four more coffee cans and handed them to me. I walked over to the tractor and set those cans on top of it.

Dad was checking our weapons as I walked up to him. He looked at me and smiled. "You know why I like to use the frying pan and coffee cans for the targets?"

"Because they're about the size of someone's head." I rolled my eyes at him. "You know you tell me that every couple days, Dad. And it's not even a nice way to talk. Mom says it's not."

"Sorry, princess, your old dad doesn't know too many jokes. Well, of course, that's not actually a joke, technically speaking. The pan and the coffee cans are about the right size for what we have in mind. Even if it's not nice, it's what we're training to do, so we might as well come out and say it." He winked. "And I really like the sound the pan makes when you hit it."

He'd laid everything out on a blanket on the grass. There was a .38 S&W Model 10. That was the handgun I practiced with the most, both because it was the easiest to service, and also because it was a little smaller and easier for me to handle. Next to it was a .40 Beretta 96. I had only just started shooting that one this season. The size, weight, and recoil made it hard for me, but I had gotten decent with it. Next to them were two rifles—a Ruger Mini-14 with a scope, and an M16. We used the former sometimes for hunting, and the latter was another new addition to my training. My dad had put some jury-rigged deflectors on both the rifles, to keep the ejected casings from hitting me in the face, since I'm left-handed.

My dad set himself down on the grass behind the blanket, pulling his knees up and resting his forearms on them. He reached up and scratched me between the shoulder blades. "You like shooting, princess?"

"Yeah. I'm good at it. I have to be." I scanned all the nasty, oily black metal at my feet. I could hate the idea of the weapons, and I could even hate the look of them—dully glistening there like shards of the body armor from some gigantic, evil insects—but I knew I'd had them in my hand so many times that they felt as natural as anything could. They were a part of me.

"I know you are. I tell you so every day." He scratched harder and made me laugh. "Sorry you have to be, honey. I don't tell you that enough."

"There's nothing to be sorry for, Dad."

"No?" He shrugged off his own jacket, then reached in the one pocket to pull out his boonie hat. "I know you've been talking to Milton and Jonah way too much to give such a practical answer," he said as he put on the hat. "We don't want you sounding like your old dad."

I smiled at him. "I don't think they ever want us to feel sorry for anything, Dad. They just always talk about how complicated and confusing things are. I like that."

He reached into his other jacket pocket and got out a small pair of binoculars. He cleaned the lenses on the sleeve of his jacket. "You like things to be confusing? I don't."

I had to roll my eyes again. "You know what I mean. I like it when people tell me what's what. And if something is all confused, I like for them to tell me that and not dress it all up for me."

He grunted as he put his elbows up on his knees. "Yeah, well, that's why they got me handling the uncomplicated things with you. I just give you the tools and skills to put big holes in things at a distance." He put the binoculars to his eyes and adjusted the focus. "Like we've been doing it. Show your dad how you make dead things deader, sweetie."

I knelt down and put on the protective ear muffs I used when shooting. I loaded the .38 from a box of ammo next to it, working quickly to slip the six rounds into place. I swung the cylinder back into place as I stood up. I raised the gun smoothly, holding it with both hands, my left forefinger on the trigger. My breathing was steady. My palms didn't sweat like they used to, either. The frying pan was plenty heavy enough that the breeze didn't move it at all; even the shots wouldn't set it swinging enough to throw off my aim, unless I hit near the edge and started it spinning. I knew that wouldn't happen. I squeezed off the six rounds, quickly and methodically, but not hurriedly. There were six low, satisfying clangs.

I knelt again and set down the .38. I took up the Beretta, which was also unloaded. The night before I had loaded a bunch of magazines with five rounds each, but my hands still weren't strong enough to load a full magazine of ten, so my dad had put the last five rounds in each one for me. I picked up one of the magazines and slid it into its place in the handle. I moved the safety to the fire position and racked the slide to chamber the first round. I stood, turned to my right, and brought the gun up with both hands. The weight was definitely still cumbersome, but I had gotten used to it, and had also gotten over the intimidation of such a big gun.

It took me seven of the rounds to hit the four cans on the fence. I turned to the tractor. With the three remaining rounds I knocked down two more cans. The field was in a slight depression, with the ground sloping up around us, so my dad could usually call my misses by watching through the binoculars for where they hit behind the target.

We went through this with the handguns several times, with me setting the cans back up in between rounds. Then my dad took up the Mini-14 and the M16, I took up the bag with their spare magazines—which my dad had loaded the night before when I was loading those for the Beretta—and we walked farther from the tree, to another spot with matted-down grass and brass casings on the ground. My dad got back in his position with the binoculars, while I set the selector on the M16 to the "BURST" position and practiced firing three-round bursts at the frying pan. I almost always hit with the first round of each burst, then the recoil pulled the barrel too high.

"That's normal," my dad said. "Just keep working at holding the gun steady throughout the burst, okay?"

We picked up the rifles and ammo and went even farther from the tree, about a hundred yards, and I practiced firing single shots from the Mini-14. I was nearly as good with that as I was with the .38, even at this range, since we'd been hunting with it before.

When we were done shooting, we packed everything up and ate lunch in the shade of the big hickory. Mom had packed hunks of salty, gritty ham; it had been put up last fall. The hard-boiled eggs, on the other hand, had still been inside a hen two days before. There was a loaf of bread Mom had made from a combination of acorn and corn flour. It always came out crumbly, but as with so many things, I had nothing to compare it to. After walking and shooting all morning, I thought it tasted perfect. A little brook cut across the field, and we got cold water from that to complete our meal. It was a small enough stream and we were close enough to its source that we didn't bother with boiling it first.

After that break, we got up and took the two staffs that we had left leaning against the big tree the day before and practiced fighting with those. I knew Dad held back, but I also had enough bruises to know he was making me work for every time I'd catch him with the big, heavy stick. After a long bout with the staffs, we had some more water from the stream and lay down under the tree to rest before the long walk home.

I loved looking up at the leaves, how they danced and melded into all different patterns against the sky. "You tired?" my dad asked.

"Yeah."

"Good. You gonna take a nap?"

"No, I'm fine."

"Even better, 'cause then I can." He folded his hands on his chest and closed his eyes. This whole area had been cleared of the dead years ago, but it was still way outside of the central fence and wall network, so dad never let us be completely off guard here.

I watched the leaves. "Why do we practice with the staffs, Dad? It's not like the dead can use things like that against us."

He kept his eyes closed as he answered, holding up two fingers. "Two reasons. The first one is tactical." He folded his middle finger back. "One—it's not as much fun for anybody if you just whack me with a big stick all afternoon."

I swatted his arm down. "I don't know. That sounds pretty fun."

"Hmm-mmm. Just like your mother." He extended both fingers again. "The second one is strategic."

"Strategic?" I'd heard the word before, I just didn't see how it fit here. "How so?"

"It means the big picture, not just what's going on at the moment."

"Okay. What's the strategic reason?"

"You take a vow to protect the living. The dead aren't the only threat. So you don't learn to fight just the dead."

I turned my head to look at him. I'd always suspected the answer, but it still made me feel cold inside. The wisecracks about the frying pan and coffee cans being head-sized didn't seem so funny in light of that answer. I first tried to find some factual inconsistency to object to. "But why do you always tell me to go for a headshot? That wouldn't matter if the person were alive."

He folded his hands back across his chest. "If someone is bad enough for you to kill them, then they're bad enough that you want them to stay dead. I don't think their behavior's going to improve much if you leave them dead and walking around with a hole in their chest."

Now I tried to assail the logical inconsistency of it. "You kill the living to protect the living?"

"I didn't make the rules. I just teach you to play by them."

I paused. "You ever kill anyone? I mean, someone who wasn't already dead?"

He shook his head a little, still without opening his eyes. "No. I was lucky that way. You might ask your uncle Jonah, and he can tell you about it. I hear it's very complicated, because when you're actually doing it, sometimes you get to liking it a little too much. And then when it's done, you don't like it at all and you feel sick. That's how he's explained it to me, and I think he's probably right." He opened his eyes and looked at me. His eyes were a bright, lively hazel, unlike my dull, dark brown ones. I always wished my eyes were pretty like his. "But I do know how you think about it before you do it, how you have to think about it every minute of your life."

"How?" I whispered and looked back up at the leaves for some guidance.

"You see anyone trying to hurt you or anyone you know, then it doesn't matter if they have a pulse or not. All you think of is how you can put them down for good, as quickly as possible. Bullet, blade, stick, run over them with a car, set them on fire—

hell, it doesn't make the tiniest bit of difference. You do it without thinking or hesitating or considering any other option. That's as much a part of your vows as anything else. That's as much a part of who you are and who you have to be now." He reached over and squeezed my bicep. "You talk to Jonah and Milton about dealing with the complications, but you believe that part through and through, without question. Okay, little girl?"

I nodded and bit my lower lip.

"Hey, I got something for you." We both sat up and he reached in one of the bags we'd been carrying. He got out a small handgun in what looked like a homemade leather holster and handed it to me. "I stitched the holster myself, so sorry it looks rough. I know your mother sews better, but you know she doesn't like... you know, guns and even stuff related to guns."

I carefully slid the small gun out. It was a dull blue-black, curved and perfectly formed, though still graceless and brutal. But it fit in my small hand like it had been sculpted just for me. And when I squeezed the grip, the hammer cocked; I released it, and it uncocked. "Snazzy, Dad. Thanks!"

"Heckler and Koch P7M8. 9mm, eight-round magazine. Pricey gun, back when it cost money to have a gun. Small, but decent stopping power. It fits your hand well? I know you still have trouble with the Beretta."

I nodded. "Perfect." I racked the slide. The best thing was that it was a completely ambidextrous gun. "And it's better for a lefty."

"Yeah, I was lucky to find it. You like it? I don't mean like, I guess. I mean, is it a good gun for you to carry around and have as your own? You need that now."

"Yes, Dad."

"Good." He reached over and gave my shoulder a squeeze. "Don't tell your mom, okay? But it's yours now."

"Okay, Dad."

"Can you sit there a couple minutes while I catch a few?"

"Sure."

He lay back down on the grass. "Thanks, sweetie."

I studied the 9mm for a few minutes, then slipped it back in its rough little holster and put it in my jacket pocket. I spent the rest of the time watching the butterflies and listening to my dad's steady, reliable breathing, till he awoke and we walked home.

Chapter 4

Milton came inside the fence with us and shooed the other people away from the little building near the gate. That building was different from the others. It had windows and a sign over the door that read "OFFICE." With the other people at a safe distance, Will came inside the fenced area as well. He broke the glass on the door and went into the office. He came out with keys and, staying behind Milton, he unlocked all the other doors. Then he and Milton left and locked the gate again.

It's funny, but now that the doors were unlocked, I felt embarrassed to open them, especially in front of the two men who could talk. It was like I was doing a trick or passing some kind of test they had set up. But I didn't see how to make them go away and give me some privacy, so I slid one door up.

Inside the dark compartment were bicycles and furniture and boxes piled to the ceiling. Some of the other people with me went into the compartment and started pulling stuff out, and I wanted to stop them, because they didn't seem to appreciate or respect the things; they just tossed them all around. But I knew they had as much right to these things as I did. The stuff didn't belong to any of us, we were just taking it, and if that's how they enjoyed the objects, then I had to let them. If I wanted to rearrange the things or use something myself, I could just wait till they lost interest and wandered off, which all of them did after a few minutes of going through the things in the compartment.

Inside the compartment was a sofa, and I sat on it and examined some of the things that had fallen out of boxes. There were all sorts of little things. Some I could identify, some looked vaguely familiar, and some were a mystery. But I liked all of them and was glad to have them. It wouldn't be so bad here, if I had some objects to look at, some things to learn about and study. My heart leaped as I thought there might be books in some of the boxes; I had been able to read the signs outside, so I thought I could probably read more complicated things, and even if it was hard, getting more practice and learning to read better would give me something to do.

It still made me a little sad to be locked in here, but as I sat there looking at an album full of pictures and running my hand over an old quilt, I had to admit that even if the gate were open, I wouldn't know where to go. I had no idea what was out there. There could be things that were dangerous—wild animals or violent people or even fire. I shivered when I remembered that Will and Milton had built a fire at night when we were walking here. It had scared me almost as much as being near Milton. I looked at all the boxes, and I thought that for a while, maybe a long while, this would be a really nice and safe place to stay and learn about the world. Maybe later I could go out and see other things, once I'd learned what was safe and how to get around better, and if they'd let me.

I looked sideways at Milton and Will, trying not to let them notice that I was looking at them, letting them think I was focused on the things in the compartment. They, on the other hand, made no attempt to conceal how fascinated they were by watching my every move.

"Why's he different from the others?" Will asked Milton quietly. "It's like he remembers things from when he was normal,"

I didn't know what he meant by that. I know more now, but I still don't understand everything that happened or why some people are different from others. I don't remember enough of it to understand. I still think I am normal, even today. So are these people in here with me. We're different from the people who can talk, but we're all different from each other, and they're different from one another, too. I didn't like the way they watched me, and talked like I was so different, or even that there was something wrong with us. I remembered that we'd killed and eaten some people, so maybe we deserved to be punished, but there was something else in how they talked that made it wrong. I'd forgotten the word, but I read it in a book later—"condescension." It made me feel a little angry and insulted, but I had to admit that whether or not one could talk seemed to make a big difference in how one got along with others. Maybe it was an accurate measure of our worth, and whether we were good or bad people. Besides, Milton and Will had opened the doors for me. Maybe they weren't so bad. I didn't want to be angry at them.

"I've been studying them more than you have, Will," Milton answered him. "I've had more time, since I started rounding them up. I'm out here with them for days and days." He shook his head. "It seems to affect each one differently. Some of them are worse than the wildest animals. They're violent, completely alone even when they're in a crowd, lashing out at others and even hurting themselves. And others—they look at me and at each other like they love and trust everyone. I know it'd be different if they saw a normal person and their hunger took over, but with each other, at least some of them are peaceful and content."

Now Milton was confusing me even more, because he said we were nice around him, but not around "normal" people—but then what was he?

"For all we know, some of them are gentler and more humane now than when they were alive."

I still didn't understand—was I a nicer person now than before I woke up? But what was I before then? If I were alive then, what was I now? I'm still not sure.

"And some of them seem to remember a great deal. They recognize each other, and they hold on to things, and I think they're happy, in a way. That's why I wanted to keep these ones apart. I think they'll be happier here. And the violent ones can do what it is they like to do somewhere else—biting and scratching and tearing at things. And the living can be safe. Things are the way they should be, I think."

Will shook his head. "If you say so, Milton. Just seems weird to me."

"It's not that different than what we've been doing with our own dead. We don't put them down or just herd them in with others—we put them somewhere safe."

"I know, Milton, but we knew those people. You said it was just too mean and impersonal to treat them like the others. But even that's a lot of trouble and danger to go to, even if you knew the person. For these ones we don't even know, it doesn't seem like it's worth it."

Milton smiled and shook his head. "I think sometimes you sound more like Jack than Jonah. Don't you see that it's no real trouble for me to take care of these people more carefully, spend more time with them? And if it makes them happier, then of course it's worth it."

I wanted to nod, and I really wanted to say something out loud, but I also didn't want them to know I was listening.

"I don't know how happy dead people can be, Milton."

Milton smiled again. He had the most peculiar smile, and he seemed to smile a lot. "That's funny, Will, because I often wonder the same thing about living people. I haven't noticed much difference. I believe Jonah will remember better than I do that there's an old saying somewhere that we can't be sure someone's happy until he's dead." He waved the younger man away. "Come, let's leave him alone. It seems rude to stand and stare at him. If you choose not to call him happy, that's fine. He's at least safe from us, and we're safe from him, and that is certainly a good thing."

They walked away and left me with all the new things I had found. I spent all that day going through boxes, and I didn't even finish with everything in that first storage unit. I could see that there must be dozens more in all the buildings, so I knew I'd be busy for weeks or even months. I cleared a space near the door, so I could sit on the sofa there, and I put a couple chairs in front of the sofa, though none of the others seemed to want to sit down, or really look closely at anything I'd found. They would just wander in, pick something up, drop it, and wander back out. After a while, I hid all the breakable things, or there'd be nothing left but broken little bits all over. I wasn't sure what we'd ever need glasses or dishes for, but I got tired of seeing everything just shatter on the concrete into useless little pieces.

I found some clothes and I could finally get out of the bloody, torn ones that I'd been wearing for so long. As I took off the bloody jacket, a wallet fell out of the pocket. I picked it up and looked at the contents. It held money, and I thought I understood what money was for, but I couldn't fit it into how things worked in the real world. I knew you were supposed to give money to other people to get things from them, but I didn't see how or why that was possible. Like the stuff in the storage unit, things just sat around and people could pick them up—why would you have to give someone something in order to get what you wanted? I understood trading: I'd already enticed some of the other people to give up a fragile object by offering them something else in exchange for it, so I could get it away from them before they broke it. But I really couldn't understand why someone would give up something in exchange for these little pieces of paper. The pieces of money were sort of pretty, but there were lots of prettier pictures you could trade.

In the wallet, I also found a couple of little plastic cards with numbers on them. I remembered that these were like money, only their operation was even stranger and more mysterious, because when you gave one of these cards to people, they wouldn't keep it, like they would money. Instead, they would give you what you wanted, plus give the little card back to you. Both the money and the little plastic cards made me feel uneasy in some way, and I stuffed them back in the wallet and then stuck the wallet between the cushions of the sofa.

Besides these, there were two other plastic cards with a picture of a man on them. I had found a mirror among all the stuff and I looked until I found it again, which took me a minute, as I had hidden it with the other breakable things. The picture was of me, though I had to touch my face, it looked so dry and grey compared to the picture. But it was definitely me. Both these and the other cards also all had the same name on them—"Wade

Truman." It was my funniest experience yet, as I concluded it must be my name, but of all the things I'd seen and heard so far, this one held less familiarity than many others.

I tried to make the sounds of the name, in case hearing it would help me remember, but of course it didn't come out right, so that was no help. I just had no connection between the name and myself. I thought the first name reminded me of water and I thought that was good, as I always felt so dry and thirsty all the time and it'd be nice to have a name that sounded like something as good and pure as water. And I knew there had been a president named Truman, but that was a long time ago, and I wasn't even sure what a president did and I was pretty sure there weren't any anymore, at least not around here.

One of the cards had "Department of Motor Vehicles" at the top, and the other read "Stony Ridge College" above my picture. I knew the general implications of these places, but not how they specifically related to me. I knew what a car was and that this card proved I knew how to drive one, but I didn't remember if I had a car, or what it was like, or how it felt to drive it. And I knew what a college was, but I didn't remember being in one or what I did there, but I suspected, since I knew so many strange facts and ideas, that maybe I was a professor. That seemed kind of nice, though I suspected that, like presidents, there probably weren't any of those around anymore.

Unlike the other cards or the money, the ones with my picture didn't make me uneasy. In fact, I sort of liked them, so I put them in the pocket of the new pants after I put them on. I felt a little funny, getting undressed there in the open, but once Milton and Will had left, I didn't really feel like I was being watched, even though the other people who couldn't talk milled around near me. The other clothes I put on weren't new, of course, but they were old clothes that had been packed in big plastic bags, so they were dry and clean, and not all stiff from caked-on, dried blood, like the ones I discarded. These clothes smelled nice, too, like soap, and I had to admit that everything on me and on the other people around me smelled foul. Our clothes were dry, dusty, used up, like dead leaves—not even the wet, slimy kind you find in puddles or under other leaves, but the dry, brittle kind that are getting closer to being dust than they are to being leaves anymore. I was glad to have new clothes.

They were kind of loose on me, but I thought they looked nice enough. There was a flannel shirt and some pants and they felt coarse, but also comforting, like a scratchy blanket. It took me forever to negotiate the buttons, both on the clothes I was removing, and even more so on those I was putting on, because with those, I didn't want to tear any buttons off as I fastened them. I got so frustrated when I'd gotten part way through and saw I had more buttons than holes left to match up with them, so I had to undo them, line them up right, and start over. But by the time the sun went down—which was pretty late, because it was getting to be almost summer—I had everything on, even some comfortable shoes.

I would've said it was time for a walk, to show off my new outfit, but I still wasn't very good at walking. Also, there wasn't anyone around who would show the slightest interest in my appearance, so there seemed to be little point in such an exertion.

I dragged one of the chairs outside the storage unit and sat down. It was an old lawn chair, the kind with green and white webbing across an aluminum frame. The frame was a little bent, and some of the nylon straps were torn, but it was still usable. After the day's discoveries, it seemed the perfect night to sit outside and dream of all the things I would find and learn in the days to come. I looked up into the purplish dusk as the sun's light faded and the stars came out. I wondered if I'd ever know what kind of a professor I was. Maybe I was a janitor at the college, or a security guard, or a cook in the cafeteria. Without anyone to see whatever was wrong with my smile, I went ahead and smiled at that thought, as it really did seem quite amusing.

I folded my hands in my lap, and as I did so, I suddenly tensed and my body seemed more numb than normal. It was another of those things I hadn't noticed, another obvious thing that hadn't occurred to me, like leaving the city hadn't occurred to me for so long. I felt a ring on my left hand. I felt it with my fingertips and it was smooth, just a plain band, without any stone or setting. And unlike the college identification card, that could mean only one thing: there was a Mrs. Truman, and, quite probably, even little Trumans. Or at least there had been at one time, back in that time and place and identity before I woke up. And even more disconcerting and far less amusing than not knowing if I were a professor or a janitor, I realized I knew nothing of these people. Even if I could look for them, I wouldn't know them if they walked right up to me. Maybe it was just as well. Milton had said some of us were nicer now than we had been before. Maybe I hadn't been very nice, and the rest of the Truman family would remember that. Or maybe they were violent and angry now, like many of the other people I had met.

I tilted my head back to look up at the stars again. They looked very small and cold, and in an odd way, mocking. I wondered who or what it was that could be punishing me by taking away the memory of myself, my life, and my family, and leaving me only with such random, disorganized, but most of all, meaningless knowledge.

Chapter 5

School was not quite over for the spring, so the day after I went shooting with my dad, I was back in class. Our community didn't have enough kids to divide us into age groups, or "grades" as our elders called them. Since there weren't many people born right around the time the old world ended and ours began, bigger kids like me were in classes with anyone ten or older. We used part of an old school building for classes, so I had some idea of the enormous scale of the old world, but I still find it hard to imagine that those rooms were once *filled* with children. To multiply that by the thousands of towns and cities I see on an old map—that makes it harder to grasp than the idea that there were once billions of people on the planet.

It almost frightens me, the idea of all those people jammed into cities, all those children packed into schools. I know I'm not supposed to say it, but I find myself wondering if things are better now. Only the dead are crowded, and we're free, the way I like to be. Again, I don't know. Maybe people back then liked being all crowded together. Still, the idea frightened me, and I liked the way I was living in my world.

Even though all of us bigger kids were in the same class, we did go to different teachers for different subjects, which apparently is how it's always been. Mr. Caine, Vera's dad, taught English. I always liked him. He was quiet and intense, not easy-going and cheerful like my dad. I thought it was nice how he was so different from my dad, yet they were such good friends, like they needed each other for balance or guidance in some strange way. I hoped I could find a friend like that someday, but only with the transition to Piano Girl did I begin to have a normal social life, so I was a little behind on forming friendships with the other kids.

Vera and I used to play more when we were little. I always envied her light brown complexion; her dad was white and her mom was black, so in the winter, her skin was the color of wheat, and in the summer it would darken all the way to a walnut brown. Mine varied between porridge white—all mottled and pasty—and steamed crawfish pink. And of course, there were all the ugly freckles across my cheeks and nose. But the two-year age difference now seemed more of an obstacle between us than when we were younger.

She still believed boys were gross and smelled bad. That summer when I was twelve, I could begin to see how they were strangely interesting, even compelling, though I still wasn't sold on the idea of having them or their smell around all the time, or too near. Sexuality was something my mom had explained to me soberly and clinically, and something about which the kids at school constantly tittered, lewdly and ignorantly. But either way, it was something I understood only vaguely and abstractly. For that year, I was content and intrigued to observe boys from a slight distance, but I knew things were different now than they had been when I was younger.

Of course, none of those vague feelings that boys might not be smelly little toads applied to my younger brother, Roger, even though, overall, we had the kind of playful competition and bickering that siblings always have, with no real harsh feelings between us. He had always been the extrovert I never could be, and the cheerful, boisterous personality of my dad was much less appealing or even bearable in the smaller package of my little brother.

Tall for his age and athletic, he barely tolerated the piano lessons to placate our mom. For me, the piano had been part of salvaging my social life. For him, it was an impediment, though even back then I knew he was being an unusually good sport to go along with it for our mom's sake. A lot of kids wouldn't have, or would have complained even more bitterly and frequently. Of course, Dad had something to do with keeping the complaining to a minimum, as he didn't take much off us two kids. He kept us in line, and made us as strong as we needed to be in this world.

But Mr. Caine and Milton both made us strong, too, even if their methods and the strength they built were wholly different and even hard to pinpoint or describe. As I had tried to articulate it to my dad, and as I have since come to understand it better, his was the strength of certainty, of facts, of tools and guns; theirs was the strength of curiosity, doubt, mystery, and awe. I was lucky that I thrived on both, and by my twelfth year, I sought them out like they were food or water. A book felt as right in my hand as a pistol; the anxiety and frustration fed by some of the books Mr. Caine assigned were as satisfying to me as the pistol's report and the clang of the frying pan as I punched another round into it. I was lucky, even if that luck and the gratitude for it only dawned on me gradually as the years passed.

Mr. Caine had all of us bigger kids finish the school year with a play by Shakespeare. The youngest of our group, the ten- and eleven-year-olds, had read *Julius Caesar*. The rest of us, twelve and up, were split between *Macbeth* and *King Lear*. Since not everyone had read each play, we went in groups, giving class presentations on the plot and characters and answering some basic questions of interpretation or historical background. I presented on *Macbeth*, though I had read both of the others in my spare time. As I said, I was like that back then, reading and studying whenever I could.

Looking back, the plays other than *Lear* were straightforward enough, and the theme tying them together was accessible enough even to adolescents—kings gone bad, corrupted by personal flaws and bad decisions, turned into familial and national tyrants, bullies, and murderers. But there was something unreal about all the plays, and as often as I kept things to myself, sometimes I could find a voice for my frustration, as I did that morning. "I don't understand why we read these, Mr. Caine. The plays, they're all set in a world even before yours. They talk about kings and queens and empires. I can look all those things up in a book, but they're not part of our world. I mean, there are even witches and ghosts in these books—those never existed, they're just made up. None of them matter to me. Nothing in these seems real."

I had read enough books about mean teachers—I'd already read *Portrait of the Artist as a Young Man* on my own—to know how far out of line I might be considered, and how cruel and wicked people could be. But I had known Mr. Caine my whole life, and I had as little fear with him as I had with my dad. I knew he loved good questions—not frivolous or nit-picky ones, though he would patiently answer those, too—but challenging ones, ones that got to the *why* of what we were reading or discussing.

He just nodded, then looked out the window. "I see your point, Zoey. Maybe I shouldn't have picked all plays about kings. I should've seen how the very concept of government—let alone something as ancient as kingship—would be too distant and alien for you."

It was how he always answered a question, I realized later—by agreeing with the questioner and admitting to being wrong. The only person more disarming with rhetoric was Milton, and both men had always held me enthralled. "But let's think if that's the only thing these plays are about. Zoey, the play you read, *Macbeth*, what was it about? I mean, the main character was a bad king, but what is it about, besides what a bad king is like?"

I had read enough on the play to know the basic answers. "Ambition. Power corrupts. Revenge. What's appropriate for each sex." There were some snickers. "Some people think he wrote it in support of the Tudors."

Mr. Caine smiled. "Everyone—ignore that last one!" There were chuckles from the people who were paying attention. "Reductionism, Zoey? I'm shocked!" I almost smiled too, but held back, as it was another of the things—like my hair or skin or voice—that I found especially ugly and awkward that summer. "As though I would assign you something that was just about some bit of historical trivia, as though a work's beauty could be boiled down to something so mundane! But the other themes—

yes, they're all in there. And maybe we're blessed with not having to worry about those today. Nobody has too much ambition, or too much power. We're all just struggling to survive. So maybe those themes are irrelevant to us, too. But I think you missed one theme, Zoey. It's biggest in *Lear*, but it's in *Macbeth*, too."

He had me caught without an answer. He was so good at that, but it was never mean—if I'd had the answer right to hand, he would've praised me for that, and if I didn't, like now, he'd coax me along. He didn't want to prove me wrong, he wanted me to be right. So all I could do was shake my head and wait for his help.

"It's in probably the most famous speech in the play," he hinted. "'Out, out, brief candle.' I know you know what that speech is about."

I was surprised then that I'd missed it. "The meaninglessness of life."

He nodded. He smiled at my success—he always did, and the smile's sincerity was complete and made you feel like you were as tall as the ceiling—but I also saw the sadness in his eyes, the sadness of an old-timer. "I imagine you've thought of that more than once, haven't you? Maybe more than we ever did in my time."

I nodded. What else could one say in a world where life was so small, brief, and fragile, and death was so terribly large and durable?

"I think we all have." He looked back out the window. "And what about the supernatural parts in all the plays? You said those things aren't real, they don't exist. When I was your age, we thought like that, that the things people used to believe in were superstitious and silly and science would solve everything—every disease, every problem, every fear would be gone, even death. I think we stopped believing in monsters, and that was our mistake. What we got was quite different than we'd expected or hoped for. And I think what we got was much closer to what Shakespeare thought the world was like—a world where there are many things we don't understand and can't explain, things that frighten and amaze us. And the biggest one of those mysterious and frightening things is right here." He tapped his chest. "It's us. And I don't think that has changed much, either. Even the people out there, the ones who are dead, they're still us, they're still threatening us because they're like us and they remember what it's like to be human, and we know a little bit what it's like to be dead inside."

"Like Banquo," I said quietly.

He turned back towards me and nodded. "Quite. Or Lady Macbeth, who wastes away so slowly and painfully. I don't think ghosts and monsters are as unbelievable as I used to think when I was your age." He paused again and looked out the window. "Well, I'm monologuing again at the end of the day, aren't I?"

"Like in *The Incredibles*!" my brother helpfully offered, and all I could think was "knucklehead," though I kept my reaction to an all-purpose, dismissive eye-roll.

Now Mr. Caine really smiled and the laughter was throughout the room. "Zoey and Roger, perhaps sometime you can explain this to us. When your father, in all his infinite wisdom and care, finally splurges and fires up the generator, why is *that* the only kind of film he ever shows to the rest of our wonderful community?"

"It's one of his favorite movies!" Roger informed us.

Mr. Caine kept smiling. "I thought that was *Die Hard*."

"He's showing that in a couple weeks. He promised us when school was out he'd show all five of them in a row!"

"And I'm sure that'll be worth every precious ounce of fuel and every minute of your valuable time. Well, with that wonderful treat in our future, class dismissed."

The other kids scrambled out of the classroom for lunch. Mr. Caine stopped me and Vera before we ran out and asked if we'd have lunch with him. We often did this, since he was her dad and he and I talked a lot now, getting ready for my vows. On the way outside, we passed Mr. Enders at his little station by the door. He was the school guard. I doubt he could've done much to stop anyone, living or dead, but he was an older man, and it made him feel useful to sit there with his nightstick and whistle and sign-in sheet. He waved us by as he and Mr. Caine started their back-and-forth, which I had heard with very little variation, most days, for the last seven years.

"Morning, Mr. Caine."

"How's it going, Mr. Enders?"

"Oh, can't complain."

"That's good. No one would listen to you if you did."

Chuckles followed. I had always wondered how they decided on the script, because when my dad walked by Mr. Enders, it was always, "Hey—working hard? Oh, no, hardly working!" Even back then, I marveled at Mr. Caine's ability to segue seamlessly from the highest speculation and analysis down into meaningless banter. It was another of his charming ways of putting people at ease, because he did enjoy his quips with Mr. Enders, for what they were. There was never any condescension or fakery in it.

We went outside and sat on the ground in the shade of the school building. Mr. Caine talked to Vera first, asked how her day had been, what she'd done in her other classes. She was kind of at an awkward age at that point, because she both did and didn't want to be treated as a child, but Mr. Caine was always flexible with her moods and listened to her carefully. Of course, I was no less awkward, as I only wanted to be treated as an adult, but lacked the experience, strength, or discipline always to act and respond as one. But again, I never felt nervous or anxious around him.

All our lunches were meager at this point in the year, before new food was harvested in the summer. I was chewing on some jerky that required extensive application of saliva before my teeth could have any hope of defeating it, even if the odds were 28-to-1. I also had more of Mom's crumbly bread and some dried nuts. Mr. Caine had a bunch of apples from last fall that required extensive surgery with his pocket knife to get out all the bad spots. He shared the good pieces with me and Vera as he cut them out. They were mealy and slightly tangy from having fermented some in the skins, but eating is mostly about the company, I knew even then, and for that I was grateful.

When Vera had said enough about her day, Mr. Caine turned the conversation more towards me. "Ready for your vows, Zoey?"

I shrugged. How was anyone ready? It was built up as this big deal, but I still didn't know everything expected of me. "I guess. Dad says I'm really good at all my fighting skills."

He kept cutting around in his apple. "I'm sure you are. Your dad is great at that. He used to teach me all the time, back before you were even with us. I doubt I would've survived without his help."

It was the same as in the classroom. I didn't feel like what we were talking about was relevant, and I wanted him to know. "How am I supposed to feel? I just feel like I've been training, and now there's this ceremony—I went to someone's last year, but I don't see what it's supposed to mark or make different about me."

He kept at the apple, nodding as he worked the knife. A smile curled up his lips as he thought, and I knew I was in for something. "Funniest thought just occurred to me, Zoey. I remembered as clear as crystal why I wanted to become a professor all those years ago when I was working for it and studying all the time— what it would offer me, teaching older students, so that some of them could become teachers, too. For almost a decade, I prepared to answer questions like you just asked. I got all the right words and categories for it, for dealing with how complex it would be. I learned several other languages, so I could study what other people had written on a difficult topic. And now it's so funny, because I can't explain it to someone for whom the answer really matters."

He chuckled—not like with Mr. Enders, though he had been sincere then, too—but deeper, quieter, up from the place where we laugh at ourselves and still feel good about it. "So I'll try my best, Zoey, but the words are all big and wrong, so bear with me. I remember at some point, I realized that all real knowledge is relational." He looked at me for the first time since he turned serious over lunch. "It just means that real knowledge—not mere facts, like 'Zoey is a girl,' but deeper, more fundamental knowledge, like 'Zoey is now an adult,' or, 'Zoey is a good person'— knowledge like that is not some thing floating off in the mind of God, or off in a detached, objective plane that we get glimpses of if we try really hard. It's part of and made up of all the relations Zoey has with the world around her. And forget all the mundane, physical relations, like that Zoey is on top of the ground or under the sky. I mean the deep relations Zoey has—that she loves her mom and dad, and thinks her brother is goofy but loves him anyway—those relations. You understand?"

I nodded. "I think."

"Okay. So if all the deeper, more important knowledge is relational, then it means that we don't merely *know* these things—the way I know that Zoey is a scrawny little girl, for example..."

Vera tittered at her dad's joke at this point.

"...but that I *will* these things, I *decide* them to be true for me, I *choose* to have a relationship with this knowledge in this way. So that's what your vows will be about. It's not about whether you know how to fight—anyone who's seen you knows the answer to that, it's an objective fact. It's about you deciding with every ounce of your will, and then saying in public, that you commit your life to the service of others. That's a relationship. That's a vow. And how are you supposed to feel? Like you're committing to something new and different and important and scary. So is that how it feels, Zoey?"

I nodded and swallowed some of the slightly sweet, mostly sour apple. Yes, it was how I felt. It was like the change in how I felt about boys—I wanted to keep it at bay or tame it, but it was a shift that had taken place and I couldn't deny it or postpone it, and I both welcomed and feared it.

Mr. Caine squeezed my shoulder. "That's all I can do to explain it, Zoey. But you know your dad and I think you're ready, and that should tell you something. I remember the day I first saw you. We were having a bit of a bad day, let's say. There had been a lot of killing and destruction and I wasn't sure we were going to make it. I was scared, really scared, but for one moment I forgot my fear and thought only of you, how the only thing I wanted was for you to survive. And now you've not only done that, you've grown into as good a person as any of the rest of us. You'll never disappoint any of us. Just know that, and I think your vows will be the way they're supposed to be."

I nodded as I bit another apple piece. It was mushy and sour, not like you expected or wanted an apple to be. I didn't like it, exactly, but I knew it was the way an apple was supposed to taste in June, and that was enough for me.

Chapter 6

In the days that followed, I continued to explore the storage units and find useful and interesting things. Even though I was sad that I had a family I could no longer remember, I remained curious and eager to learn about all the things the world still held that were beautiful or good or true. There were a lot of tools in the storage units, and I probably could have figured out a way to get through the fence, but I'll admit I was too scared to try it. For now this seemed a good enough place to pursue my reeducation.

I found a lot of books in the storage units. I think this place was for storing things people didn't really want, or at least things they didn't want where they could get them easily and use them. So it surprised me there were so many books there, because books were just what I wanted, though I noticed the other people in there with me didn't seem nearly as interested in them. The only things that held their attention for more than a second were shiny things made out of metal, or things with buttons and knobs, and even these they just dropped after a few minutes.

Maybe the books hadn't just been forgotten in this storage place—maybe they had been put there in case of emergency, to survive whatever it was that had happened to make all the people leave the city or die. Maybe there had been a war or a natural disaster, and this was the special facility to guard against such eventualities by preserving the people's knowledge and other special items. I liked that thought better; it made me feel as if I were fulfilling an obligation to study what had gone before and keep it alive. That seemed like what a professor should do. If that's even what I was. But it was what people in general should do, I think, so what I was before didn't matter anyway.

It was then that I first tried writing my ideas down. I had found some paper, along with some pencils and pens, and though most of them didn't work, a few had useable points, and I tried writing with those. It proved as impossible as speech. I couldn't read it myself afterwards, even though I knew what it was supposed to say, so it would be completely useless for communication. Something was wrong with my body and kept me from doing these basic things. That's why it was so lucky I eventually found this typewriter, but that didn't come until later.

Some days passed. A big, springtime storm blew through and the sign above us came crashing down into our area. No one else seemed to notice, but I made a point of finding a broom and sweeping the broken bits away. Then a few days after that, Milton and Will brought more people to stay here with us.

"Look at him," Will said as he and Milton studied me. "He's changed his clothes. Like he cares what he's wearing."

I looked at what I was wearing and frowned. Well, if I *really* cared what I was wearing, I think I would have hunted around for something a bit nicer than *this*. A faded flannel shirt and some scratchy woolen pants? Hardly the height of fashion or vanity. The shoes were the only things that fit and felt right on me. But I couldn't very well walk around, crunching every time I moved because of all the dried blood on my clothes, and with that big hole in my middle making me feel cold all over. It was just common sense, though I did wonder again why I hadn't thought of it before, back in the city.

Then I looked at the other people in the storage area with me, the ones I'd come with and the ones who had just entered, and I saw that most of them were torn open in places, or had parts missing, and most all were covered in dried blood, but they didn't seem at all interested in new clothes. It wasn't like I'd kept the clothes to myself or hidden them like the breakable stuff. Once I'd found the ones I put on, I left the box out, but the other people just rummaged through it and flung the things around and I had to keep straightening it up again. But I left it out anyway. It wasn't like the breakable things. If the other people liked throwing the clothes around rather than wearing them, that was their right, and I had no authority to prohibit them. It was sort of my job now, when I wasn't reading or looking at other things, to pick up after them. I didn't mind. It gave me a purpose, more responsibilities, and I liked that.

Milton now looked at me and my new clothes. This time I didn't pretend not to notice him, so I looked back, though I had put my books away when I heard them coming. There was no sense in having them know everything about me, until I knew more about them and their intentions. Milton smiled his odd smile again. I remembered a word for it later: he had a very *eccentric* smile. That's the right word. But it was a nice smile. It made me think he cared, and while he was surprised at what I'd done, it didn't upset or alarm him. If anything, he seemed rather pleased. I half hoped he'd give me more things to do around the little compound, but I didn't know how to ask him that, or even if it was his place to do so. "Are you happy in there?" he asked.

I shrugged. I could've been a bit more enthusiastic, I suppose, but I still didn't like them feeling as though they were doing me a favor by keeping me locked up, even though it was true that it was sort of where I wanted to stay now. "We don't want to hurt you," he continued. "Do you understand that?"

I looked at Will for a minute, then back to Milton before I shrugged again.

Milton looked at Will, and then back at me. "Yes, Will can hurt you, if you try to get out or if you try to hurt someone else. It's not safe for people like you to be wandering around freely, because you might hurt someone else. But you can stay here and be safe. All right?"

This time I nodded, because I appreciated that he had gone to the trouble of explaining why I had been put there. He probably knew what I had done to the woman back in the city, and he certainly couldn't have known how I felt afterwards and how I would never do that again. Even if he had known how I felt, I couldn't blame him for not trusting me. And he must have been able to see how the other people around me pressed on the fence and tried to get to Will to attack him. As he had said the last time he had come by, things seemed to be the way they should be. And I was glad for it, though still a little sad by being lonely in here and unable to communicate with others.

Will and Milton left after that. I liked how Milton had some sense of my need for privacy and didn't stay and watch me longer. I got my books back out. I was reading a biography of Abraham Lincoln and I liked it very much. I had some of the same problems with reading that I had with everything else—my body wouldn't cooperate. In particular, my eyes kept slipping in and out of focus, like I couldn't control them. But it just slowed me down, and time was one thing I certainly had in abundance.

As I was reading, I noticed someone from the new batch of people had approached my cubicle. At first I kept reading, as the other people had always just shuffled by without really noticing or trying to interact with me. But this person stood near me, swaying slightly and looking at me, so I put the book down, so as not to be rude, and because now I was curious about this new neighbor.

I don't suppose staring at her was any less rude, but I didn't know what else to do at first. I already knew speaking was out of the question. Smiling hadn't seemed to work properly with Milton and Will, and motions of my head or shrugging could only work if she asked me something, which seemed highly unlikely. So I sat just observing her.

She was in a summer dress, faded to a grey with darker splotches so you couldn't tell what the pattern or color had been. Her left side was terribly mangled, a stretch of bloody cloth mixed with torn flesh from her neck to her abdomen. Her left breast might have been in there somewhere, but it was indistinguishable. On top of this mess, her head tilted to the left side and slightly forward. Her blond hair was pulled down on that side and was stuck to her left eye and to her neck with dried blood. Her right eye was a brilliant blue. It didn't sparkle, of course—none of our eyes do since we don't have tears to moisten them, which was something else I envied the people who can speak—but it was a couple shades darker than the sky on a sunny day. It was how I imagined an uncut and unpolished sapphire would look, though I had to admit I only remembered the word "sapphire" and that it was a kind of bright, blue jewel; I did not recollect actually seeing one myself. And this one tiny disk of perfect, living blue around a black pinprick was now fixed on me, and I could feel its intensity and vitality filling me up.

I scanned the rest of her shamelessly, I admit, and it all was as perfect as her one eye. She was slight, like most of us, of course. But the swell of her remaining breast and her hips still looked completely feminine and graceful. Her legs were far too thin now, but instead of detracting from her beauty, they made it poignant and fragile and utterly irresistible. When I first looked up at her, the sun was gushing about her from behind, setting her alight, igniting her golden hair into a crown around her half-face with its bone-white skin. She reminded me of the stars I'd seen the other night, before my thoughts turned lonely, when I had seen them as perfect needles of light in the cold dark of the sky. She was the most beautiful thing I think I'd ever seen.

I finally shook myself loose from all this rude staring and brought my gaze back up to hers. I stood up, but then I made an awful mistake. I just couldn't help myself, and I raised my right hand to pull back her bloody hair. She growled and bared her teeth as she pulled back from me and batted my arm away. I quickly withdrew my hand. I was aghast at my own behavior, and how she might not trust me now. I thought I needed to make some kind of amends, so I pushed the box of clothes towards her with my foot. She looked at it quizzically and suspiciously. Then she tried to reach down to it, but her joints seemed stiff and she let out a pained moan as she first tried to bend at the waist. Then she tried to kneel, and the sound this time was a horrible squeal. She could accomplish neither of these movements and both seemed to cause her pain—I suspected not only from physical discomfort, but from the indignity and shame of not being able to make her body do what she wanted, what she needed it to do. I could see her clench her fists and start to shake.

I knew just how she felt, so I reached over to her and—being very careful to put my hands on her arm and shoulder and not bring them near her face—I helped her sit on the sofa. Then I picked up the box off the floor—causing some significant pain to myself—and set it next to her, so she could go through it without moving around. She eyed me first, and I felt myself melt again under the gaze of that one tiny, perfect globe. She nodded to me slightly, and I was glad; it seemed I had made up for my terrible indiscretion before.

She went through the box much more carefully than the others had, even perhaps more carefully than I had, pausing over several items and not just immediately picking the first things that might fit her. She was small all over, and for some reason I estimated she was a size four, though I again had no idea from where such knowledge came. Now that she was seated, her movements were very smooth and fluid, not jerky and halting like those of the rest of us, and not pained, as her movements had been when she was standing. Her hands were tiny, and of the same exquisite hue as her face—a pure, guileless white like unfired porcelain. She could use her hands much better than I could, grasping things with just her thumb and index finger, while I had to sort of scoop them up with my whole hand. She made a pile of clothes in her lap, then went through this pile and returned most of the things to the box.

She tried to stand, but again she had difficulty. I thought she was getting up to go somewhere else to put the clothes on, and I knew there were other people now wandering all over, so I didn't think she'd find much privacy. I also didn't think she could manage to change clothes while standing up. So I stood up and waved at her to stay on the sofa. She stopped trying to rise, but still looked at me plaintively, not knowing what to do. I went outside the storage cubicle and slid the door down till the bottom of it was about two feet from the ground. I thought she'd still have enough light to see that way. I heard a wheezing sound that seemed affirmative from her, and I waited there. I could hear her moving around and moaning—some motions obviously still caused her pain. I heard the affirmative wheeze again, and I slid the door all the way open, though slowly, in case I was wrong and she hadn't finished yet.

She had managed to stand up on her own. I can't say she had chosen the things I would have picked for her to wear, but I'm sure she had her own desires and judgments of what would be comfortable or attractive. She had pulled on what looked like pajama bottoms—baggy, blue, plaid pants. On top she had a loose, black, cowl-neck sweater. I looked down and saw that, unlike me, she hadn't chosen shoes that just slipped on, but had sneakers on and had actually tied their laces. In her left hand she held a long, silky scarf of yellow and orange. I was in awe of her. Everything was too big and graceless for her delicate, beautiful form, but again, it seemed to make her happy, and that was all that mattered.

I stepped around her to a closed box where I had put the breakable things, and I got out a mirror. I held it up for her. She nodded. Then she raised the scarf she had been holding and wrapped it around her head, diagonally, to cover the left side of her face. She tied it and looked from the mirror to me. Again, it wouldn't have been my choice to cover her this way, but maybe she was self-conscious about her left eye. There was enough of her beautiful hair still spilling out from under the scarf that I didn't mind it too much. And the scarf didn't look bad, either, for it added some color to the otherwise dark clothes she'd picked out.

I nodded back at her and we sat on the sofa together. I offered her books, but she didn't seem interested in those, so we just sat. It was getting too dark to read, anyway. I wasn't even sure how many other people could read, but I was sure there was something special about her, judging by how she looked and moved. She would be one of the good and beautiful things I could find out about now. And now I wouldn't be lonely. I hoped she would be happy now, too.

I got up and with some difficulty I slid the sofa—with her on it—slightly outside the opening of the storage unit, so we could sit together under the stars. I wished I knew her name, but didn't see how that would be possible. Asking was out of the question. I thought of my cards and how I'd found out my name, but I remembered women usually carried such things in a purse, and she hadn't had one when I met her. Knowing of how captivating her eye was, I decided I would call her Lucy, for I suddenly remembered—from nowhere, as usual, with no indication of where the information came from—the story of the saint and how beautiful her eyes were and how holy she was.

We sat there throughout the night—with me gazing at Lucy, and her looking up at the stars. Now things really were the way they should be.

Chapter 7

A few days later, I went out with my mom to a smaller river nearby, partly to collect some early strawberries from the fields there, but mostly just to take a break from the normal routine. Dad was going out with Roger to hunt, so my mom wanted to do something with me. We packed a picnic and headed out in the morning, not quite as early as the men, but still pretty early.

We left our house on our bicycles and started pedaling south. We were going farther than Dad and I had the other day, so the bicycles were the best transportation. We had several cars in front of our house—most people did, since there were literally thousands of them just lying around, abandoned, and only a few hundred people in our community. Many had been wrecked when all the people had died, but most were still usable; almost all were at least salvageable for parts. But we only used them for important errands, as fuel was still at a premium, especially the real gasoline and diesel. I could remember when we began producing bio-diesel, but it still was unusable during the winter months, and we weren't able to divert enough of our food production to make the fuel in sufficient quantities. So for now, fuel was conserved, usually for driving the trucks that would gather more resources—tank trucks to gather fuel from faraway gas stations, or large flat-bed trucks if we were going to cut down trees for firewood and lumber.

Mom and I went through the old part of the city, the part that Milton first cleared of zombies when I was too small to remember. All the streets here had been cleared of abandoned vehicles—mostly by just pushing them to the side, not actually taking them away—so bicycling was easy and pleasant here, though eerie, going past so many empty cars and buildings. The streets that weren't regularly used were being reclaimed by plants growing up through the pavement. Most of the buildings were tagged with warnings, as they were unstable and would probably have to be torn down and rebuilt before people could use them. If there were ever that many people again.

We first went south because in our part of the settlement there wasn't a gate in the main security barrier. We lived in a part of the city where the people had built walls connecting a number of abandoned warehouses and other buildings, then boarded up the buildings, tagged all of them with warning signs to keep people away, and now the walls and buildings together acted as the northern border of the central city, the live zone. Guards patrolled this barrier regularly, several times a day.

Beyond this was land, like the field Dad and I had gone to, and the one Mom and I were headed to now. Milton had cleared out the dead, and then a fence had been put around it, enclosing miles and miles of empty space that now served as our source of food—by farming, hunting, fishing, and gathering. These lands were sparsely populated, and the outer fence wasn't checked as often, so these weren't considered completely safe.

Teams took turns going around it in circuits that took a couple days to complete. They often found small groups of the dead gathered, pushing against the fence, and they waited while Milton was called to round them up. They also sometimes found holes in the fence. Some of these were from burrowing animals, but some meant worse problems and dangers. Beyond the outer fence were only the dead, so far as any of us knew, and Milton was rounding up those close to our outer fence and was putting them in enclosures outside of our lands. We only went into these wild, dead areas in well-planned incursions to gather supplies, not pleasant outings on bicycles.

Mom and I got to the main street and turned east. This took us past the museum, where life as we knew it started with a few people barricaded in against the dead. Although our limits were much wider than the few hundred square feet they had had, life was more or less the same as it had been, and a quantum leap away from the kind of life depicted in the museum exhibits. For us, the airplanes and satellites in the museum were as removed from our daily lives as the cave drawings of far older tribes; if anything, the last technological achievements of humanity were far more alien and mysterious than the bows and spears of some of the museum's dioramas and display cases. In a way, though, the museum was the center of our community, its touchstone with the past, and the symbol of its survival.

We waved to some older people who were there, trimming the grass around the wall. Through the open gate I could see the helicopter on the ground among the big, abstract sculptures. The chopper was still maintained for emergencies, though its fuel was even rarer and more precious than regular gasoline.

Just past the museum was one of the guarded gates out of the live zone. As in our part of town, the buildings on either side of the street were boarded up, and they formed part of the barricade. Across the street a brick wall had been built, connecting to the walls of the buildings on either side. The building to the right had been a warehouse with loading bays. To exit our city, one of the guards would open a loading bay on this side, and the people or vehicle would enter the building, then exit though another loading bay on the other side of the wall. It meant the wall could be made stronger and permanently anchored to the buildings and the pavement, rather than being a metal gate that had to be hinged or drawn back.

A guard was on the roof of the one building, and another was on the street, holding the leash of a big dog, a Rottweiler, black and sullen-looking. The guards often used them when patrolling, and although the dog didn't make any aggressive move or bark, I still shivered a little at the sight of it. I'd always been afraid of dogs. Something about them seemed wrong, like they knew too much and too little at the same time. I didn't know how to express it, but I knew the effect they always had on me, as useful as they were.

Both men smiled and greeted us. The whole arrangement was a necessary precaution, but it was hardly run like a military operation. Dad sometimes said it was more like a neighborhood watch. "Hi Sarah… Zoey," the man at the wall said. "Where you headed?"

"The South Fork, past the bridge. We'll be back late in the afternoon," Mom answered.

"Great." He wrote down our information on a clipboard, so if we didn't come back, someone would know to come looking for us. He eyed me warily and didn't ask how I was doing. His son, Max, was a year younger than me, but he'd been known to jump in and call me names back when I was Zombie Girl and some of the bigger kids were picking on me; I don't think he ever had the nerve to hit me, though it was hard to remember some of the times I was doubled-up or on the ground. That summer I was old enough that I wouldn't necessarily have begrudged him the pleasure: if it earned him points with the other kids and kept him from being picked on, if I was going to take a beating anyway, what did it matter if he had gotten some licks in? Maybe my pain would've at least served some small, good purpose.

I wasn't sure if Mom and Dad had ever talked to Max's parents, so I wasn't totally sure what his dad's aloofness towards me meant. I always wondered how much the parents went along with their kids' ideas of who was a weird or undesirable member of the group. I mostly looked at my bike as he opened the door to the warehouse and escorted us through.

"Have fun. Be careful," he said as he opened the other door to let us out.

We got back on our bikes and pedaled away as the big door clattered closed behind us. I looked over my shoulder, back at the brick wall. There were eight small, dull-green rectangles on this side of the wall—four on the ground, and four on brick shelves built into the wall about five feet up. I couldn't read the writing from this distance, but I knew what it said on each of them—"FRONT TOWARD ENEMY." Claymores. Not the sword—

though I'd seen one of those at the museum, and not even my dad was strong enough to run around swinging that as a weapon. These were M18A1 anti-personnel mines. One and a half pounds of C-4 and seven hundred tiny steel balls behind a plastic casing. They were set to be triggered by the roof guard, rather than with anything as dangerous and indiscriminate as tripwires—or what the manual termed "Victim Initiated Detonation." Apparently, in the old days, such mines were just left lying around, ready for a victim—like a child—to detonate them. Even with the mindless dead wandering around, I couldn't imagine being that callous and brutal. Dad, of course, had pointed all this out to me; he made me read the operations manuals for nearly every weapon we owned, and for many we didn't. As with learning to fight with sticks, my knowledge of lethal—or even just harmful—things extended far beyond what was only useful against the walking dead.

Pedaling between the two buildings, for the next few seconds Mom and I would be in this gate's kill zone, or what the manual termed "the area of optimal lethality and coverage." If every-thing—and I mean absolutely everything—fell apart and there was a real horde of thousands bearing down on us, the guards were supposed to try and lure them into this area between the two buildings and in front of the wall, rather than let them bang away on the softer targets of the building walls, which even undead hands could probably break through pretty easily at this point, given the inevitable rust and rot from twelve years of lowered maintenance. Considering how the dead herded together, this would pack a few hundred walking bodies into a rectangular area that would then have thousands of little steel balls flying through the length of it at very high velocity. No guaranteeing how many would hit heads, but definitely some, and enough of the rest would just ruin someone's day, as my dad would put it. I was proud to know all this, and glad to have it here, just in case, but I was also really glad when Mom and I cleared the edge of the buildings and were in a land of less lethal constructions and more living sights.

The roads out here weren't completely cleared of wrecks, so we slowly weaved between them as we pedaled down the road. Plants grew up through the pavement everywhere. The decaying suburbs and industrial parks around the perimeter of the city trailed off into farmland and countryside, dotted with partly collapsed hulks of buildings being reclaimed by the land. Some of the fields here were cultivated, corn mostly, with some wheat and a little bit of cotton, and some fields were left to grow as grass for livestock. On the right the rows of an orchard stood out. The grass between the trees had been kept down, and there were even rows of smaller trees, planted recently to replace the old ones as they gave out. Butterflies and moths flittered everywhere, and a few cows and sheep grazed in one field, but we didn't see or hear any people.

My mom looked back at me and smiled. She was always so busy at home, I knew she liked going out like this. She didn't even have her hair in a ponytail, and it cascaded, unfettered, behind her in the breeze. Such a concession to being carefree always meant she was feeling happy. Even with a few streaks of grey, she still had the most beautiful brown hair, especially compared to my dull, black locks, which neither curled nor shone like hers. I was glad she was looking so happy.

We turned left down a road, and after a little ways we came to a bridge across a small river. The bridge had collapsed into the water, and logs had been washed down in successive floods to accumulate around the partially sunken, crisscrossing bands of metal. We turned right to follow a smaller road alongside the river. For a while we were under trees, which felt nice, as the rest of the ride had been under the warm, early summer sun. Then we came out from under the canopy into an overgrown parking lot by the river. The river at this point was backed up behind a small dam, over which it spilled; on the opposite side of the river you could see the remains of a run and a mill building that had used the falling water for power.

We parked our bikes and looked around. There was a line of trees next to the water, but otherwise the area was open on this side of the river. There were the remains of a small building at the far end of the parking lot, and you could still see the metal frames for swings and slides sticking up out of the grass. There were some picnic tables made out of concrete under the trees, and we put our stuff on one. I had my jacket and I draped it over the concrete bench; the HK 9mm was in one pocket and the magazine was in the other. Mom didn't know about that yet, but out here especially I knew to have it nearby.

We took the two cloth sacks we had brought and started looking for strawberries. We'd been to this field before, so we knew there were lots here, and we weren't disappointed. Oddly, strawberries were one of the things every old-timer swore was better in the old days, even though food in general was something which many found to be superior now. Older people would go on about how much better milk tasted now, or how much bigger and juicier blackberries or corn were now, but apparently human agricultural science had found one of its few victories with the strawberry; I thought it was strange that that was the best they'd been able to do, but I was also sure allowances had to be made for the faultiness and selectivity and wishfulness of people's memories. Either way, the small, bright red berries seemed fine to me, as tart and firm as they were. But long before we had exhausted the supply to be picked, we had worn out our backs; strawberries are one of the worst things to pick, since you're either doubled over, or on your knees the whole time. We grimaced, then laughed as we stood up and went back to the picnic table to rest and have lunch.

Mom and I ate some of the berries we'd picked as we got out our lunch—crumbly bread and hard-boiled eggs again. We'd brought our own water, as the river could be muddy this time of year, and there were enough animals out here that giardia was always a worry, especially with runoff into bigger streams like this river. We ate in the shade and listened to the water cascade over the dam.

"It used to take just a few minutes to get here by car when I was little," Mom said. She could get wistful, too, like Mr. Caine, but now she seemed mostly happy as she ran her hand over the gritty top of the picnic table. "We'd have picnics here when I was little, with my parents. And when I was bigger, like in high school, this is where you'd go when you wanted to be alone, you know, with other kids."

"With boys?" I mostly wondered about them to myself, but since she'd brought it up, I thought maybe I could get some more information on the mysterious other half of humanity.

She blushed, but not as much as I thought she might. "Well, yes. Things were different back then."

"Boys were different?"

She smiled. "Um, no. I'm afraid boys will never change much. But yes, when I was a little bigger than you, sometimes I'd like to be alone with a boy."

"What did you do then? Did you, you know, kiss? Was that different back then?"

She looked a little shocked, but she also smiled. "Zoey! And what do you know about kissing boys?"

Now it was my turn to blush, and with my skin, which I was convinced was so gross and ugly, I knew the florid pink showed a lot more and a lot less attractively on me than it had on my mom. "Just, you know, kids talk about it, that you're supposed to do it."

She watched me as she nodded and chewed slowly. "Well, yes, when I was your age, and a little bigger, people would talk about kissing all the time, how important it was that you do it. So I guess that part isn't very different. And people talk a lot about things they know very little about, Zoey. I think that's the same now, too. You shouldn't ever do something just because people are talking about how you're supposed to."

"I know, Mom."

"I know you do. You'll be fine. Those little shits—pardon my French, but they still make me so upset—all beat you up when you were little. I don't think anytime soon you'll be doing anything for them because they tell you that you're 'supposed' to."

I smiled, not at the real content of what she was saying, but at the funny expression about French; I wondered if there was anyone left anywhere who still spoke French. I doubted it.

"But anyway, what I meant is how different it was when we'd come here to be alone, because when you left town back then, this was about the first place you'd come to where there weren't many people. The whole way out here there were restaurants and gas stations and houses and you'd see people and cars everywhere; and just now we came all the way out and didn't see anyone. And back then, there'd have been a bunch of people even way out here, especially in the summer. If we were here back then, the parking lot would be full. There'd be hundreds of people here, more than we have in our whole community."

I nodded. I was more interested in boys, but I hardly wanted to press the point, and she had put some of my questions into perspective. "It doesn't sound so nice, when you talk about it that way."

"Hmm, I suppose not—not to someone who's not used to those kinds of crowds. But it was nice, in a way. Like when all different people were having picnics—my gosh, the things you'd hear and see and smell. I would walk around while my parents fixed lunch, and I could go walk all around here for several minutes without hearing any English, just all kinds of other languages. And the food—I mean, we'd have sandwiches, and some other people would have other regular stuff like hamburgers, but I'd also smell curry and lamb and chili and all kinds of spices I didn't know, things I'd never expect to see at a picnic. I remember Indian women in their colorful saris, and one time, over on the other side of the parking lot, I saw a whole crowd of maybe thirty people, all facing the same way. I thought they were posing for a group photo. Then they all fell to their knees at the same time. They were Muslims, and it was time for their prayers. I sometimes wonder if there are any Indians or Muslims left anywhere. Do you ever think of that?"

I nodded. In school, Mom taught us Spanish, and Mr. Caine did the best he could to teach French—though he admitted it wasn't what he was good at; I often wondered how many other languages were now gone forever, every last speaker of them reduced to mute undeath. But most of the time, speculating about what might have happened to other people made little sense when we were busy enough here.

She shook her head. "I hope there are. I miss all those wonderful differences between people. It's just that life is so plain now." She smiled and ruffled my hair with her hand. "Except you. You're as fancy and beautiful as anything I ever need."

I frowned and pouted. That summer I could be insufferable, which I half-realized even at the time. "Stop it, Mom. My hair and my skin and everything looks funny. I wish I looked different. And I know after the vows, I'll look even worse."

"No, you stop it. We just talked about not listening to what stupid kids say who don't know anything."

There was a moist, slapping sound off to our right. We both turned. A wet sneaker had made the sound on a large, flat rock next to the river. The sneaker was on a foot, which belonged to about three-quarters of what had once been a man, sometime back before I was born. Now it was a shambling, slimy bag of clothes and flesh. And death. It had plenty of that, and was eager to share. It rose up as it brought its other foot out of the water and turned towards us. It grinned. Well, let's say it opened its mouth in a way that made me think it was very eager to get closer to us, though the normal, human feelings of joy or humor were long gone. It took another step, slowly but very deliberately and somewhat more dexterously than I'd been taught to expect.

My mind went completely over to my training and the cold analysis of the situation. I scampered around to the other side of the table, where my jacket lay. Mom had jumped almost as fast and was rummaging through the picnic basket. "Shit," she muttered, a little alarmed, but overall much more in control than I might have expected. "I know I put a .38 in here. Here it is!" She brought up a short-barreled revolver, not the standard four-inch barreled one I usually used. "The ammo is in my jacket pocket."

"Don't worry, Mom."

"We'll have to shoot it. We can't leave it wandering around this close to town, inside the outer fence. Milton is way out in the wilderness."

"I know, Mom." I had the 9mm out and was sliding in the magazine. I racked the slide and chambered the first round, just as Mom slapped a handful of cartridges onto the table. By the time I turned and raised my weapon, the thing had taken another two steps; as I said, it was way faster than I liked, and I was glad we wouldn't have to load the revolver in this situation. Its right arm was gone, but otherwise it was in better shape than most, unless they'd been hiding in buildings and protected from the elements. This one still had some clothes and both its eyes and ears. When it grinned, I had seen that it still had most of its teeth. I made a note to ask Dad if maybe the water preserved them better, so we could plan accordingly. I squeezed the grip as I sighted. Then I squeezed the trigger as I exhaled.

I placed my weapon on the table. Mom and I sat down, still looking over at the wet pile of clothes and flesh. "How'd it get here?" Mom asked quietly.

I shrugged. That was not part of my training. I noticed my hands shook now.

"Maybe it was pinned under water until it could tear its own arm off and get loose," Mom said. "Maybe it washed downstream with the spring floods. I guess there's no telling." She looked at the 9mm on the table, then at me. "When did you get the gun?"

"Dad gave it to me. Don't be mad."

"I'm only a little mad you didn't tell me. I knew you'd need a gun of your own soon. You and your dad will pardon me if I wanted to put it off as long as possible."

I got up, thinking of everything I'd been trained, remembering my duties. "You think we can burn it in the parking lot without starting a brush fire?"

She shivered as she gathered our stuff. "I guess we have to."

"Honor the dead. It's our duty."

We dragged it over to the parking lot, so it could dry in the sun while we made a pile of grass and sticks. We placed the body on top, and I ignited the pyre with a knife and a piece of flint. We unfortunately could not stay upwind the whole time it burned, as we had to keep moving around to stomp out the little fires where sparks had blown off the conflagration. It was a smoky, nasty affair and it took much longer than either of us would have liked.

When it was done and we left, I wondered whether we were supposed to honor the dead man by coming here more often to gather strawberries, or if, instead, we were to honor him by avoiding this place for anything as frivolous as gathering bright, little berries right by his burnt bones. Desecration and sanctification seemed so close in life. As I watched my mom's back, I also wasn't sure what she would say; she had somewhat surprised me with how calm she had been during the whole attack, how composed and resigned to what we had to do. And though I had some preference for the kind of honoring that would include berry-gathering, I couldn't tell if that was only because I liked strawberries. I would have to ask Milton about it, as I was unable to decide which was right. Perhaps both were. Perhaps neither.

Chapter 8

In the days that followed, Lucy and I explored other storage units. I found so many books I had to prioritize them, deciding which I would like to read first, and which things—like books of tax laws or computer programming—could just be left out for the others to rummage through, since they seemed to like that. We hadn't found anything yet that Lucy liked as much as I liked books, though I felt sure that soon we would.

She wasn't as visual a person as the rest of us. Shiny, bright, or colorful things didn't seem to interest her. This would explain why she'd picked an outfit of completely mismatched, dark colors. I liked this about her because it made her different from the others, but it also seemed sad, since her one good eye was so much clearer and prettier than those of the rest of us, yet it didn't seem to function as well for her. I couldn't remember the word for that at first, but then I found it in one of my new books. It was *ironic*. But not funny in the humorous way, I don't think, just sad.

Lucy seemed serious and not given to humor in general. And she really seemed to be searching for something in the boxes, intent on finding something we hadn't uncovered. Every afternoon, after looking all morning, I'd settle on the sofa to read, but she would keep looking. I didn't mind; I knew she'd be careful with everything, not like the others, and she'd put everything back where it had been. Sometimes she'd bring me a book, and I thought that was nice of her. Then later in the evening, as it got dark, she would join me and we would just sit. She would sit closer to me now, leaning against me, and I liked that. Like pain or tears or speech, I understood what sexuality was, but I knew it was not a part of me now. Nonetheless, I liked Lucy to be near me, and I wished I knew what she was looking for, so that I could help her find it.

Then one afternoon, as I sat reading, Lucy sat down next to me with a small black case. In it there was a violin and bow. She tuned the instrument, though my hearing was either not trained, or sensitive, or perhaps undamaged enough to distinguish the difference or improvement. Then she held the violin between her chin and shoulder and started to play.

Again, I'm no expert—I'm not even sure whether or not I like violin music—but from Lucy it sounded divine. In a way it was the perfect complement to her stunning, feminine beauty, that she could make such captivating and enchanting music. And best of all, I could see how happy it made her to play like this.

I looked past Lucy to where the others were shuffling around. They continued moving restlessly about, occasionally stopping near us, seeming to listen for a moment, the way they would occasionally grab something from a box, examine it for a second, then wander off. I understood how lucky Lucy and I were to have at least some of our senses intact. It also helped me understand why we didn't have the same preferences. Lucy's sight and her ability to process or understand visual images must have been diminished, along with some of her ability to move her whole body, while her hearing and her love of music were still acute and her dexterity with her hands was exceptional. And I had trouble focusing, I wasn't very dexterous, and my hearing was not especially attuned, but I had retained the ability to read.

And the other people? I still wasn't sure what they were capable of. I suddenly felt scared and sad that each of them might have some little part of themselves that still worked perfectly, but they couldn't express or share it with others because of all the clumsiness and inertia of their bodies, the same reason poor Lucy had struggled for so long before she'd found her violin.

As for Milton and Will, they were a complete mystery to me, what their abilities or deficiencies were, beyond their ability to speak, which all of us here seem to lack. Maybe they had fewer deficiencies overall, and that's why they were in charge. Or was it just because they could hurt us, the way Milton had implied when he'd seen me looking with fear at Will? But he'd also said we were locked in here to keep us from hurting other people. Overall, the situation confused me, but at the same time I felt much better than before, now that Lucy was happy.

Lucy and I would still spend our mornings together, searching through the treasures in the storage units, though she didn't have the same urgency and frustration as before. Mostly she would find more books for me, and sometimes she'd find other things she liked, especially if they made some sound, like music boxes or other musical instruments, though everything that needed electricity or batteries was useless. We found an old bicycle, and although neither of us was coordinated enough to ride it, it had a bell on it that made the most welcoming tinkle, so Lucy wheeled it over to our area so she could ring it now and then. Then we would spend the afternoon together on the sofa, though now we both had something we liked, and that made it so much nicer.

One afternoon as we sat there, I could hear the others getting more agitated and making noise. I put my books away, because I suspected it was Will and Milton. I gently touched Lucy's hand, to indicate to her that she should put down her violin too. Then I noticed she was sniffing the air, baring her teeth, and growling. I knew then it must have been Will by himself, or someone like him, someone the others perceived as both a threat and food.

I stood up and held my hand in front of Lucy as I shook my head. I had wondered whether she still tried to eat, and I had no way to tell her that she shouldn't, but I was worried for her—worried either that the others might hurt her as they fought to get at Will, or that Will would hurt her. I wanted her to stay here with me. She remained seated, but she kept sniffing and growling.

I stood and moved farther out from our cubicle so I could see the main gate, but I kept my hand on Lucy's shoulder. The gate was closed, but the other people were congregating around it and making noise.

Then Will came running along the fence and—quicker than I thought possible—he climbed it, threw a tarp over the barbed wire at the top, and pulled himself over to our side. He looked at me, then ran back towards the others, who were slowly turning away from the main gate to catch up with him. A second gate separated the area around the office from the storage units, and Will pulled this closed and wrapped a chain around it and locked it. Lucy and I were trapped in here with him, and he was safe from the other people, who were now locked in the area between the two gates. I didn't like this at all, and I helped Lucy stand in case she had to get away or hide. I didn't know what to expect.

Will approached us. I kept Lucy behind me and extended my arm to keep her from attacking Will. On her feet she moved more slowly and awkwardly than I, so I could keep her back, but it was an effort, and I was trying also to watch Will.

He approached slowly with his hands out in front, his palms towards us. I noticed his clothing more than I had before, now that he was closer. He was dressed all over in a heavy material, denim or canvas. It was patchwork, like it had been worked on and repaired many times. He also wore a glove on his left hand, and this, along with his left arm, had bits of metal sewn on to the thick fabric. It was obviously a kind of armor he'd made to keep people from biting him.

"Easy there," he said quietly, though his voice was still hard, commanding, not like Milton's soothing tones. "I just want to talk some more, and Milton keeps taking me away like you need privacy or something." I was happy to see that Milton understood what I was feeling and had been considerate. "I just want to find out what you know. You obviously understand what I'm saying. Can you speak?"

I shook my head.

"All right. But we're communicating okay so far. Is this your girlfriend?"

I looked back at Lucy. I didn't want to embarrass her, as obviously I had never referred to her as that before. But she took her eye off Will and stared straight at me, and I knew she wouldn't mind. I nodded.

Will shook his head. "Wow. That really takes some getting used to. You don't...?" He shook his head more vigorously. "No, never mind that. I can see where Milton was right about some things being private. Okay. You don't seem to want to eat people, is that right?"

I nodded again.

"It doesn't look like she or any of the others have the same tastes."

I shook my head.

"All right. Milton's always talking about how you all are still part of our community, and we should respect you. And most of the time, I see all of you just bumping into each other and trying to eat people, and I think he's lost it, and we should just shoot you all in the head." Lucy got very agitated at this. I really didn't know how much speech she understood, but something insulting and threatening seemed to have gotten through at that point.

With an inhuman snarl that rose to a shriek, she shoved past me and lunged at Will. She was far too slow and clumsy to catch him by surprise or overpower him, and I was sure she'd be dead in seconds. Will stepped into her lunge and brought his gauntleted left hand up; her mouth clamped down on it. He was big enough and strong enough that from that position he could hold her at bay and keep her arms from reaching him. Given how muscular he was, and how obviously used to fighting, I suspected he could snap her neck from that position too.

I stepped towards him, and even though I was faster than Lucy, I hadn't even taken a full step when the barrel of an unbelievably huge revolver was in my face. I didn't know much about guns, but I was pretty sure that when the hammer was pulled back—as it already was when Will raised it to my face—then it was really bad to be where I was, in front of this end of the barrel.

Besides its size—which was beyond belief, so much that I couldn't believe Will could hold it rock-steady at arm's length like he was—it was also an exceptionally shiny revolver, which starkly contrasted with the infinite blackness inside the barrel. For the first time that I could remember, I realized what death was, and that I did not want to die. But I also knew I had to defend Lucy.

Will shook his head very slightly. "No," he said, staring me right in the eye. "I'll paint that wall with your brains before you twitch, Mr. Smart Zombie. And then I'll do the same to your girlfriend. So why don't you explain to her—however you explain things—that it'd be a good idea for her to let go of me. All right?" He clenched and unclenched his teeth from the pain her bite was obviously causing him.

I kept my eye on the gun and took a step back. I didn't understand the thing he had called me, but I understood what needed to happen. I placed my hand on Lucy's shoulder and held her gently as I gave her the low wheeze that we used to express something indistinctly positive or affirmative; we hardly had the exact vocabulary for what Will wanted me to communicate, nor for what I really wanted to say, which was that I loved her and didn't want her to be hurt. She was unbelievably taut, vibrating from the anger and exertion of clamping down on Will's hand. I squeezed her shoulder more, but still gently, and I kept up the low sound until finally I felt her relax slightly. Will's hand slipped from her mouth, and she and I stepped away from him.

Will took a step back as well. "Okay. Now the gun stays out when we talk. I was trying to say something nice, lady zombie. I said that I think of shooting you all because you act like animals, or worse. Having a whole pen full of you is too much like having a pen full of rabid, starved wolves. I don't like it. But you two seem to be different." Will tilted his head to indicate me with his chin. "He doesn't eat people, and you both seem to understand it when I talk. And you seem to like each other. He almost got his head blown off just now, trying to defend you. There are plenty of real people who wouldn't do that for a girlfriend, or anyone else, and there are plenty of real people who'll hurt and kill for less than food."

Again, I didn't understand in what way Lucy and I weren't "real," but there was hardly a way for me to pursue the issue. "So I'm trying to say that maybe you two aren't so bad, and I can take you out sometimes to see other stuff. Would you like that?"

As happy, indeed idyllic, as things were here with Lucy, I had been thinking that eventually we would want to go out and see what else there was, once I got over my fear of wild animals, violent people, and other dangers. From what I had just seen, few people could be more dangerous than Will, so it might be useful if he came along with us. Lucy still seemed sullen and aggressive, but I could tell she'd been thinking along similar lines. We both looked back to Will and I nodded.

Will nodded as well and holstered his gun. He looked more closely at me. "You remind me of someone. I think it was my fifth grade social studies teacher. He was my teacher that last year, when we still had a real school and subjects and books." He shook his head. "Social studies? What the hell is that, now? Things that don't exist." He looked like Lucy, almost snarling. Then he relaxed a little. "But he seemed nice, is what I'm trying to say. You look a lot like him." He looked even more intently at me, squinting his eyes. "No, couldn't be, that would be too much of a coincidence. Do you remember who you were?"

I took a very slow step towards him as I reached in my pocket and offered him the identification card from Stony Ridge College. He took it and glanced at it, and looked more closely at me, then handed the card back to me. "Yup, that's you. The people who raised me after my real parents died, the man used to be a college professor. He's nice too. But it's not like having your real parents." He shook his head. "Well, Truman, I hope we can be friends. Does she have a name?"

I wasn't about to mangle Lucy's name with my voice, and even if I did, she'd never heard herself called by that name anyway. It applied to her only in my dim mind. Still holding her, I pointed to her eye with my other hand.

"What?" Will asked. "One Eye is her name?"

I shook my head.

He looked at her more closely. "What? Blue Eye? Yes, it is unusual, not like the eyes you all usually have. So, lady zombie, may I call you Blue Eye?"

Lucy nodded slightly. I think she even smiled a little, and coyly.

"Thanks. The next time I come back, we'll go somewhere. I'll check a map. It'll be fun for a change."

He went back to the gate that was holding the others back. He unlocked the chain he had put through, yanked it off, and ran back towards us. He tossed the chain over the fence, then he was up and over it before the other people could even get the gate open. I watched him walk away and wondered what I had gotten us into.

I led Lucy by the hand back to the sofa and we sat down. I felt so drained from the intense and conflicted feelings of fear and devotion I'd felt when Will had drawn his gun. But at the same time, I knew I owed him a debt of gratitude. Because as I gazed down into Lucy's perfect eye, I could see she knew my feelings and commitment better than I ever could've explained them to her on my own. We leaned against each other and I felt closer to her than I ever thought I could feel towards anyone ever again.

Chapter 9

Finally, the day arrived when I would take my first vows. I dressed in the plain grey pants and sleeveless shirt that Mom had sewn for me. I spent most of the day alone, away from others, according to the custom. I had read up on rites of passage enough to know it was standard to separate the inductee from the community before she is reintegrated with her new status. The intellectual understanding of it from books and the real experience of it were as different as reading a cookbook and eating, for throughout the day I could feel how inappropriate it would be for me to be around others right then. I didn't just understand the necessity of my being alone, I craved the loneliness as much as I both craved and feared the rites I knew would come at the end of it.

During these hours alone, I fasted and tried to prepare myself mentally for the commitment and devotion necessary. I had also read enough to know that my time alone and my attempts to contact the higher, non-physical or metaphysical powers of the world would have been called "prayer" in the old world. It was still a fair enough label, if one could subtract all the trappings of organized religion—which I knew about only from the books I had read, and a few scattered comments from older people, who seemed ambivalent about it, overall. Organized religion was as alien to our life as were the concepts of state and government and money. But just as we retained the need and desire to be in a community with others, so also we yearned to commune and unite with something more than our own weak, mortal selves, even if every creed and sect that had ever promised such a union were now dead, so far as we knew. And on the day of my vows, this longing was acute, filling and stretching me much more than the physical hunger compressed and tightened my small body.

As I prayed, I asked no questions, made no requests, but only felt the deepest gratitude and vulnerability before the world. And from somewhere both within and beyond me, I felt the certainty that those feelings were directed towards something that would never ignore, scorn, or abuse them. Such feelings have filled many of my days before and since, but I remember vividly that it was on that day I first became fully aware of them.

Finally, a couple hours before sunset, my parents came and we climbed into the big SUV Dad used for longer, special trips, when fuel conservation was not an issue. As we drove away, people lined the streets and waved, sending us off. The guards at the gate ushered us through the two bay doors, and then we were on our way into the countryside. Dad and Roger were up front. Mom sat in the back with me, and she'd squeezed my hand when we first got in, but then she'd retreated slightly to the other side of the vehicle, and we were all quiet for the trip. As Mom had said on our bicycle trip, we covered a lot of land quickly with the truck, reaching the very edge of our domain in far less time than Mom and I had taken for a much shorter trip on our bikes. We arrived at a grove of trees on one side of the road, with two other vehicles parked under them, and some people standing and sitting around. Dad pulled up beside them and turned off the truck.

We got out as Milton, in his "dress" white robe, strode up to us. It was always amazing to me, how much energy he still had at his age, and living the life he did, out among the dead most of the time, living off the land. The other people there included two sets of the guards that patrolled the outer fence; this far out, and expecting to stay after dark, extra precautions were always in force.

There were also two families with children who would be up to take their vows next year; Max and his parents were one of these families.

Milton smiled at me and laid his hand on my left shoulder. "Welcome, Zoey. Please be at ease as much as you can." He turned to the other families to include them also. "That goes for you other children as well. Nothing here is meant to frighten or upset you. It is only meant to teach you of the world we live in, and our responsibilities in it, and to do so in a reverential way—for of all feelings, reverence is the one most appropriate and necessary in our world. And now, everyone, please follow me."

We all followed him into the woods a little ways, my mom and I at the front of the group behind Milton. My dad had taken his MP5 submachine gun out of the back of our truck; it was a small, nasty, indiscriminate weapon that I'd never trained with, but like every weapon, I knew its use and capabilities—in this case, throwing lots of slugs around in a short amount of time at close quarters. Dad slung it over his shoulder. The other men were similarly armed with submachine guns or assault rifles, the kinds of weapons one wanted when near so many of the dead bunched up in a group.

The steps of the ceremony had been explained to me, and last year I had attended one as preparation. I felt a freezing stab to my heart when the moaning began off to our right, though I didn't miss a stride or flinch. Neither did my mom, so far as I could tell, watching her out of the corner of my eye.

As we walked on, the moaning did not crescendo, but stayed steady; it was a rather subdued and calm sound. Slowly the chill released my heart and I could begin to feel what Milton had described—reverence, not fear. Stepping slowly and deliberately, I could tell clearly that if anything demanded reverence for its power and ubiquity, it was death, which was calling to us that warm summer night—constantly and incessantly, with neither malice nor love, but only with complete and patient inevitability.

We stopped in a small clearing in which there was a large, flat rock, about the size of a small, low table. Some of the other men handed out and lit torches. Dusk was rising around us. With every passing minute, the trees closed in nearer and nearer to the clearing we were in. I sat down on the rock, with my mom standing behind me, facing in the direction of the moaning. At first, I could almost think I saw shapes moving in that direction, but in just a few moments, no matter how hard I strained to see, there was only darkness there among the trees.

Milton now stood before me and addressed us briefly before the actual rites began. "At one time, when I was much younger, in a different world, when people thought of rituals or religion, they most often thought of something called faith or piety. I'm not sure I can tell you so much about those virtues in our world today, for we who have seen so much have little inkling or desire for things that are unseen, and we have little to put our trust in, little to believe is steadfast and reliable."

He looked right at me, and I felt as if he could see the things I'd been thinking during the day when I was alone. "Zoey, if any among us have faith, it might be you, I think, as I look at you now. But if you do have this mysterious, precious quality, then all the rest of us can do is look upon you with awe and rejoice for your wonderful and unknowable gift." He returned to looking at the others, but the memory of his gaze and the strength it gave me lingered. "But I can say that tonight we celebrate two other virtues that I know all of us can share with Zoey—hope and love. To me, she has always embodied these, as a sign of hope and love's triumph over despair and wickedness. So Zoey and Sarah, if you are ready, we will begin."

Milton handed my mom a pair of hair clippers—old manual ones, not electric, so they would still work. As he handed these over, he spoke the first words of the ceremony proper: "Hope for the future often requires a sacrifice in the present."

I felt the cold metal touch my scalp as my mom intoned, "And love for others always requires a sacrifice of oneself." I felt the slight motions as she started to shave my head. I stared straight ahead, all my muscles tense, too tense. This, too, I knew from my reading, was a pretty standard part of initiation rites, marking the inductee as physically different from the rest of the group, with strange markings or clothing. It also tended to erase gender distinctions and put the inductee in a threshold state outside of normal social conventions.

Again, the experience was quite a bit more vivid and consuming than the theory. With each motion of the clippers and each tickling tumble of my hair down my neck, I felt colder and more alone and vulnerable. And with the first pinch, followed by the moist warmth of blood on my head, there was considerable discomfort to the operation, which I countered by biting my lower lip and gripping my knees with my hands as hard as I could. I knew it was a tradition that the rite was considered especially auspicious if the shaving were done without a drop of blood being shed, or with a lot of blood. Therefore, after the first nick, the person clipping felt a strong temptation to make more "mistakes." I knew my mom would do anything to avoid hurting me, and I knew that both she and my dad were especially practical and non-superstitious people, but I also knew—and more importantly, I respected—that tradition drives much more of what we do than many of us would like to admit. So once I felt the first accidental cut, I expected—even craved—more. And I was not disappointed.

With my head bloody and bare, I sat as Milton and my mom gathered up as much hair as they could from the rock and the surrounding ground. Again, from a purely objective, intellectual perspective, I was sure that drawing some blood was intended to help with the next part of the ceremony, but at the time, gripping my knees and trying not to shake or cry, the only thing I felt was the most intense hope that my hair and some of the blood on it would work and the rite would continue well.

Milton, holding the pile of hair in a fold of his robe, walked off into the darkness in the direction of the moaning. The sound diminished slightly for a few moments, then it rose to a shriek and a howl. I relaxed my grip on my knees and nearly wept at the sound; it was the first positive accomplishment in the rite, meaning that my offering was acceptable.

Though it was too dark to see, I knew Milton had gone to the fence behind which the dead of our community were kept, unable to hurt us or be hurt by us. The area had, appropriately, been a small cemetery with a high, wrought-iron fence around it. This fence had been reinforced with more bars, so the smaller among the dead couldn't squeeze through. On a night of first vows, Milton would cast the initiate's hair in with the dead. Their reaction to the touch and smell of something that had so recently been in contact with warm, living flesh was usually wild and enthusiastic, as it was that night. We had no way of knowing whether this was only their ravenous, physical hunger for our bodies, or some residual longing and remembrance of what it had been like to be near us and touch us in less animal and destructive ways; the latter seemed too sentimental for the horrible reality of undeath, the former too cold and objective to grasp. Whatever it was that drove them, it was a connection they craved, and we owed it to them.

As Milton returned, the noise from the cemetery calmed back down to the persistent, welcoming moan. Now was the final part of the rite. My dad took my hand and we walked with Milton to the designated spot, just at the edge of the light and away from the other people.

In a loud voice, Milton continued the words of the ceremony. "Zoey, you come before us tonight of your own choosing, and with the full permission of your parents?"

"I do," I said, and my mom and dad agreed at the same time. My head was bowed slightly, and my dad was right at my side, his big hand on my right shoulder. I don't think it would've mattered much if I had looked up, it was so dark now in the woods, but the path had been laid and measured out so that as long as we took the steps at the right moments in the ceremony, we would be where we were supposed to be.

"Good. Then lead her forward, Jack." We took two steps as Milton spoke the next part. "Zoey, you are at the beginning of adulthood. You must tell us what this means to you and how you will follow your new path."

We stopped. It was hard to make my voice clear and loud, with my head bent down and being so nervous, but I took a deep breath and forced the words, as harsh as they sounded to me at the time. "Death is easy; life is hard. Childhood was easy, now life will be hard. I vow to put away childish things and always follow what is difficult, right, and just, as written in the laws of our community."

"You speak of what is right, Zoey, but there are many laws. On which two are all the others based? Tell me the first and most important." Two more steps.

"To protect the living."

"To protect the living requires much training and dedication. Jack Lawson, is your daughter ready for such responsibility?" Another two steps and we stopped.

I could hear in his voice Dad was nervous too, and he wasn't the sort, but Milton always made him a little uneasy, in a good sort of way—the uneasiness that comes from an intimacy full of difference and mystery. And in the dark woods that summer night there was plenty besides Milton to make anyone nervous in more physical, visceral ways. "She has trained long with staff and with gun, in all weather, at night and in the day. She is as ready as any of us to face life and serve her people."

"And the second great law of our community, Zoey," Milton continued, "the one we affirm this night most of all?" Two more steps.

The moaning right in front of me had not crescendoed, but I was so much closer that it was a palpable trembling throughout my head and body. Without tilting my head up, I rolled my eyes up as high as they would go, so I was looking in front of myself. The darkness was a blank curtain. I could hear the rustling of their clothes, and I began to smell them—no longer rotted, but simply musty, worn-out, like forgotten, useless things dissipating until only vapors remain. I over pronounced each word in a hoarse shout, casting it at the wall of dead sounds, "To honor the dead."

Milton paused. "That is correct, Zoey, and if it is the second most important law, it is often the more difficult. Take your final steps, Zoey." Two steps and our feet were touching a line of stones set in the ground to mark off this point as precisely as possible.

I could barely hear the snick as my dad flipped the safety on his MP5. "Anything goes the least bit funny, little girl, just get out of here while I take care of it," he whispered.

"You vow to honor the dead, Zoey," Milton called out from behind us. "Then receive from them their benediction. Let them welcome and bless you in the only way they know how."

I leaned forward and closed my eyes. With every inch I tilted forward and down, my dad's grip tightened on my shoulder more and more. He had explained beforehand how they always made sure the dead's fingernails were thoroughly trimmed; a few days previous he had been out here, yanking their arms between the bars of the fence and cutting the nails himself. But even so, as I felt the ghostly touches on my wounded head, all I wanted to do was throw myself back and scream. My empty stomach seemed to tighten even more and collapse downward to my pelvis, as though it too were fleeing the deathly fingers.

As the touches became more palpable, however, I relaxed slightly and let them glide and dance across my skin. There were no claws or calluses or scabs, but only papery skin that slid across mine, sought a purchase, slipped, and slithered back. The fingers were urgent, restless, mechanical, but also soothing, loving, and, most of all, pitiable. And so I willed them to be for a few seconds, as I let them grope me. Whether it was with human love or a hellish hunger, I knew I owed it to them and could endure it for their sakes.

"The dead accept and honor you, Zoey," Milton called out behind me. "Now return to the living." My dad pulled me back up, and we walked back toward the torches in the clearing.

My mom hugged me tight, sobbing quietly and whispering apologies in my ear for the cuts she'd inflicted on me. Milton and the others congratulated me briefly, mostly silently, with hand-shaking or pats on the back.

On the way back to the city, my mom and I huddled together in the backseat, just holding each other. She only spoke once on the ride, to whisper, "Your dad and I are so proud of you. And so are your birth mom and dad."

As Mom could so often do, she'd intuited the right thing to say, for I had just had my only sad thought of the evening—of all the dead behind the fence, I knew my mom and dad were not among them; they were gone from my touch forever, and that made them both safer and better than "regular" dead, but also far less real. My mom was showing how she had not forgotten them, and neither had I.

I sank into Mom's warm body and let myself nuzzle her. She caressed my head and neck. There was nothing to apologize for, or congratulate, or mourn over that evening, and I realized Milton was right—there was only a great deal to revere, and I knew how much I revered both my sets of parents. It was another feeling I've had many times before and since, but which first fully overtook and enveloped me that night.

When the truck stopped in front of the museum, I stepped out to perform the final denouement of the ceremony. I had asked that Mr. Caine be my vows-father, the member of the community who welcomed me back after my vows. He had helped me mentally prepare in many ways for what I had just undergone, and especially for taking in the meaning of it. Mr. Caine took my hand and led me to an enormous pile of wood in the parking lot in front of the museum. The petroleum smell coming off the wood was pungent and bracing, but welcome in a way. Everyone from town had gathered, some holding torches. Mr. Caine beamed down at me with his kind and reassuring smile. As in class, I never liked to smile, and in front of so many people it would've been unthinkable, but it was dark enough, and his smile filled me with enough confidence that I risked raising the corners of my mouth to acknowledge his encouragement.

He stood behind me with his hands on my shoulders. "Citizens of our city," he called out. "Zoey left us with great joy a few hours ago, and she returns with even greater joy and promise. She has returned with all the rights and responsibilities of a woman. She will serve and love others with all the courage and patience and strength a human being can, in good times and in bad. And we will continue to protect and love her as we have since the day we were blessed to find her. She will help light our way to a better future, as she will now light this fire."

He took a torch from someone nearby, then offered it to me. I instinctively reached for it with my right hand, as I had learned to shake hands and do most polite, social things like a right-handed person. Mr. Caine withdrew the torch and gently moved my right hand away. "With your left hand, Zoey," he said, softly enough that I was sure no one else could hear. "Don't pretend."

As I took it with my left hand, he smiled again.

"Being a part of a community should never be denying or hiding who you really are, Zoey, so don't start with that kind of a gesture." Then he turned from me and called out louder, "The light, Zoey, the light of this night is yours to give us."

I touched the torch to the wood and it flared up quickly. A cheer went up from the congregation.

Mr. Caine took the torch from me and handed it back into the crowd. Then he stooped a little to hug me. "Don't ever be embarrassed of who you are, Zoey," he whispered. "That should be one of your vows tonight."

He let me go, and scores of other people came up to congratulate me, their hands reaching for me as eagerly as those of the dead. But if anything, the hands of the dead frightened me less than these more lively and unpredictable limbs, especially when I saw some children my age whose parents forced them to "make nice" with the Piano Girl on the night of her vows. Though as the greetings wore on and the calm and honesty induced in me by Milton and Mr. Caine took hold, I could fully embrace this night's truth: all my fears were ultimately unfounded. I would serve the living and the dead, and they would let—or even help—me be happy and be myself. And we would do this, sometimes in spite of ourselves, and sometimes because of who we were. But as I felt the heat from the huge bonfire, as I felt dizzy and flushed from hunger and all the extremes I had gone through, I knew all this would always, somehow, happen because of that ultimate object of gratitude and vulnerability that I had intuited earlier, sitting by myself. I had truly returned to the community a changed person; or, I had returned to a community that had changed, so far as I was concerned. Either way, there was an intense feeling of awe, wonder, and vitality that night.

Finally they led me to food and drink laid out on tables under the stars. As I ate, people became more interested in eating and drinking, or in talking to others, or flirting, or dancing, and little by little I was left more alone at the periphery of the crowd, chewing and thinking. And as my stomach filled and hurt less, the cuts on my head tingled more—not with pain, but just with excitement and awareness. After the feast, we went home and I slept, more full and content and alive than ever before.

Chapter 10

A few days later, Will returned. I could tell by the same commotion among the other people locked in with me, though this time the commotion did not move toward the gate, but gathered off to the left of our little storage cubicle. I couldn't see Will over the other people, but I heard him shout, "Truman, take Blue Eye to the gate while the rest of them are here!"

I took Lucy's hand and we moved behind the others. Almost all of them were pressed against the fence and oblivious to us, focused only on Will, except a boy and a girl near the back of the throng, whom we had to push past to make our way to the gate. They growled at me, but Lucy growled back and they turned quiet and sullen. I didn't understand that other side of her, but I was always so happy she showed her beautiful side to me while all the others missed it.

After a minute of shuffling, we were at the gate. As we waited, I looked down at Lucy. I hoped this was not a bad idea, going out with Will. She looked up at me, and her hand squeezed mine as she gave a low, throaty purr. I knew she approved and wanted to go outside, too, so my fears were gone; I was doing what she wanted, which was the only thing that mattered.

After a couple minutes, Will ran around and let us out the gate. As he resecured it, he kept an eye on Lucy.

Will was wearing his usual protective clothing. "I was in town for a couple days," he said. "I had to see some people and catch up on what's going on there. But now, let's go where you want. I think I've seen everything around here, since I'm usually out here every day, so you go ahead and take the lead. Why don't you just start walking down the road? There are a few buildings, then it's fields past that. Go ahead."

We did as he suggested, walking down the cracked, over-grown macadam, the moaning of the other people fading behind us. I could hear birds singing, and I saw some fly by. Insects buzzed and flew everywhere. I even saw a deer before it bounded into some nearby trees. Lucy seemed enthralled by everything around us. When we had walked a little ways, Will came up along-side me and walked with us, though he still kept a little apart. I understood it was difficult for him to be near us since we were different, and I knew he still had to be cautious, as Lucy had attacked him before. But I was glad to be out, and I was very grateful he'd made the effort to help us and be nice to us.

As Will had described, the storage facility was near other buildings, or what remained of other buildings. With so much pavement around it to keep plants from growing, and with build-ings made of cinder blocks, brick, and aluminum, the storage facility had survived much better than others. Most of the other nearby buildings were made of wood, and more than half of these had collapsed in whole or part. A few seemed to have burned down, with dirty, cracked chimneys and skeletal, blackened spars of wood pointing up at the sky. But even these barely diminished the joyousness of this early summer day, as flowering vines had climbed up most of the structures, yearning for the sun. I felt sorry for all the people that had lived here, and I wondered what had happened to them, but I still had to feel grateful for the beauty all around us.

Near the end of the little group of ruined buildings, we came to one that had been a gas station. It had suffered much worse violence than the others. All the windows had been smashed, and at some point the canopy that had been above the gas pumps had collapsed. There were several burned out, wrecked cars under the canopy and around the building. "Besides the gas, there probably was a convenience store in there," Will explained. "For a few hours, that would've been a battlefield, with people trying to get gas or food. But then it was all over. You all won." I wasn't exactly sure what he meant, nor did I know what to make of his tone, which seemed accusatory, sad, and resigned all at once, as it did most of the time.

On part of the canopy's white sheet metal, which was now tilted down and visible from the road, someone had spray-painted "DRY" in bright orange paint. Will gestured to it. "When we get all the fuel from a station, we mark it, so people don't waste time on it later. That's partly why you all are here—we've gotten everything we can use out of this town, so no one will come to this area anymore. Now it'll all just sink into the ground and be covered over with plants. A whole town, just disappeared. And of course, they're all like that. Do you remember the town where you used to live, Truman?"

I shook my head. I thought it was nice of him to ask, though.

"That's funny, how you remember some stuff, but not things that relate just to you, like where you lived. What about you, Blue Eye?"

She stopped and considered the buildings around us. She shook her head, then raised her arm with her hand bent and the palm down, as if indicating something taller than herself.

I thought I knew what she meant—we had been able to communicate a little using similar pantomime—but I looked over to Will to see if he understood.

"You lived in a city," he asked, "in a tall building?"

Lucy nodded.

"It must've been the really big city east of here. That's where we found you. That's where Milton has been clearing you all out for the last couple years, but there are so many there, I don't know when he'll ever finish."

At the end of the little town, the road extended into the fields beyond, barely distinguishable beneath the plants. In the cracks and in the fields where the grass wasn't so high, I picked some dandelions and wanted to put one in Lucy's hair. Even after we'd been together and close for a while, sometimes she didn't like to be touched, and with someone else around I really wasn't sure how she'd react. I approached her carefully and showed her the flower. She smiled a little and I knew it was all right. Almost the same yellow as her scarf, the dandelion looked nice behind her ear. Out in the sun, she shone so beautifully, even more than at home, I thought.

Will smiled too. He definitely still looked rather serious, alert, dangerous, but not at all mean or angry as he had on previous visits. "Those dry up so quick, Truman," he said. He picked one of the ones that had gone to seed and blew the little parachute seeds off to float over the grass. "I used to pick them for my mom all the time. They'd be all closed up by the end of the day. Funny isn't it? They grow so fast, and take over the whole yard and choke the grass, but when you pluck them, they don't last as long as other things. Funny."

Among the tall grass in the field beyond the road, some lilies had grown. Their trumpet-like flowers were big and orange, with little black flecks, like brushstrokes. Will pointed them out to me. "Tiger lilies. At least, that's what I was told they're called. They'd last longer once you pick them. Go ahead. No reason for her not to have more than one flower." I did as Will suggested, and now a lovely pair of yellow and orange flowers peeked out from under her scarf, just above her blue eye, underlined by the pure, innocent white of her skin.

"But you know, Truman, you may be right," Will continued as he considered her. "Maybe dandelions are a good choice too. You could grow some where you live in that little patch of ground by the office. Here, pick some of the seedy ones and put them in your pocket."

All three of us started picking them until the two pockets of my shirt were stuffed. I could just barely tell that Will kept me between himself and Lucy, and I don't think she noticed. I appreciated his subtlety.

"Come on," Will said, beckoning us farther into the field. "There's a river over here."

There were some trees there as well. Lucy and I sat under one. Will jumped from rock to rock to cross the water and started gathering sticks and grass. "Guys, I'm really thirsty, but I need to boil the water before I drink it or it might make me sick. So I'll need to make a fire."

Lucy nudged me and I realized we should help. We made a little pile of kindling on our bank, but neither of us was nimble enough to jump across the water like Will. He saw us and laughed. "Go ahead and take your shoes off and step in the water. I mean, I guess you all don't get hot like regular people, but it might feel nice. Go ahead, if you want." He had a nice laugh, I thought.

I looked to Lucy, and we sat down under the tree. With her grace and dexterity, she untied her shoes quickly, almost as fast as I slipped off the ones I was wearing, which didn't have laces. Then we sat back down on the bank and let our feet touch the water. At first it felt too cold, like it would hurt us, but in just a second, it was delightful. Lucy gave the braying kind of hiccup that I knew was her laugh. To be honest, it was not the prettiest sound she made, but I accepted it the way she accepted my wrong-looking smile, for the emotion it contained, rather than its appearance. We sat there as Will gathered up all the grass and sticks into one pile, a little upstream from where we were. He sat next to it and raked a large knife across a dark piece of stone. Sparks flew out, and these startled me, but when the grass and tinder caught fire into a bright, orange blaze, I felt the heat and smelled the smoke, and I remembered how much flames frightened me. Lucy gave a little shriek and grabbed my arm.

Will put his hands out in front of himself, in a calming gesture. "Hey, hey, you two. It's okay. It's way over here, and I won't let it get any bigger. Just sit still and enjoy the water." Lucy and I both calmed down and nodded.

Will got out a large metal cup from a pocket of his jacket and dipped it into the river, then placed it at the edge of the fire. With a bigger stick he piled some embers around the base of the cup. As he waited for the water to boil enough, he took his boots off and put his feet in the stream. I moved my feet to splash Lucy with some water. She gave her odd laugh, and Will laughed some more, too.

Using a piece of cloth as a pot-holder, he took the cup from the fire and blew on it till it was cool enough, then he drank the water. It took him a couple minutes, sipping it like tea. Then he dipped the cup back in the stream. He walked in the water towards us and offered me the cup. "I guess I've never seen you all drink, but would you like to try?"

I took the cup. It felt nice in my hands—cold and smooth, calm and reassuring. It was a big measuring cup with a bent band of metal as a handle. The gradations were marked on the side with little indentations in the metal, and I ran my fingers over those, feeling them like Braille. I raised it and poured some water into my mouth. It didn't feel like when I'd tried to eat that horrible thing before, not at all. It felt like a part of me was a little bit more alive right then, like it had been deficient or wounded before, and now it was healed. I wanted the feeling to spread through me, but it didn't. I couldn't even master swallowing the water; most of it spilled out on my chin.

"Try again," Will said with surprising patience. I had been afraid he'd laugh. "This time close your mouth when you try to swallow it."

I did as he suggested, and managed to get some down. The sensation was not as intense as it had been in my mouth, but it definitely felt like something was more complete, less broken in me than it had been before, though the feeling was faint and it passed quickly. I handed the cup to Lucy. With her better control and coordination, she was much more successful than I had been. She looked surprised and elated, and she smiled at Will as she handed the cup back.

We sat there a little longer, before Will stamped the fire out and we put our shoes back on. We slowly made our way back home.

"I hope you two had fun," he said as we shuffled through our gate (Will had already led the other people to the opposite side of the enclosure). He looked happier than he had before, like he thought the outing quite enjoyable. I was glad.

He locked up the gate. "You two seem all right, like real people. *Better* than some real people, even."

I was always confused when he referred to us this way, but I was getting used to it.

"I got something for you." He pulled out a glossy, colorful brochure and pushed it through a tiny gap in the fence. I took it and read the cover: "Stony Ridge College—Where Learning and Character Grow Together." I lowered my eyebrows a little, for the motto wasn't quite what I expected, even as high-minded as it seemed. I certainly hoped I had lived up to it when I had worked there, but it sounded so grand I wasn't sure if it were humanly possible to do such things for people, at least not at school.

I looked back to Will.

"I don't know if you can read, Truman, but it's your old college. I went out there the other day to check it out." He glanced at the other people as they moaned and approached. "Some of the buildings are falling apart, but I found one office where they had these brochures and they were all boxed up, so they were still readable. It's quite a ways, but we can go there next time if you want."

As the first of the others began to push and jostle me out of the way, I nodded, touched by his thoughtfulness. Will nodded too as he stepped away from the fence.

I moved back through the crowd, so I could get away from them. Lucy came with me, and we retreated to our little cubicle, where we sat together on our sofa. I opened the brochure to examine it. Inside there were pictures of ivy-covered, brick buildings and smiling, pretty young people of every race. None of them were bloody or missing parts, I noticed. None of them even had a deformity as minor as crooked teeth or scraggly hair.

Looking at such perfect people, I wondered if any of their learning and character had grown because of me. I also wondered where they all were now, and if any of them still remembered anything I'd taught them—again, even assuming that I'd been a teacher there. I thought of all the other people in the storage area with us, who couldn't speak or read, who didn't seem to remember much of anything, and I wondered what difference I had ever made. I was grateful for how thoughtful Will had been, but I almost wished he hadn't brought the brochure.

Lucy touched my arm and leaned over to look at what I was reading. She tilted her head up at me, and I pointed to the brochure, then at myself. She furrowed her brow and shook her head. I pointed to my pile of books near the sofa, then to a picture of books in the brochure, than back to myself. This time she nodded. She put her finger on my chest, then turned the finger back to touch her breast. I put down the brochure and took her hand; with one finger of my other hand, I touched her breast and then my own chest. She nodded and leaned her head against me.

After a while, Lucy sat up and took up her violin. As she began to play, I thought of how some teacher must have taught her, probably many years ago. As I leaned back and again enjoyed the overwhelming beauty of Lucy's serenade, I knew that teacher's work had at least made my meager life more tolerable, even joyful, whatever else it might have accomplished. Perhaps some of my students were somewhere, doing something similarly beautiful or good. It was only a hope, I suppose, but that summer night it was enough that I felt good about the day's events and I could sit beside Lucy as happy and content as I had been on the previous nights.

Chapter 11

Only a few more days of school remained after I took my vows. The littler kids were already done, and the bigger kids like me were taking exams. During the final exam in Mr. Caine's class, a little girl came into the classroom and ran up to Mr. Caine. They whispered, and then Mr. Caine called me to the front of the class.

"Zoey," he whispered, "leave your exam on your desk. I'll pick it up and keep it for you for later. You have to help your mother with a delivery. Go and meet her at the street corner. Good luck."

I nodded and left the school building. I went to the street corner, and Mom came running.

"Who is it?" I asked her as we started to walk, almost at a jog. "Who's in labor?"

"It's Rachel," Mom said. "Ms. Dresden."

That's what I had thought. I knew it was almost her time.

"Zoey, remember what I've said. Rachel has had a hard time. We're not here to judge. She needs our help."

"I know, Mom."

I had always found Ms. Dresden a fascinating, if somewhat troubled, presence in our community. She was a young woman, only nineteen or twenty. She was extremely pretty, I had always thought—short, a little stout, but muscular and well-built, with full hips and breasts, perfect teeth and skin, a sprinkling of freckles across the tops of her cheeks, and remarkably red hair the color of some fall leaves—vibrant, undulating, and free. She kept her hair longer than most women, just down to her shoulders, but not as long as my mom did hers. She smiled and laughed often, though she seemed more impish and sardonic than cheerful, I thought later. Her parents had both been killed in the initial onslaught of the dead, twelve years ago. Rachel had managed to hide until she saw the people in the museum; she had scrambled over the wall to safety with them.

As with many people her age, she'd had difficulty adjusting to our way of life, more difficulty than most people who were either older or younger. When I was little, she was the wild girl parents warned their children about—smoking cornsilk cigarettes (or even marijuana, I had heard people accuse), wearing suggestive clothing and garish makeup, staying out late with boys her own age or older. Hanging around boys and men all the time, she'd learned to operate heavy machinery—loaders, forklifts, excavators—and she spent much of her time going past the fence to haul lumber or other supplies back to our city. Of course, hanging around men all the time inevitably led to the situation my mom and I had to help with this day.

Even though my parents encouraged me to be more circum-spect in my own behavior, they kept the blame and ostracism of Rachel to a minimum; they said she was so hurt and alone by what had happened that she compensated by taking risks and behaving in unacceptable ways. The important thing, they always insisted, was that she never hurt or lied to anyone, and therefore her behavior was not immoral in any substantive, important way. I of all people knew about ostracism, so I did not want to ridicule or criticize her.

My mom told me Rachel had not—or, the gossips confi-dently asserted, *could not*—name her baby's father, but this made no difference to us that day. She was alone and in pain, and all we needed to think about was how to help her.

Ms. Dresden's house wasn't far from the school. We went right in. There were old rock posters on the walls, dead flowers in a vase, and lace and bead curtains in each window and doorway. A large pistol sat on the end table next to the couch, and leaning on the wall between the end table and couch there was a shotgun. She'd stuck a big, plastic flower in the barrel of that. On the mantle she had a rifle, a box of ammo, and a bunch of partly burnt candles, all under a picture of Jimi Hendrix superimposed on a marijuana leaf. I thought it was the most delightfully scandalous room I had ever seen.

We followed her grunts to her bedroom. Ms. Dresden was on her bed, panting and sweating, her belly impossibly huge. She didn't greet us, just sort of nodded as she breathed, puffing her cheeks out with air. She threw her head back, grimaced, and let out a howl of animal agony.

Mom took a towel out of her bag and unrolled it on a chest at the foot of the bed, revealing a row of medical instruments. She pulled on her rubber gloves, then handed me a pair; I put them on.

"Easy, Rachel," Mom said as she pushed the woman's knees up and back, then pushed the big gown or t-shirt up around Rachel's waist. The sheets under her were wet; her water had broken. Rachel gave another howl. The contractions were really close together. This would be done pretty soon.

"Thanks for coming so fast, Sarah," Rachel managed to pant in response, before another contraction wracked her body. "I appreciate it."

"Of course. You knew I would." Mom kept her eyes on Rachel's as she reached inside. "You're not dilated enough, so try not to push. I know it's hard."

Rachel went through another contraction, this time with her mouth open but silent, trying to work the uncooperative muscles and fight the urge to push. All the drugs used to induce or inhibit labor had long since expired. So had the ones for pain. Sometimes the woman would bite something, like a strap or a rolled up towel. Mom would usually run the generator to power an ultrasound machine twice during a pregnancy, but other than that, births took their course with little interference from technology. Mom just had to keep encouraging her and checking how dilated she was.

Ms. Dresden let out a string of expletives with most of the contractions, cursing the world and herself, but it was pretty normal by birthing standards. This went on for a while, but not nearly as long as some of the more difficult births I'd been to. In less than an hour, Rachel was fully dilated and could push. Mom guided the baby and coached Rachel, and I got ready to catch it with a clean towel. But after it had crowned, I could see there was a problem. Its shoulder caught a little, and the baby was a pale blue. Mom kept working, but she looked to me. A stillbirth was an extremely traumatic and dangerous procedure and I'd never been with Mom during one—until then.

"What's going on?" Ms. Dresden demanded, picking up on the change in our demeanor. "What's wrong?"

Mom was working to maneuver the tiny corpse out of her. "Your baby's not alive, Rachel. I'm so sorry. But we have to work quickly. You know that. Keep pushing. Zoey, get ready to cut the cord."

I grabbed a pair of shears from the tools Mom had brought. Gleaming, stainless steel—I never liked handling medical instruments. I found the oily, black sheen of guns far preferable; they seemed more human somehow, while such shiny, pristine utensils as these looked alien and otherworldly, taken from out of science fiction and dropped down onto our simple, dirty, broken planet.

Ms. Dresden let out another howl as she pushed, and this one was followed by two small sobs. The tiny body finally slipped out of her. Mom held up the cord for me. I cut through it, surprised again at how tough and gristly the flesh seemed, like a chicken neck. Mom handed the body to me and I wrapped it in the towel, trying to keep my back to Ms. Dresden so she couldn't see it. I made the wrapping as tight as I could, covering its face, and set it on the floor where I thought Ms. Dresden wouldn't be able to see it. I turned back to Mom, who was working to get the afterbirth out. "Keep pushing, Rachel." Mom was sniffling too, I could see, and she bent her head down to wipe her eye on her sleeve. "We've got to get everything out. We don't want infection. And you know we have to do it quickly now."

Ms. Dresden's sobs crescendoed to the most perfect, keenest wail that cut down from my head to my abdomen and resonated there, making my diaphragm spasm into choked, restrained sobs. She took a wheezing gasp and then cried, "Who the hell cares? Just leave me alone!" She let out another string of expletives, then started thrashing her legs, kicking at us. I grabbed her right leg and held it as best I could so Mom could finish.

After she had done everything she could, Mom balled up a towel with all the fluids and tissue and shoved it to the side. "Okay, Rachel, okay, we're done." She looked down at the bundle I had put on the floor. She nudged it with her foot. It slid just a little, then started to move on its own, the towel pushing out in one spot, then another. Mom scooped up the bundle and her bag. "Zoey, stay with Rachel. I need to take care of this."

Ms. Dresden sat up as Mom hurried from the room. I tried to sit next to her, to comfort her, but she was already thrashing and pushing me away. I got her around the shoulders, but she was strong.

"Get off of me, you bald, little freak!"

She wrenched her body away and tried to follow my mom. I thrust my left arm over her shoulder and across her chest, then snaked my right arm under and around hers to press my hand on the back of her head—a half nelson, my dad had called it. It was a better hold, as I didn't think she could shake me off as easily, but I didn't have as much purchase with my legs. I could feel her well-muscled back and shoulders; with the adrenaline pushing her, she could probably stand up with me still clinging to her. I braced my right foot on the floor and twisted my body to keep her from standing.

"I said get off me, you little, zombie, freak girl!" She elbowed the side of my head, but I held on. I was crying because I was fighting this poor woman, not because of the pain.

"Sarah, you bring my baby back in here!" she bellowed as she got one foot on the floor and started to turn. "You got no right to do anything with it!"

"I have to take care of it, Rachel!" Mom shouted from the other room. "You know that!" I could hear a small moaning—plaintive and angry—and then repeated tearing sounds.

I leaned back as hard as I could, but Ms. Dresden was getting her other foot around to stand.

"You leave my baby alone! And you and your little freak girl leave me alone, too! You always think you're so high and mighty, Sarah, 'cause you're married to the big, boss man of this little shit hole! Screw you!"

Now she had both feet on the floor. I grabbed the headboard of the bed with my left hand as I twisted and wrapped my right leg around her waist. She slid a little and lost her balance and we were wrestling on the bed again as she screamed more at my mom. "Yeah, the big man! Piss off, Sarah! Maybe it was him that knocked my ass up! Maybe hubby's been screwing me 'cause you're such a cold, heartless bitch, and now you want to take it out on my poor baby! Is that it, Sarah, you sick cunt?"

"Rachel, stop it," Mom said in loud but measured tones. "I know you're devastated, but stop it. Zoey doesn't need to hear that." There was a thud from the other room, and Ms. Dresden went slack and slumped back on me.

I slipped my arm and leg from around her. "Mom?" I croaked, my voice sticking in me. "You're going to bring Ms. Dresden's baby back in here, aren't you?"

"Yes, Zoey, I just dropped my bag." She came through the door carrying the bundle, which she had wrapped with white cloth tape. The head was poking out, moving a little side to side and moaning. "Zoey," Mom said, "go to my bag and get a surgical mask for Rachel. Sometimes they spit."

I nodded and went to get the mask. Once I'd put it on Ms. Dresden, Mom handed the bundle to her. "It's a boy," she announced.

Ms. Dresden nodded a little and rocked the thing that would've been her child in a better, kinder world. Unlike a normal baby, it watched her intently, its cloudy eyes filled with that mixture of forlornness and bestial hunger that one can always imagine in the eyes of the dead.

The tears came slow and steady now from its mother. Not the previously violent sobs of denial and rage, but the calmer bathing as her soul sank down into abiding sorrow, accepting the small comfort that comes from embracing enormous pain.

Mom brushed Ms. Dresden's sweaty, red hair off her forehead. It was so red and glistening that for a moment it looked as though she had removed a bloody gash from there. Mom smoothed the hair back, then gently stroked her pale face, swollen but still so overwhelmingly pretty, and now so weak and vulnerable. "I'm so sorry, Rachel. I'm so, so sorry."

Ms. Dresden looked up at my mom, and pulled the mask a little away from her mouth to speak. "I shouldn't have said those awful things, Sarah. I don't know what to say now. Please forgive me."

"Of course, Rachel. I've heard a lot from women in labor. Don't worry about me. I've always said you were a nice girl. I know you are."

Ms. Dresden turned to me. "You too, Zoey. I'm so sorry I said those things and hit you."

"It's okay," I said.

"You hold him a while, Rachel," my mom said. "You need to. It's natural. And when you need to put him down, I'll put him in the other room, so he's safe. I think Zoey should sit with you for a while, if that's okay. It's harder when you're alone."

We both nodded.

Mom and I sat in the living room among the guns and rock posters for what seemed like a long time while Ms. Dresden held her baby. Afterward, Mom put the baby in the bathtub and closed the bathroom door. She and I gathered the bloody towels and made a clean bed for Ms. Dresden, propping her up with fresh blankets and pillows. Mom left, and the two of us sat alone, not speaking, just sitting there, Ms. Dresden in her bed, me in a chair next to her.

"Zoey," she said, breaking the silence, "I know it sounds funny, when so much has happened, but I can barely see straight, I'm so hungry. Someone left some stuff for me. It should be on the stairs down to the basement, where it's cooler. Please bring me something. It doesn't matter what."

I went to the kitchen, where the door to the basement was. There was still enough daylight coming in that I could see a few steps down into the darkness. Hanging on the wall was a large haunch of smoked deer meat, and on the steps was a bag with berries in it, and another with hard, dry bread. In the kitchen, I found a knife to cut away some of the hard rind on the meat, and to slice the bread into smaller chunks. I picked through the berries to get out the moldy ones, too. I took the good parts to Ms. Dresden and we sat on her bed, chewing silently till we were full. Then she lay back. I put the food in the bags and returned it to the basement stairs. Then I sat back down on my chair next to her.

I lit a candle when it got darker. More light might've been nice, but most of our candles were tallow, and the smell wasn't pretty.

Ms. Dresden spoke up again. "That was gross what I said about your dad. I know your mom and dad are nice and they don't talk about me. I should've remembered that, and I also should've respected you and not tried to hurt you, especially not that way. You've always been a nice girl, too. I'm so sorry."

"It's hard, when you're sad and in pain, to be nice. I know."

"I guess that's right. But still, I shouldn't have." Though the candlelight made the room look slightly sinister, Rachel's face looked serene and softened. "I need to sleep." She scooted over a little on her bed. "Sit next to me if you want, if it'd be more comfortable. Or I'll be okay if you want to leave."

I sat next to her. "It's okay. I could stay a while. Mom will come get me later."

Protect the living. Honor the dead. I had done what I had trained to do, what was necessary for survival. Survival meant life continued, and life was hard. This was true, and I now saw how difficult truth was.

As she finally sank into an exhausted sleep, Ms. Dresden's breathing fell into a rhythm that matched the frail wheezing from the thing in the other room as it struggled against its bonds. Though identical in rhythm, the latter had the ragged pant of desire, frustration, and restlessness, while poor Rachel's spent body was only soft, yielding, finally without struggle or pain. I leaned against her as she slept and just breathed in all her feminine, fecund, and profane scent—warm, solid, and enduring. Though there was a pain in my heart so cold and bitter I could taste it, metallic and sharp, slowly I felt my bones soften and settle onto Rachel's small but powerful frame, till I too fell asleep.

Chapter 12

It rained on and off for the next two days, but after that we saw Will again. It was early in the morning, with the sun just breaking over the horizon. I was glad he was back so soon, but also apprehensive about going to this place supposedly associated with me.

After he let us out, we followed the road for a long time, at the slow pace Lucy and I could maintain. Will told us about life with the other people like him, how they grew food and protected themselves from us, the ways they had relearned how to do basic things like make paper and cloth and generate electricity and drill wells for water. He seemed pleased and proud of everything they'd built and done, as well he should be. I was almost glad to lack speech at that point; I could hardly come up with a list of even the most meager accomplishments in our group, and it would've been quite embarrassing to admit it out loud. I was a little proud that Lucy and I had planted some of the dandelions in little flower pots by our storage unit and set out more containers to catch the rain water, but even that had been her idea.

In the middle of the day we stopped to rest in the shade of some trees. Nearby, some bushes and vines grew over an old fence, and as Lucy and I sat, Will picked some berries there and ate them.

After that he sat down with us. He reached in a pocket and got out a little handmade leather pouch, from which he got a cigarette and a lighter. The cigarette was obviously handmade— the ends were rolled and pinched shut and the paper wasn't a pure white, but grayish-beige.

"It's a lot easier than the flint and tinder, especially for a smoke," he said as he lit the cigarette, careful to cover the flame so Lucy and I couldn't see it. "But I guess eventually we'll run out of all the lighters and matches. Maybe by then we'll make our own." He blew the smoke away from us, which was considerate. "It's cornsilk. I saw one of the old-timers doing it when I was younger. Some of them get so desperate for cigarettes. Real ones ran out years ago, and we haven't found any plants or seeds to grow our own tobacco yet. I don't know if there are enough people to make it worth growing, though some of the old timers talk about it all the time, how they want a real cigarette or some dip.

"But I remember how when I was little—you know, in the 'regular' world—all you heard was how you should never, ever smoke or chew, it was like the worst thing for you. Funny that people thought this was so dangerous and deadly." He considered the tiny little roll of paper with the glowing end and shook his head. "They didn't know shit about dangerous and deadly. And I know our world is all messed up, Truman, but sometimes I wonder if the old world was messed up in its own way, or if nothing's changed."

I couldn't offer any better response than a shrug.

Will looked like he'd gotten an idea. "You want some? I really doubt it'd hurt you at all."

As with everything else, I didn't remember if I were a smoker or not. I had some image of professors smoking pipes, but that was all imagination and mystique. Will's musings had me curious enough about it to try. I looked to Lucy. She shrugged. I looked back to Will and nodded.

He smiled a little. "Okay. Not this one; it's too short already and you'd burn yourself." He inhaled deeply from his, then dropped the end on the ground and crushed it under his heel. He lit a new one and handed it to me. "Careful. Hold it with your fingers as far from the lit end as you can. I have no idea how it'll taste to you, so just go easy."

I inhaled it cautiously, afraid the smoke would be hot and burning, like when I had tried to eat, or like the fear I always had of flames. But for whatever reason, it felt only slightly warm and a little tickling. I tried inhaling it deeper, and the sensation was a little more pronounced, but really no more profound than if I'd sat out in the sun. I held the cigarette away from my mouth, looked to Will, and shrugged.

He took it back and crushed it under his heel like the other. "That's what I figured. It's all about the fruit being forbidden. I only like them because I was told not to. You try it, with no one telling you one way or the other, and it's nothing to you. Interesting." He got up. "Well, let's get moving. We won't have too much time to look around."

As we continued down the road, a group of red brick buildings became visible in the distance. After a while we passed through gates with the school's name on the side. As Will had said, some of the buildings were collapsed, but since most were brick, the majority had survived.

"I don't know if you remember, Truman, but it happened in the summer—I mean that's when the world ended—so there wouldn't have been many people here. And I can't think why anyone would try to escape to here, so that's partly why the place is in such good shape."

I didn't remember, but I nodded.

Will gestured to one building. "That's where I found the brochures. It must be the administration building. Does anything look familiar? Do you want to go in that building?"

Things did look vaguely familiar, but I had to shake my head tentatively at the first question, since I really couldn't identify anything. I shook my head more definitively at the second question. If the people in that building had made up the brochure with the vague and hyperbolic slogan I couldn't quite fathom, I didn't want to go in there.

We continued among the buildings. The gymnasium had been a newer building, but its huge, flat roof had collapsed under years of rain and snow accumulation, pulling down part of one wall with it. The library was in much better shape. The doors were locked, of course, and being an older building, the doors weren't glass, but heavy wooden ones, so I thought we might not be able to enter.

"You want to go in here, Truman?" Will asked.

I nodded.

"Wait here."

The windows on the bottom floor had metal bars across them, but Will clambered up these with amazing agility and soon he was hanging onto a rain spout, kicking in a window on the second floor. He climbed in, made his way down, and opened the main door for us.

Lucy and I entered. The entryway was dark, since there weren't many windows there, but the room off to the left had high ceilings, with enormous windows extending the full height of the room. Sunlight fell upon scores of wooden bookcases full of books. I ran my hand along the spines and realized how poor my collection at the storage facility was. No longer did I have to sort through tattered books of how to program in Pascal, or inspirational novels based on the Bible: here I had copies of Pascal and the Bible! Now an anthology of selected and abridged works was not the best treasure I could hope for—the complete books were here before me! *This* was a room and a feeling I did remember—not vaguely, but vividly, as if it had happened many times and with particular intensity. This was a *real* library. And now it was mine. Carefully, I selected a few volumes to take back today. There'd be time to come back for more, but I wanted a few right away.

Will was also marveling at the library, looking up at all the books stacked high around us. "Milton and Jonah are going to love this!" I must've growled reflexively, because I didn't mean to, but I couldn't stand the thought of someone taking these from me.

"Oh," Will said. "You don't want me to tell them?"

I hung my head a little. I hadn't written these books, and I hadn't worked for them; I'd just found them, so I had no right to snatch at them like I was doing.

"It's all right," Will said. "I can put off telling them if this place is special to you, Truman. But does this mean that you can read, too?"

I nodded, still keeping my head down.

"Wow. That's more than I had expected or thought possible. But if you can read, you should have first dibs on the books. I think you have little enough at your place. Don't worry."

I was quite overwhelmed that Will, like Lucy, was so much more kind and willing to share than I was. I vowed to be a better person in the future.

It was getting late and we had to start back. On the way to the door, on the librarian's desk, I noticed an old manual typewriter. All the other desks had darkened, useless computer screens on them. I wasn't positive why this desk had a typewriter, but I thought I remembered libraries and other offices using paper forms, some of which could be filled out more easily with a typewriter than a computer. I tried to pick it up. It wasn't too heavy.

Will saw me with it and came over to help. "Wait, Truman. There's probably a case for it somewhere here. It'd be easier to carry. There might be some spare ink and ribbons too."

In the cabinets, we found the case and the extra supplies. Will fit everything inside the case, which had a handle, like a suitcase or Lucy's violin case; it was easy for him to pick up and carry.

Near nightfall, we returned home. Will gave the typewriter to Lucy, and he led the others to the far side of the compound while we waited at the gate. Lucy seemed troubled, as though I might like her less for having seen things from my other life. I looked deeply in her right eye, and even put my hand on her right cheek, and I think she realized she was mistaken. I hoped so.

Will let us inside and began to wrap the chain around the two metal poles of the fence and the gate.

With a high shriek, two small people lurched from behind one of the buildings. They looked to be about a foot shorter than Lucy, not small children, but pre-adolescents, one boy, one girl. I remembered pushing past them before our previous outing with Will. Maybe because of their age, they were much quicker than the other people in the storage area. They seemed to have waited for us behind the building. They also seemed to move in concert, as though they had planned this together. They crashed into the gate, throwing Will off balance and making him take a step back. The girl wriggled through the opening in the gate as the lock and chain clattered to the ground.

The others in the storage facility slowly approached us, filling the space between the fence and the one building, as well as the area between the buildings. I dropped the books and for a second I didn't know what to do. Both children were now through the gate. Will grabbed the girl by the throat with his gauntleted hand and pistol-whipped the boy to the ground. Will kicked him in the face, then stepped on his throat, pinning him.

I took a step toward the gate—I had to secure it—but Lucy put her hand on my shoulder. She dropped the typewriter as she shook her head at me. Though her eye was as tranquil and lofty as ever, the snarl on her lips shocked me with its morbid hunger—and perhaps even with its cruelty.

Will, holding the two children at bay, glanced between me, Lucy, and the crowd approaching the gate.

"Truman," he said in a voice that sounded surprisingly calm, "I know you're scared, but you need to close that gate, whatever happens. You need to do it *now.*"

I looked into Lucy's eye for what seemed a very long time; I needed to know what she was thinking. Was she trying to save me or the children from getting hurt? Or had hunger driven her to it?

Even over the increasing moan of the crowd, I heard Will pulling back the hammer on his gun. It had the mechanical finality of a clock before an execution.

"Blue Eye," he said, "that gate is going to be closed and locked now. If you and Truman don't do it, I'm going to kill these two and lock it myself. If you do it for me, I promise I won't kill them."

Her gaze moved towards Will, and their eyes met.

"Please trust me," he said, sounding more concerned for us than for himself.

I looked to Lucy and thought she nodded slightly. I took her hand and pulled her to the gate. I was too clumsy to handle the lock myself anyway. Lucy helped me thread the chain through the fence, then she locked it.

As the crowd reached us, I let it carry me forward and push me up against the fence. I lost Lucy in the crowd.

"Remember," Will said, "trust me. I'll be as careful as I can, but I'm not going to be gentle." He tossed the girl as hard as he could, and she flew several yards before landing on her back. She immediately rolled over and began to get up. Will trained his pistol on her. My eyes widened and I let out a wail, but it was nothing compared to the cry of rage, despair, and betrayal that Lucy sent up from somewhere in the crowd. The others droned on with their meaningless, emotionless moaning.

The pistol exploded, louder than I could've imagined, and Will's arm jumped upward a little. A dark, chunky spray shot out of the girl's knee onto the cracked pavement and weeds. She collapsed with a groan, then rose up on her hands and slowly pulled herself towards Will. But without her one leg she could get little traction and could barely move.

Will holstered his gun. He lifted the boy by the neck and one leg, then swung him a couple times and threw him part of the way over the fence. The barbed wire there snagged the boy's remaining clothes and he was stuck.

"Truman," Will said, still very calm, "you're going to have to pull him over. Hurry. I have to get her over too."

As Will walked over to the girl and picked her up, I tried to push through the crowd to where the boy's head and right side hung over. Everyone else reached for Will and followed his motions, ignoring the boy, even though the barbed wire seemed to cause him pain as he struggled and it tore into him. I noticed something I'd seen before with us—there was no blood on the cuts; we had none left in us, it seemed.

I finally got close enough to grab his flailing right arm, and I pulled on it with all of my weight; he tumbled over on top of the crowd.

Will threw the girl over the fence. She was smaller than the boy, and she got farther over before her pants snagged on the barbed wire. It only took a slight tug on her arm to bring her all the way over to our side.

Will walked over and sat under a tree. He finally looked shaken and exhausted. "Truman, we're going to have to be more careful," he called to me. "You two aren't the only smart zombies in there. And Blue Eye," he called louder, "I can't see you, but I'm sorry I scared you. I don't want to hurt you all. We take a vow not to, unless you're going to kill one of us. I hope you'll trust me now. Thank you both for your help."

And with that, he rose and left again. The crowd dispersed.

I found the typewriter and the books; nothing was badly damaged. Lucy and I went back to our sofa and sat there as night came on. I looked once more into her eye, and I was as captivated as before, but there was deeper meaning, complexity, and regret to my feelings. I could see the terrible truth Milton had spoken: we needed to be locked up. Even someone as good and beautiful as Lucy, or as seemingly innocent as the two children, could be willing, even desirous, to hurt and kill another. I remembered the word "bloodlust," and thought painfully that it was more like a blood-need: it wasn't a lustful urge that overwhelmed us and then abated. It was more like a dull, hungry ache, conniving and malicious.

It was then that I resolved to type up everything that happened, as fully and honestly as I could. If, as Will had described it, the people on the outside looked upon us just as animals to be put down, I should describe how things were different, more complicated. Of course, part of the complication was created by confusing, frightening scenes such as today at the gate—where hunger, anger, and fear had been almost too powerfully arrayed against a new and fragile trust.

I wished that evening Lucy would play her violin and remind me of gentler, lovelier things, but I was almost glad she didn't, for that would make it too easy to forget the bad events. Instead, I just gazed at her and knew I could—I *would*—love her regardless, in spite of the imperfections I now knew were in all of us, and not just in me and our uncommunicative neighbors, but even in her.

As we sat there, even without the violin, I became convinced—I hope because of Lucy's love for me, but perhaps only because of my own love for her—that she really had been trying to protect me and the two children, not just trying to hurt Will. As with my thoughts the other night about my former job, it was only a hope. But such a hope was as persistent a need, deep inside me, as the bloody hunger and violence I had just witnessed. And once again, such a hope seemed enough.

Chapter 13

It was funny how things went on pretty much as normal, both after my vows and after the death of Ms. Dresden's baby. I always wonder if it's a resilience or sturdiness that we all have, or the kind of hope that Milton talked about, or just stubbornness. Sometimes I think it's more a kind of inertia of living matter—a gross, wet weightiness that keeps life flowing or rolling forward like a flood or a glacier, depending on the situation. The living stay alive; they even keep living after they've died. It's not good or bad, it's just the way it is, and you have to plan on it and work around it.

So we kept going as we had, through the mundane but sometimes pleasant activities of our lives. School was done for the summer, but I had one more ballet lesson with Ms. Wright. On my way to class, I walked by Mr. Enders at his little desk. He had dozed off on this hot, sultry day, leaning against the cool, plaster wall with his eyes closed and his mouth open. I went past him quietly, since there was no need to bother him.

I joined Ms. Wright, Vera, and the other girls in the classroom. "Hi, Zoey," Ms. Wright said. She was much more stern and intimidating than her husband, Mr. Caine, but I still liked her. She always looked comfortable in her body, which was the opposite of how I felt that year. Her skin was a very dark brown, rich and mysterious. Like my mom, her black hair had some grey in it, but unlike my mom, she kept it closely trimmed. Her body was muscled in the way a dancer's is—an average or even slender torso with powerful, toned legs.

Besides her skin, her big, brown eyes were the most strikingly beautiful thing about her—they were large, open and frank, but always a little serious. Not sad, but keen and hardened, like they had seen and absorbed far too much of the world's mystery and pain.

"Hello, Ms. Wright," I said as I set down my gym bag.

"You okay?" She touched my shoulder and looked at my blackened left eye.

"Yeah, I'm okay." Bald, pale, with a purple-yellow bruise around one eye—it was everything I could do to go out in public at all.

She gave a hint of a smile. More of her seriousness, I thought, that she seldom smiled and never laughed. "You did good, Zoey. You always do. I hope you know that."

The room we used for dance had windows along one side, so it was brightly lit now in the afternoon, and with the windows open it remained comfortably cool. Most of the tables had been moved to other classrooms, but a few were left under the windows. Sometimes we'd use them as props when we practiced scenes.

On the wall opposite the windows, there were two doors—one near the front of the room, one near the back. They were old-fashioned, with a smoked-glass window on the top half, and wood on the bottom half. For some reason, no one had scraped off the names painted on the glass parts of the school doors, so we could tell that twelve years before, this had been Ms. Thele's fifth grade class.

One day when I was younger, I'd been allowed to rummage around in the cabinets in the back of the classroom. Among other things, I'd found pictures of Ms. Thele and her classes over the years. Through the pictures I could even watch her age from a very young woman, to one in early middle age. In two of the pictures, I thought she looked bigger. Pregnant twice. At least two children of her own. Hundreds of students. It was unnerving, not just because every one of them was almost certainly dead, but because they had almost certainly killed many others after they died. Their classroom was a better tribute to them than their actual physical selves had been.

After some talking amongst the girls, Ms. Wright began the class. As we practiced our steps, all of them with French names, I again found myself wondering whether there were any people left who spoke French. The repetitive motions of the dance drills—long since trained and pressed into my muscles—gave my mind the freedom to wander into such abstract, non-practical speculations. It was one of the things I always liked about dancing—the mental freedom of practice, as well as the physical beauty of performance. I thought of France, of the maps I'd seen and the descriptions I had read in books, and I couldn't see how anyone could have survived there. Too crowded and not enough guns. Same for all of Europe. Gone. I'd read about the Louvre, Versailles, and the Vatican. A few of the older people had visited these places and said how strange and lovely they were, the same way Mom had reminisced about all the people and their foreign, exotic picnics. All gone.

Even if there were other people left somewhere and all our little cities grew and grew until one day our descendants walked across Europe again, they would only find ruins, things for archaeologists to dig up and decipher. We'd have better copies of the Louvre's artwork in our books than the rotten tatters they'd find in the original museum.

I remembered some Caribbean islands had been French colonies, and I thought they had a better chance of harboring survivors. I didn't know if the survivors I imagined would be doing ballet, though, and that made me think of something else I'd read, of how there'd been this ancient form of dance in Cambodia (another place I thought had a better chance of surviving than Europe), and then some people there had killed all the dancers. They thought that kind of dancing represented the aristocracy. (Here again were some of those concepts of society and government that were very hard for me to grasp—the idea that one group would think itself superior to another, or that one group would try to murder another group because of this misguided belief.) And since they didn't like the aristocracy, they thought they needed to get rid of the dancing, and therefore the dancers. The living dead had probably been more thorough in wiping out all kinds of human things, but it didn't seem as bad as the tragedy in Cambodia. I thought, not for the first time, how zombies made more sense than people, some of the time.

As we went through our steps, the window on the door at the back of the room exploded inward, the glass flying in and shattering on the floor. Two fists crashed down through some shards at the top of the window, this time flinging thick splotches of blood on the shattered glass all over the floor. Mr. Enders leaned through the window, his dead eyes seeking us out.

The broken glass had cut several long gashes in his skinny arms. He snuffed the air and licked his lips slowly, his grey tongue snaking around. I froze for just a second and imagined how he might have already been dead when I walked by him in the hall, how his cold hand could have shot out and grabbed me.

But then, as when Mom and I had been attacked a few days before, I just started doing everything automatically. Most of the other girls were younger, and some understandably had let out a shriek when they first saw the dead man. The older girls, who had taken their vows, began to herd the smaller ones toward the front of the room.

"All of you, out the front door and down the hall," Ms. Wright said loudly, but matter-of-factly. "Get outside and get help."

She went for her gym bag. I had already reached mine, and we both pulled our handguns out at the same time. Then we started rummaging for the magazines. We loaded our guns and racked the slides at almost the same moment.

I was closer to Mr. Enders, who was still half-in and half-out of the room, fumbling with the handle on the inside of the door. This was one of those bizarre moments of the undead mind at work: the door wasn't locked, so why hadn't he just turned the handle on the outside? And if he didn't remember how door handles worked at all and had smashed through the glass in blind, uncomprehending rage and hunger, why was he trying to open the door from the inside? I could again see how zombies usually made much less sense than people.

I knew not to stand in Ms. Wright's line of fire, so I took two steps back. We both had our guns pointed at the floor. "Zoey, leave," she said quietly as she raised her pistol. It was a Glock, and I remember thinking it was way too big for my hands, as useless as such an observation was right then. "I know you took your vows and you want to help, but you don't need to see this. Believe me."

"We don't need to shoot, Ms. Wright," I said quietly. "It isn't what we're supposed to do."

Mr. Enders figured out how to turn the handle, and the door opened unexpectedly. He stumbled and fell forward, supported only by his arms through the window as his feet slid on the floor, trying to get purchase, like he was drunk, or like when I'd first tried to ice skate and my feet had slid all over till I fell on my butt. But Mr. Enders wasn't drunk, and he would never try anything new or fun again; he was just dead.

"I heard you put one down the other day," Ms. Wright said, still aiming her Glock. "This needs to be done."

Mr. Enders stood up and dragged his arms out through the broken glass at the edge of the window frame, opening up more red, flowing furrows in his flesh. His left arm flopped down to his side and dripped blood from his fingertips. He moaned and lurched toward us. You could distinctly see the blood pour into his palm, then down to his fingertips, where it dripped onto the floor.

"Mom and I were alone," I said quickly. "There was no one around for miles. I guess one of us could've stayed and kept an eye on it while the other one went to get help, but it was dangerous. And it wasn't Mr. Enders that day. You know it's not right to shoot now."

She looked at me, back to Mr. Enders, then over to the windows and the tables under them. "All right," she finally agreed. "Keep your gun on him. And careful, because I'll be in the way. Just be sure you aim high. I trust you, Zoey."

I raised the pistol and kept Mr. Enders' forehead in my sights as it bobbed from side to side. Ms. Wright hauled one of the tables away from the wall and slid it across the floor.

Mr. Enders, who had been focused on me, stopped and wavered, confused, growling slightly, and then he turned towards Ms. Wright. She ran forward, gaining more speed, and shoved the table into him, hitting him right in the middle. He bent over the tabletop and could almost reach her, but not quite. He wasn't a big man, and he had no coordination or leverage now. Ms. Wright pinned him against the wall with the table. He flailed about, though only his right arm seemed to have any controlled motion. I found myself wondering uselessly whether he had died of a stroke.

"Go, Zoey," Ms. Wright rasped, "get the restraints and the gloves out of his desk and bring them back here. Hurry."

I ran out the door at the front of the room and went to Mr. Enders' desk down the hall. I pulled open the drawers until I found what Ms. Wright had asked for—a muzzle, metal handcuffs, and two pairs of heavy, leather gloves that could not be bitten through easily. They were standard equipment in any public building, the way I'm told fire extinguishers used to be.

Back in the classroom everything was as I had left it—Mr. Enders struggling weakly, Ms. Wright pushing against the table to keep him contained.

She told me to set the muzzle and cuffs down, which I did, and she braced the table with her hip as I helped her put on the gloves. I put my pair on as well, and she looked around to figure out how best to contain Mr. Enders.

"All right, Zoey. Stand back and be ready with the muzzle and cuffs. This isn't going to be pretty, so just be ready for that."

She let go of the pressure on the table. Mr. Enders started to push it back, but he was slow and he was only working with his right arm. Ms. Wright stepped around quickly and shoved the table out of the way with her left foot, tipping it over. Then with a snarl she smashed him in the side of the face with her fist. It wasn't a jab, but a powerful roundhouse, her whole body uncoiling deliberately since there was little chance of a zombie blocking a punch. It took me by surprise—how fast, strong, and savage a blow she could deliver. As dangerous as Mr. Enders now was, it was pathetic and brutalizing to see him beaten to the ground. Worse still, in a way, was how gracefully and beautifully Ms. Wright attacked, little different in form, if not intent, from the dances we had been practicing. I suppose that's one of the things I learned that afternoon—that life is not just heavy inertia, but equally the mesmerizing, beautiful dance of violence.

The first blow knocked Mr. Enders off balance, and Ms. Wright followed up with another roundhouse as she stepped forward and tripped him up with her leg.

He landed facedown on the floor, and she straddled his back, looking to me for the restraints. She grabbed his writhing right arm and pushed her knee against his right leg, so he couldn't get the leverage to roll over.

I quickly stepped over to them. As I knelt in front of Mr. Enders, his clouded eyes seemed pleading, but the snarl that he now gave was only bestial rage.

The muzzle was simple—a sack made of heavy cloth. I forced it over his head and tied the bag's drawstring tightly. Ms. Wright handcuffed him, binding his hands behind his back. I was glad the whole thing was over quickly.

We stood Mr. Enders up and dragged him into the hall. I tossed the couple of mops and brooms out of a janitor's closet, and we were shoving him in there when more people finally showed up. They barricaded the closet door and set a guard on it till final arrangements could be made.

Two days later, much of the community gathered at the cemetery where I had taken my vows. Mr. Enders and Ms. Dresden's baby were taken in a special truck for safety reasons, and we drove Ms. Dresden. I saw many people in the crowd I had not seen in a while, including Will. It was nice of them to show their respect, though I suspected most of them were there because of the kindly, harmless Mr. Enders, and not for the scandalous Rachel and her illegitimate child. I tried to tamp down my anger as useless, misspent energy.

The ceremony was not nearly as involved as my vows ceremony had been. Most of the preparations or ways that we eased the transition from life to death seemed futile and ineffective, especially for those still alive; they had to work through the grief on their own, and in their own way, for a long time after the actual funeral. And we had to admit, I think, that our situation took a lot of the mystery out of death. It was hard to imagine the elaborate rituals or speeches at funerals that I had read about in books, when our funerals include the dead person, thrashing against his bonds and trying to kill us. In our world, the dead demand some respect and attention on their own; we've tried to find a way to give them that, without causing more pain and killing. Whatever we did seemed far preferable to killing them outright once they were restrained, which sounded utterly monstrous and inhuman to me.

Milton ushered the dead away from the cemetery gate. Dad and another armed guard led the restrained Mr. Enders into the graveyard, removed the muzzle and handcuffs, and let him take his place with the others, as he fled into the crowd to get away from Milton.

The interment of dead children was trickier. It had to be done quickly and carefully, but the parents were allowed to set the child down among the dead themselves. My dad handed Ms. Dresden her baby, wrapped just with a towel and not taped up like a mummy. With my dad and the other guard flanking her, Ms. Dresden quickly moved into the enclosure behind Milton. They led her to a small mausoleum near the entrance, where she could lay her baby at the door, under the stone overhang. Milton had made a little bed or nest out of leaves and flowers to make it as gentle and easy as possible on the mother, even if there was little reason to think it mattered to the baby. Though there was no telling what would happen to the creature in its new home, the dead were unlikely to hurt one another, and the ones herding away from Milton were fairly careful, if clumsy, around the smaller ones among them. Ms. Dresden bent down, kissed the middle and forefinger of her right hand, and pressed them to the baby's forehead. The men led her out of the cemetery and locked it up.

Milton's speeches were always simple and very short at funerals. His talent was for uplifting messages, encouragement, and flights of speculation and hope. He believed it better to leave people with their private thoughts and pain, perhaps to remind them of their responsibilities before they went back to their regular lives. I've always thought he was quite right in this, and that day was no exception.

"My friends," he began, "two of us are now a part of our community only with their bodies, for their spirits—or most of their spirits—have left us. But whatever is left, we will honor and remember and protect. We owe that tiny bit of reverence and gratitude, for all the joy they gave us. Mr. Enders had no family, but the children of the community saw him every day, and I know you'll remember him fondly. Rachel's child would've had a loving family, and I can imagine how much you all will want to comfort her after this loss." I thought I detected more accusation or admonition in Milton's statement about Ms. Dresden than in his comments about Mr. Enders. "Let us go, and remember, and help one another heal."

We dispersed after that. Ms. Dresden stayed to cast a handful of flowers over the wrought iron fence, onto the more or less uncomprehending heads of our deceased. We waited patiently and discreetly for her by our truck. After she left the fence, people offered their condolences. Will spoke with her briefly. I thought it was nice of him, as he didn't usually say much, but her situation was so sad I imagined anyone would be moved by it.

On the way home, Ms. Dresden sat between me and my mom, silent, though she squeezed my hand when she first got back in the truck. Inertia or not, I looked in her small, sparkling green eyes and wondered whether I could ever have as much strength, or even if that was something to hope for. I vaguely remembered a line I had read somewhere, that to the one who has much, more will be given, and I thought how some people had a lot of sorrow, and sometimes they were given even more sorrows. Perhaps that was Rachel, and I could hardly envy her, but only marvel, and squeeze her hand, our eyes locked for a moment of perfect understanding and compassion.

Chapter 14

Over the following days I was anxious that Will might not come back after what had happened. I certainly wouldn't have blamed him. It was nice enough of him to take us out, when, from what I could tell, the outings didn't offer him anything tangible. Unable to speak, I couldn't imagine Lucy and I were much company, though I think we had tried our best. But for him to be with us when it was positively dangerous to do so, I thought very unlikely.

After the incident, Lucy seemed especially nice, always letting me get close to her or touch her without objecting, as though she were making up for what had happened, or showing me that she wasn't as savage and violent as she had appeared that day. If Will didn't come back, it wouldn't be so bad to stay here with her and her music and my haphazard collection of books. I did have to admit I was a little disappointed. That library had really filled me with hope. There was little point in dwelling on mistakes or false hopes, however, so I enjoyed our days there in the storage facility as best I could. I spent much of the time typing up our story. I was happy with the progress I had made on my journal, and how my writing seemed to improve with practice, coming to me more naturally the more I put down on paper.

After that day, I had also decided on a special project that I needed to do. I would need Lucy's help, especially her better coordination. Finding the supplies was the easy part, there were always so many miscellaneous and useful things around where we lived. From one unit, I grabbed a rope and some wooden slats, about two feet long, and in another cubicle, where I'd seen some medical equipment, I handed Lucy a crutch.

We roamed between the buildings until we found the girl Will had shot. She had not been able to stand since, but pulled herself along with her hands, agonizingly slow. Some of her fingernails had torn off with the exertion. Even though she no longer bled, the wounds looked horrible, and it was impossible to know how much pain they caused her. I knelt next to her, and Lucy followed my lead. I, of course, couldn't make the girl understand what I was trying to do, so she growled and tried to push my hands away. She seemed to trust Lucy more, as Lucy made soothing sounds to her, and gradually she struggled against me less, so I could put four of the slats as a brace along her wounded leg. I was very glad Lucy was there, first to calm the girl, and then to help tie the slats to her leg. I didn't have the dexterity to do it on my own.

When it was done, I thought she might be able to stand, as her knee wouldn't just immediately give out, but I didn't think she'd be able to put all her weight on it, so walking would be difficult, compounded by not being able to bend at the knee. Lucy and I helped her stand, then slowly loosened our grip till she was standing on her own. She grunted her approval, then tried to take a step and faltered, but we caught her and held her up. I tried to put the crutch under her shoulder, but it was too long. There were two bolts with wing nuts near the bottom of the crutch, so you could slide the bottom strut in and out to adjust the height. I held it up and fumbled with those, until Lucy put her delicate fingers on them and loosened them while I braced the girl. Lucy slid the strut in to its shortest position, threaded the bolts back into their holes, and put the wing nuts back on. We put it under the girl's shoulder, and I put her hand on the crutch's handle and pushed on her fingers till she had tightened her grip. Now we could let go of her completely and she was able, slowly and with difficulty, to hobble around. She looked at us and nodded.

I took Lucy back to our cubicle and she snuggled up to me. I felt good about what we had accomplished, and more reassured that Lucy had acted to protect the girl and the boy the other day. At least, mostly. Certainty was a luxury which I lacked now in most things, even assuming I or anyone else ever had it as much as we hoped or liked to believe we did.

Eventually, Will returned. I heard the usual commotion as the people in the storage facility milled to the fence near our cubicle. A lock and chain flew over their heads and landed near Lucy and me. The crowd then shuffled to the other end of the area, farthest from the front gate. "Truman," I heard Will call, "if you want to come out, then take the chain and lock and secure the inner gate, so the others are kept at this end. Then go to the main gate with Blue Eye."

I looked to Lucy. She nodded. We did as Will had instructed. When he met us at the main gate, he looked behind and around all the buildings, and we did the same, making sure no one was hiding again. Convinced it was safe, he opened the gate, let us out, and locked it behind us.

He looked at us a minute. "We okay?" he asked. "No misunderstanding or bad feelings? Well, I don't know how you'd express them if there were, but I kind of like you guys. I don't want you to think I'd do anything to hurt any of you all. Okay?"

Lucy and I nodded.

"Good. I thought you might want to see more of your old school, Truman. Maybe we could find your old office, or get some more books. Let's go."

On the long walk to Stony Ridge College, Will told us two people had died in his community. As usual, I didn't know how to express my feelings, but I hoped he knew that I shared their sadness.

When we got to the college, we looked around at some different buildings, passing by what looked like the cafeteria and some classroom buildings. I hoped Will had a plan for searching, because I didn't know how to go about it. All the buildings were labeled things like "Adams Hall" or "Ridgecrest Commons," with no indication on the outside of whether they were offices, class-rooms, or classrooms, or something else. At one point, Lucy and I rested on the stone steps of one building, while Will went inside. I at least was very tired from all the walking in the hot sun, though it felt good to be out and good that Will trusted us.

He came back out soon after. "Well, Dr. Truman, please come in. We've been expecting you." He smiled as he held the door open for us. He could be quite playful. It was very endearing, I thought.

On a board just inside the door, there was a list of offices, and on it, my name. I had been a member of the Philosophy Department, and my office was on the second floor. I was more dumbfounded than anything else. Philosophy? I liked the sound of it, but I didn't remember specifics, or what I did or thought or believed in. It was intimidating, like there would be more expectations and demands now that I was a "philosopher." The designation made it seem as though I had loved wisdom more than other people did. And what arrogance if I had ever thought that I did. I just had read and studied more than other people, and I had been a philosophy teacher. Since I'd forgotten most everything I'd known, I wasn't even that anymore, and certainly not a "philosopher." As we walked upstairs, I became increasingly apprehensive about what we would find in my office.

We got to a wooden door with my name on it. The building was old, so Will easily kicked in the door. He stepped aside and let me be the first to enter the small office. There were bookshelves along the wall to the right, a desk with a chair behind it and two in front of it, and a window on the wall opposite the door. On the wall to the left were some diplomas and a large print of "The Death of Socrates."

I was a little disappointed, as the decorations didn't seem too original, but I supposed it was harder for philosophy professors to find pictures related to their work than, say, art or literature professors. Besides, it took some of the intimidation away from my unknown, previous self, so I was less worried about living up to some especially august, original thinker.

Everything was neat and intact. No one had touched any-thing since the last time I had been in it, whenever that had been. I glanced at the books as I walked around the desk. I would look at them in a minute, but for right now, the desk was the more urgent object of curiosity.

There was a computer screen and a keyboard on the desk, and a pencil holder with pens and a letter opener in it, and some piles of handwritten papers and photocopies. I saw the handwritten papers had names written across the top. The last papers of dozens of students, I supposed, and wondered for a moment what had happened to all of them.

The most important things were the two framed photographs. These were the sort of things I was both seeking and about which I was apprehensive. Both photos seemed to be taken on vacations, with one in some warm place where everyone was wearing shorts, and the other in the winter, everyone bundled up in big, puffy coats, with hats and gloves. In each, I stood with a woman and two children, a boy and a girl. The woman was pretty, especially as she didn't have any parts missing or damaged, that I could see. She was fairly slender and had short, blonde hair. I automatically thought maybe that was a good thing, that at least I still liked blondes, but immediately thought what a stupid thing to have as the only connection to your past—what a trivial, useless, grossly physical detail.

The children were small, perhaps eight and ten years old, I guessed. Neither the woman nor the children summoned any affection or remembrance, beyond the usual sadness that these people were probably dead now.

But the whole scene filled me with sorrow and loss that I couldn't feel or remember anything. Even if I had done a great many more evil things than I remembered, I could not understand what I had done to deserve or cause this strange, disconnected life I had. I wondered if other people felt the same way, and that made it worse, as I realized that I had little way to ask them or express my sympathy for them if they did. I again remembered what crying was, and felt more cheated and alone that I couldn't even do that.

Lucy had come around the desk and stood next to me. She looked at the pictures and ran her graceful fingers over them. I set the one picture—the one of my family in the winter—back on the desk. I turned the other one over in my hands and started fumbling with the little clips on the back, trying to remove the picture from the frame. Lucy helped me. She folded the picture neatly twice and put it in the pocket of my shirt, closing the pocket's little flap over it. She pressed her tiny hand against me there. Then her one good eye rested on mine, and she pointed to herself and shook her head slowly and gave a very low, quiet moan. I couldn't tell exactly what was going through her mind, but I knew she felt badly, threatened, unwanted, useless. I knew the feeling quite well myself. I took her hand and put it back on my chest, on the photo, above where my heart sat silent but full. I looked in her eye. I didn't know whether to shake my head to stop her from thinking I didn't want her anymore, or to nod to show that I did want her, so I gave the little wheeze that we used to mean generally good, kind, positive things.

"Of course he still likes you, Blue Eye," Will offered from across the desk. He'd picked up the winter photo and was looking between it and us. "It's hard when you remember people you loved who are gone. It's something the people around you now can't understand, but it doesn't mean you don't like them. I know. It's just something you have to feel by yourself. Do you remember them now, Truman? Do you remember when these two pictures were taken?"

I could only shake my head.

He set down the picture. "Well, that's hard too, I guess. I often wondered what that would be like, if I could just forget the past. Meet all new people. Be off by myself with nothing to remind me of the past. But of course I can't. And it was hard, thinking of all the bad things I've seen—my mom and all the other people being killed, and all the other stuff. Maybe your way is just different, but they're both hard. I'm sorry if it made you sad, seeing them, but maybe it's nice to have their picture now, so at least there's some little connection with them." He actually reached out and patted Lucy on the shoulder, which I thought was remarkably kind. "And don't you worry. He's yours now." He looked back at me and smiled. He was going to be playful again. "*If* you still want him, all Mr. Big Smarty Pants professor now, with all his fancy books and diplomas. He won't want to hang around with us 'regular' people. What do they call that? Oh, yeah, 'putting on airs.' That'll be him from now on." He made funny gestures as he said this. Lucy looked back and forth between us and gave her tortured little laugh, and I felt a tiny bit better.

The books on the shelves were almost all about philosophy, though many had the word "ethics" in the title. None of them looked familiar, exactly, but they all filled me with the same excitement and enthusiasm and wonder as the trip to the library had. I was picking out some to take with us when Will gave a little chuckle. "Well, if we thought he was bad before, Blue Eye, now he'll really be impossible." He held up a thin volume that had my name on the cover. "Now he's even an author."

I took the book from Will. It was entitled *Virtue Ethics and the Social Contract*. I liked it better than the slogan I'd read in the college's brochure, though I found it a little daunting and cumbersome. At least I had some inkling of what the terms meant. I read the back cover. Apparently, in the book I outlined the specific implications that virtue ethics could hold for social ethics, forming a better foundation for modern society than the social contract model, and even forming a bridge or rapprochement between neo-Aristotelianism and some deontological thought. A professor from Oxford liked it, or so he was quoted on the back. I stopped to wonder whether there was anything left in England, or anywhere else, but then I went back to pondering what in the world I had written. I concluded that I would need to do a lot of other reading just to figure out what I had once thought.

"Heady stuff, Truman," Will said, putting my book and a few others into a small pack he had brought. "I was wondering if you'd written any books when we were in the library, but I couldn't figure out a way to look for them. There's no card catalogs because everything was online, and it would've taken days to search the library on our own. So I'm glad you found it. An ethical zombie? A virtuous zombie?" He looked at me and nodded. "Yes, I suppose you are, Truman. I mean it."

I supposed this was a compliment, so I tried to smile, but just a little since I knew people didn't like how it looked.

On the long journey home, Will stopped at one of the crossroads. On the road crossing ours, some of the grass and plants were crushed in two long strips. I didn't connect them to tire tracks until I saw how Will examined them with a look of concern and confusion.

"That's funny," he said. "When I was in town a few days ago there was no talk about a foraging raid out this way. Those things take time to plan and set up. They would've told me. And there'd be more than one vehicle. This is just one. It's a big vehicle, like a big truck. Maybe someone just wanted a quick fill up of fuel. But that doesn't make sense. There isn't a gate in the fence on this road. The fence runs right across it. That's weird."

In the distance, something roared like an engine. It lasted only a second. Will stood and scanned the trees and fields. He still looked concerned. "We're close to the fence. It's all farms inside the fence around here. Could be people starting up a tractor. But I don't hear anything more."

We listened a few seconds. Then there were three short, loud sounds. As with the tire tracks, I didn't make the connection at first. I had been so focused on the tracks and the sound of the engine that I thought maybe the sounds were from a vehicle backfiring. I looked at Will.

"It could just be hunters," he said, but I saw that his look had gone from concerned to worried. "But they should know not to hunt so near the farms. There are lots of kids out there this time of year."

I looked in the direction Will had been looking and suddenly realized what we had heard: three gunshots.

Chapter 15

With all the anticipation before and tragedy after my vows, I was very glad to get away from the city. It was a tradition that after school was done, the bigger children would spend a few weeks out in the country, working on some of the farms. The older people called it "summer camp," and although there was a lot of work involved, the farmers did always make it into a fun, vacation-like atmosphere for us. We worked in the day, then stayed up late at night, listening to stories of what the world had been like, about cities in Europe and Asia that the older people had visited, or places in the United States like the Grand Canyon, Yellowstone, Las Vegas, or Disneyworld.

I always had the funniest notions during these stories. Usually I'd have my typical sad thoughts of how all the people were dead and gone and we were stuck here in our little world and could never see those places again. Such places might as well be on another planet if they were more than a few miles past the fence.

Sometimes I'd think how the animals must like it. Without people to bother and kill them, there must have been thousands of buffalo and wolves roaming freely all over Yellowstone and the

Grand Canyon, alligators and tropical birds all over Disneyworld, Gila monsters and coyotes all over the crumbling ruins of the luxury hotels on the Vegas strip. It's not a nice thought, exactly, to think how it's good in a way that there aren't people anymore, but it was always a fantasy that filled me with wonder more than dread or loss.

We'd read books late at night, too. And sometimes, when we worked really hard during the day, the grownups would treat us to movies at night. They'd use fuel to fire up a generator and we could watch an old movie on the television. The older people would tell us how they used to watch television every day and how there weren't just tapes and DVDs, but new programs and movies that constantly came to the television from all over the world through an antenna or a cable. We would just look at them in disbelief. When I was really little, it had seemed like they had lived in some paradise of treasures and luxuries, being able to do something every day that we were rarely allowed to do now. But by the time I was twelve, it sounded more like some kind of strange excess and waste, like an addiction. I couldn't imagine watching television every day. But I'm sure we do lots of things now that people from the past wouldn't be able to believe, things they'd find odd or enviable or grotesque. And again I thought how hard it must be on the people older than me, that they had lived to see both worlds, and all the ugliness and senselessness and pain of each.

The old people told us that they used to drive for hours, so they could go somewhere else to work. And they'd work there all day, five or six days a week. Some would have two different jobs. I figured that was why they watched so much television, because they were so tired from all the work and driving; it made me glad that we could just watch a movie once in a while and have fun, and I definitely no longer envied them for being able to watch television every day.

The older people even said that many people would be at work so long and so far away that they'd pay someone to take care of their children. I asked why their neighbors didn't take care of their kids, the way we did now, and they couldn't exactly explain it; they just said you couldn't do that back then, that you didn't just ask other people to do things like that without paying them. They said sometimes you could ask family members to do it, but often they lived too far away, which also was hard for me to fathom, even if I knew in the abstract how spread out people were all across the country back then.

Even when we worked on the farms in the summer, we didn't work as much as they described. It just wasn't necessary, to work so many hours to get everything done. And it certainly made no sense to live so far away from where you worked that you had to spend hours a day driving, never mind all the fuel you'd be wasting. I couldn't understand why they hadn't lived closer to where they worked, or why someone would work and then give the money to someone else to take care of their children so they could work some more. They'd tried to explain that sometimes houses were too expensive, or the schools were better somewhere else, or you bought a house and then had to change jobs, and it all got too confusing and complicated and just too far away from reality for me to understand. It again made everything from before seem completely alien, and even slightly ugly and absurd.

As in the couple of years previous, I went to summer camp with Vera. Away from others, our slight difference in age seemed to matter less, and we could play more and enjoy ourselves without the roles or expectations of others. We'd build dams in little streams or race little boats we had made out of sticks. We would make cornhusk dolls and put them through all the tribulations of their tiny lives—keeping house, raising children, plowing fields, fighting zombies. And for us, there were berries to gather and can, meat to hang and smoke, ditches to dig and maintain to water the crops, weeds to pull, manure to spread. Every day was the most invigorating mix of leisure and work, with nothing dutiful or lazy, burdensome or distracting about either.

We worked a farm with a woman named Fran Clark. Unlike any other adult I knew then, she always had us call her by her first name, and I didn't feel uncomfortable or naughty doing so. Around her a first name seemed more appropriate, even though that didn't mean she was friendlier or more compassionate than other adults. If anything, she seemed slightly awkward and gruff around kids and had never had any of her own; she was just more forthright and direct as a way of dealing with the awkwardness, and calling her by her first name was part of that.

She was slightly younger than my mom and was one of the tallest women I knew. Her hair was blond and she kept it very short. Though her hair and bright blue eyes made her quite pretty, she was definitely less feminine than either my mom or Ms. Wright. Fran was athletic and muscular like Ms. Wright, but her body type was completely different: long and evenly muscled all over. As I often felt that summer, I was constantly in awe of how comfortable Fran was with her own body, especially when we'd swim in the pond near the farm; she showed no hesitation or embarrassment at being naked, while I tried to get in the water as quickly as possible, just to be covered up.

Fran would take us hunting and she was as good with a rifle or bow as anyone I've ever seen. The weeks with her and Vera were always exhilarating and calming at the same time, the three of us removed from society in our version of summer vacation, and yet so busily supplying our city's physical needs. Every night I'd fall asleep completely exhausted and fulfilled, content that everything was right and balanced and whole.

Like all of the farmhouses in the countryside beyond the live zone, the one we shared with Fran was a small, one-room house on stilts. It was the only kind of structure that made sense in an area where the dead might still be roaming around. If they found the house, you could easily kill them—if it unfortunately came to that—or you could fire off a flare and wait for help.

The actual room we lived in only contained our beds and a few other simple pieces of furniture. We did all our cooking and cleaning outside, near the building, before we climbed up into the house at night. The whole structure was only used during the summer, so it didn't need a fireplace or other source of heat. The generator and toilet were in separate little sheds, the former right under the house, the latter farther away, obviously.

All in all, it was a lot like living in a tree house, and there was even a tradition where the kids and adults gathered most nights to read stories like *Swiss Family Robinson*, *Robinson Crusoe*, or *Tarzan*. Reading ancient books that described people surviving or even thriving in rustic, primitive living arrangements made our own situation seem less like an oddity or burden of our harsh existence, but more like a treat—a fun, carefree adventure. (Of course, by that summer I'd already read *Lord of the Flies* on my own, so some of the romanticized notions of "the wild" had taken on other, more sinister implications for me.) Hard work aside, when they were ten or twelve, all kids thought the summer camp farmhouses were the greatest places to live and sleep.

Our particular farm was growing all kinds of vegetables, so it needed a lot of water. The large pond right by the house was a perfect supply, and had only required some minor construction to irrigate the plants. It also spilled over in a little waterfall into a stream below, making a constant roar that was soothing and—along with the drone of the summertime insects—a delight to fall asleep to. I was eager and relieved to be in such a peaceful place, after so much death and so many things fraught with meaning and sadness.

One day after working hard in the fields, we cooled off in the pond, ate lunch, and climbed up into the house. We'd often go inside during the hottest part of the day, and either take a nap or play board games or read. This day we were all tired enough to sleep a little bit. We got dressed in our lightest, coolest cotton clothes, and we all lay down for a rest.

Sometime later, I awoke to a roaring, tearing sound. I wasn't fully awake, and looked around to see the whole room tipping, completely dreamlike and unbelievable. Our beds slid across the floor and crashed into the far wall, and that sensation, along with Vera's shriek and a curse from Fran, jarred me completely awake.

I stood up among the remains of my bed. Standing was difficult, the floor was tilted so steeply, and I was stepping on wreckage with my bare feet.

"Girls," Fran said, making her way through the broken furniture, "find the guns. Find the flare, too." She picked up an aluminum bat out of the rubble. "There must be a lot of them, if they could pull out one of stilts. No moaning, though. That's weird."

I felt icy cold at the prospect of that many zombies outside, but Fran's voice was so even and calm it took away a little of the panic and made me search carefully and methodically.

I climbed down to the floor and rummaged among the pieces of a little table, which had stored a loaded handgun.

Vera shrieked again, and from the window came an animal roar. A hairy, unkempt man was climbing into the house. He held a huge knife and was dressed in a hodgepodge of skins and various bits of fabric. He definitely wasn't dead, he moved too fast and fluidly.

He made for Fran, but the tilted floor was just as awkward for him, and she'd already seen him. As graceful and sudden as Ms. Wright had been, she struck him in the head with the bat. There was an arc of blood and a rasping groan as he spun and fell.

I saw the handle of a gun among the wreckage and grabbed it. The gun's cold, solid weight sent confidence surging through me. It was Fran's magnum, so I'd only have six shots, and it was hard as hell for me to fire it at all, since it was so big and heavy and the recoil would nearly knock me over.

I was trying to stand as two more men dressed in skins came through the window. At the same moment, another man crashed through the door. They had Fran from two sides now.

She stepped back and swung the bat at the man who had come through the door. He blocked it and groaned as the metal slammed into his forearm, and the other two men threw themselves at Fran, knocking her down. It'd be risky to shoot with them on top of her, but I tried to take aim.

I raised the magnum as two more of them came through the window and started towards me. It was good to see the hideous, animal lust in their eyes turn for the briefest moment into fear as they looked down the magnum's barrel. You never got either of those looks from the dead—just blind incomprehension, like a fish—and it always made killing them seem wrong, unfair, culpable. Tightening my fingers on the pistol's grip that day, I didn't feel any of that, but instead a sudden rush. Later I wasn't sure which feeling was worse, but I knew both were necessary.

The magnum exploded and jerked way up above my head. I was deafened and my ears started ringing. Both the ceiling and the man nearest the window were splattered with brains as the bullet tore out the back of the other man's skull. Fully awake and armed and well trained, I felt no fear or confusion. I was clearheaded enough to wonder, briefly, why Fran had loaded the bedside gun with hollow points.

I brought the gun down as quickly as I could, but the brain-splattered man swatted it to the side. I twisted and screamed and tried again to bring it back up, but he had grabbed my hand. Training or no, there was no way I would win, wrestling with him for the gun.

He smashed his left fist into my face. I was stunned and could barely see. He'd hit me so hard it bent me down almost double. I dropped the gun and it fell among the debris.

He still had a hold of my left hand. I raised my right to block as he punched down again. The blow hurt my arm like hell, but at least I'd deflected it. Another punch like the first and I doubted I'd be able to see or stand at all.

It was hard to keep my balance, but I kicked him with my right foot, as hard as I could, right in the groin. He loosened his grip on my left hand and I wrenched it away.

With a shriek, Vera jumped on the man's back. She wasn't well trained, but it was an unexpected attack and it kept him distracted and off balance. I rummaged around on the floor for the magnum. It must have slid or been kicked away, because I couldn't find it. I saw that a piece of wood had splintered off from a table leg or a slat from the bed. It was about a foot and a half long and very pointy. I grabbed it.

The man had pulled Vera off his back and had flung her away. As he turned to me, I shoved the wooden spike as hard as I could, upward, beneath his ribs on his right side. He grabbed my hand and let out a shriek. I'd heard pigs slaughtered before; this sound was a lot like that. I could feel his grip loosen on my wrist and he staggered back and collapsed. The wood had probably slid all the way through his liver; he'd bleed out after a couple minutes of intense pain. Of course, he'd get back up then, but we had more urgent problems.

I looked to Vera, and she was getting up and looked okay. I was turning back to see what had happened to Fran when there was another explosion, audible over the ringing in my ears. Some-one else had a gun out. Fran was on her stomach on the floor, still struggling, and two of the men had her pinned, punching and elbowing her intermittently as she fought them. The third intruder was standing, and he was the shooter. His gun looked like a 9mm semi-automatic pistol. "All right, cue ball," he said evenly, lowering the barrel till it was pointed at my head. "That's about enough out of you."

Staring at him and panting, I felt sorry I'd failed Vera and Fran and I hoped they could forgive me. Vera came up next to me and put her hand on my shoulder. It was good to have her there, but I really hoped he'd just shoot me, so I wouldn't have to see her suffer. I had a somewhat fuller concept than I thought she did, of what they would do to us.

I raised my left hand. I was up to my knees in wreckage, and I knelt down slightly, leaning to my right and feeling around as inconspicuously as possible, hoping the bed would hide what I was doing. I still hoped for the magnum or perhaps one of the other guns in the room, though I doubted I could move fast enough even if I found one.

The shooter stepped towards me. "Other hand up, missy," he said with that same dry, measured tone. "You crazy bitches have way too many guns and shit lying around here."

I had the very cold and unpleasant realization that his tone probably wouldn't change much during our brief, violent relationship—whether he was threatening me, mocking me, raping me, or beating me to death. I put both hands on top of my head.

"Good. Better." He told his cohorts to take Fran outside and tie her to the bumper of the truck, and they dragged her, still kicking, out the door.

The shooter stood staring at us, panting, until one of the other men returned. "All right. You—the nappy-headed little one. Go with him or I'll blow your friend's head off. Now."

Vera looked to me and I nodded slightly. She climbed over the wrecked furniture and the other man dragged her out the door.

"Good. Now we can have some fun."

The shooter finally looked over to check on the man I had stabbed. He had collapsed on the pieces of one bed, clutching at his wound. Blood had soaked through his clothes from his chest to his knees, and it had stained the bedclothes all around him, still creeping outward from his body. He had been wheezing, slowly and wetly, with decreasing frequency as Fran and Vera were taken outside.

"Bart? How you doing over there?"

"Not so good, Rhodes. Kid's a crazy little bitch."

"She sure is, Bart." The shooter aimed his gun at the other man, though he was still watching me from the corner of his eye.

Bart, the dying man, didn't look scared like when I had trained the magnum on him, just resigned, as if this was boring and predictable, which I suppose it was to him. "Can't even wait for me to turn?"

Rhodes smiled. It was cold, reptilian, though also grotesquely flawed from years of neglect, more like the grin you saw on dead animals as their flesh pulled back over their rotted, broken teeth. It didn't express emotion, but tension, like a spring or a bow. Like his voice, I felt sure it would serve as his all-purpose expression for all manner of cruelty and abuse. "Nah, I'm not that patient. But hey—at least I'm using a bullet. I thought that'd be nicer— quicker and cleaner than a shovel or axe. I know you'd do the same for me, buddy."

The other man blinked once, slowly. "Yeah. You're a real saint." He looked at me. "This is all your fault, you crazy bitch. I hope this psycho here turns you out worse than you can stand for laying me up here to die."

I stared back at him, evenly and placidly. I didn't feel hatred or anger; I didn't feel sympathy, either. He was the first living man I'd ever killed. It's always surprised me, in all the years since, that I didn't feel much beyond the tiniest, almost tickling sensation of disgust and the slightest, almost imperceptible chill of pity. "People used to believe that things turned out better for you if you thought something a little nice right at the end." It was the only response I could think of, and I thought it was apt.

"Screw you, bitch."

Rhodes eagerly seconded the dying man's sentiment. "Oh, don't you worry, Bart, my man. We've got that part covered."

I watched impassively as Bart's brains sprayed onto the wall behind him and he fell backward into the warm, wet stain of mortality on our floor.

Rhodes turned to me. He took a step closer. Fran must've hit him a few times; his face was florid, and blood still poured from the side of his mouth. Good for her, I thought.

"Yeah, you are a hot, feisty little piece of ass. Too hot for poor Bart there." He ran the tip of the gun barrel down my left cheek. It was slightly warm from being fired. "But not too hot for me, baby doll." Again the sick, soulless smile. "Yeah, that's what you look like, all bald and shit—a little baby doll!"

For once I thought how my eyes weren't so ugly, as his were a sicker, paler shade of brown, tinged with yellow and rimmed with red. They seemed unusually small, especially the pupils, which was odd since it wasn't that bright inside the cabin. He slid the gun barrel down my left side, then across my belly. Training would let you withstand levels of pain you never thought possible. Training would let you watch a man have his head blown off and not blink an eye. But there was no training for humiliation and degradation; that was always personal and real and undiluted.

I thought of grabbing the gun, but he would have just added a pistol whipping to the inevitable "fun" he had planned for me. And there was that inexorable inertia of life that I had seen with Ms. Dresden, and I knew it would keep me conscious during way too much of the beating for it to be a preferable option. Though as Rhodes' stink of years-old sweat stung my eyes and made me nearly gag, I thought that passing out might come blessedly sooner.

The gun barrel slid up my belly, between my small breasts— which I had only just begun to notice in the past year or so; the barrel lingered under my chin, and then he traced my mouth with it. I still didn't feel fear so much as regret, though it was no longer just a feeling that I had failed Fran and Vera, but also a bitterness about my own impending loss—regret that I'd never have children, never hold hands with a boy, never know so many of the meager but precious joys of our world. The thought still wasn't exactly fear, but an intense pang of remorse and worthlessness and hopelessness, enough to make me hiccup a little as I caught a rising sob in my throat.

Rhodes rested the gun barrel on my lips. "Not much of a talker, either. I like that. That's the main thing I don't miss about bitches—all that talk before and after. I can go weeks out there with the boys and not hear ten words. But don't get me wrong—I do miss bitches' mouths. I sure do. You're gonna find that out, so long as you want to stay alive."

All I could do was glare at him. Rhodes took a step back, and I thought maybe his version of "fun" had been postponed. Then he smiled again, and I knew it hadn't. It still surprised me, though, when he kicked me in the stomach. It seemed such an odd gesture—not obscene like his fetishistic poking of me with the gun, and I could tell he hadn't kicked me as hard as he could have, so it wasn't a blow intended to hurt me badly—but as I staggered back, doubling up and choking, it occurred to me what it was. It was how some people could kick a dog, how they would use casual violence to show something smaller and weaker that they were the boss and its pain was only amusement, its needs or feelings as unimportant and worthless as air or dirt.

He bent over me, close enough that I felt the bloody spray of his words on my cheek and ear, smelled the rot of his teeth and whatever vile, diseased thing he'd eaten recently. "I don't think you're old enough to realize what a hard-on I have for you, bitch, but you best learn one thing: that won't stop me from putting your brains all over the ground if you don't jump when I say jump. Now get up and let's get going."

Once I'd stood, he shoved me out the door, then stepped up behind me and shoved me again, so that I fell on the hot, dry dirt in front of our wrecked cabin. I landed on my knees and fell forward, catching myself with my left hand. I stayed there, panting with rage and humiliation. Bart's punch must've cut my face a little, because blood mixed with my sweat and ran down to the tip of my nose. Three long drops fell into the dust, turning it an ugly, loveless brown.

Chapter 16

Will moved fast down the other road, following the tire tracks, as Lucy and I struggled to keep up. He gave us a second to catch up. "I don't have time to take you back to your place," he explained. "And I don't want to leave you out here by yourselves. Someone might see you and shoot you, or even other zombies might attack you. So you've got to follow me. And do what I say. I don't know what's going on, but I think it's bad. So just follow me and be careful."

We kept following the road. Up ahead a fence led off as far as I could see to the right and the left. But straight ahead, a section of the fence had been removed. The tire tracks were a jumble there. They went off to either side, along the path of where the fence had been, and they also continued along the road we had been following. The fence itself was lying on the ground, the support poles bent over.

Will said, "It's like they just drove along the fence with a big vehicle, crushing it as they went, like they just wanted to destroy it for no reason. Then they went back to following the road." He looked at us. "There are good people down there. This time of year there are lots of kids out there, too. They're all armed and careful, but the farms are spread out, not close to each other. And they're not expecting people to attack them, only zombies. I need to help them. Can you keep up and help me if I need you?"

I looked to Lucy and we both nodded immediately. Will had been so nice to us that, as frightening and unexpected as all this was, I couldn't imagine refusing his request for help, especially if people were in danger. I still couldn't conceive of what might be going on, but we followed him regardless. When the road and tracks turned slightly to the left, we kept going straight into some trees. Lucy and I had a hard time negotiating the roots and branches in our way. "It's not much farther," Will whispered. "Stay quiet."

I heard voices off to our left, and we moved more slowly until we were at the edge of the forest, looking out on an open area. I couldn't tell exactly what had happened there, but the way the people sounded and looked, it seemed clear that they were being uncaring and violent in ways I couldn't understand or imagine.

There was the wreck of a building in front of us. Two big, wooden poles held up the right side of the building, though the poles had bent over and the house had tilted so far to the left it touched the ground; the stilts on that side stuck out from under the building, connected by a large chain to a dump truck. The truck had a snowplow, and sticking out of the back on a pole, a white flag rippled in the breeze. I could make out two wavy blue lines down the middle of the flag. On one side of the blue lines was a red handprint, and on the other a red sun.

More telling and alarming to me were the people I saw. Among them were two girls. The smaller of them was sitting on the ground, and the larger girl was on her hands and knees. Oddly, the bigger girl was bald. Further from where we stood, there was a tall, blond woman with her wrists tied behind her to the back of the dump truck.

Both the girls and the woman appeared to be hurt, especially the bald girl. She breathed hard and her face was bleeding. A man stood near her, holding a pistol. He didn't seem the least bit concerned with her injuries, and he made no move to help her.

Two other men came out of the house, carrying things to the truck. They ignored the two girls, but stopped a moment to maul the woman in a gross and sexual way. Though I couldn't make out what they were saying, I could see her kick and struggle as they pawed her and laughed. Then they went back into the house. I assumed they were getting more things, whatever the things were.

"I don't think they've killed anyone yet," Will whispered, "but those men are going to start hurting those girls soon. I don't know if you remember what men like that do to girls, and I know that zombies don't do that kind of thing, but it's a very bad kind of hurting, believe me.

"I'm going to circle around to the back of the house, because if I shoot from here they might be able to make it to the house or the truck before I can get them all. I only see the one gun, but they may all have them, and I'm sure they have more in the truck. You two just stay here. Don't come out, don't make any noise. I'll come and get you when it's done. If I don't, then just run back the way we came."

All we could do was nod. I felt so sorry we couldn't do more.

Will disappeared off to the right and I returned to watching the people. After hauling out another load of stuff, and after another round of pawing the woman tied to the truck, the two men joined the one holding the gun in front of the house.

"That's just about everything," one of the scavengers said. "These people don't seem to know how to live much. No booze, no weed, not much food—just a bunch of books and guns."

The man with the pistol nodded. "Yeah, some people's priorities are all ass backwards. They got a generator? I didn't see any vehicles."

The third man nodded. "They had some diesel for a generator. Dickhead here said I could have dibs before him if I was the one to siphon it." He spat. "Shit always burns your mouth like hell."

The other two men laughed, and the gunman said, "Yeah, well, he likes to watch anyway. Gets him all worked up for his turn. I figure we got a little time to break these bitches in right before we get a move on. So, ladies, nice little place you have here. We don't usually get up this way, but pickings have been getting a little thin. I'm sure glad we came." He ran the barrel of his gun across the back of the neck of the bald girl on the ground. "We're real sorry we broke your little tree house, but we were afraid you might not welcome us with open arms—or legs."

More laughter, low and dry.

"That's a real big fence we passed on the way here, so there must be more of you people around. I was wondering if some of them might be coming by?"

"They're supposed to drop off supplies this afternoon," the woman tied to the truck shouted. "Real men, not some pieces of shit who beat up little girls."

The man with the gun smiled. I couldn't imagine mine looked worse, his was so ugly, and I didn't sense any happiness behind it. "Funny how people who don't know how to live right don't know how to lie good, either. Just got to take our chances, I guess. Oh, and I can be as gentle or rough as I need to be, you big, Amazon bitch. My new special little friend here is the one that likes to play really rough. Aren't you, baby doll?"

The girl on the ground didn't respond. The blonde shouted again. "A real man would want to get off with a woman. Or are you too embarrassed for me to see what a dickless piece of shit you really are?"

I think she was taunting them to distract them from the two girls. Like Will, she seemed very brave. I wondered how everyone in his community could be so good, and I was embarrassed at my own inaction and fear.

The man with the gun looked over to the woman. "Yeah, big bitch, I'm sorry you'll have to settle for one of these two sorry-ass bastards the first time, but your little friend here gave me such a hard-on, being all hot and feisty and fighting back. That was quite a show she put on in there. And you and her killing three guys kind of makes things work out perfect now—three of you, three of us. No lines, no waiting."

A chuckle from the other two men and they nudged each other.

The man with the gun stepped toward the younger girl sitting on the ground. "Of course, we don't want to leave you out either, sweetheart. Little half-nigger might be fun." He turned to the other two men and gestured at the seated girl with his gun. "You're so right that these people's priorities are all messed up— no booze or fun, ladies out by themselves with no respect for men, folks mating with niggers. Damn, what a world."

All three men shared in the laughter now, letting it rise in pitch and intensity.

The girl he was taunting stood up and glared at him. It seemed forever that she decided what to do next, but then she slapped him and spit on him.

"Don't!" the blond woman shouted. She'd managed to get partly to her feet and was straining against her bonds.

The bald girl on the ground also let out a rasping protest as she got up on one knee and one foot and started to stand.

The man with the gun grabbed the wrist of the girl who was slapping him. "Oh, boys, I am *so* glad we came up this way!" he laughed. "I didn't think there were three bitches with this much spirit left in the whole damn, zombified world! Now we just got to get them to mind!" He twisted the girl's wrist behind her back, making her howl with pain, then he shoved her away. When she faced him again, he kicked her in the stomach, doubling her over. Then he turned to the girl who was standing up. He didn't kick her; he just put his foot on her chest and pushed until she fell down.

I heard the shot then. The man with the gun spun around and dropped to his knees next to the bald girl. Blood spread out from his left shoulder, but he began to get back up.

Will emerged from the bushes to the right of the house, walking forward steadily—not running, just marching with his arm stiff and steady in front of him, sunlight glinting off his gun. His arm barely flinched as he fired again. This shot hit one of the other men, and as he fell, brains and blood sprayed from his head.

I hadn't remembered such blood and fleshly destruction since the woman we had attacked in the city years ago. I wondered why other people like me didn't bleed so much, and I could only stare in wonder as this man's life eased out onto the dirt. I could never have imagined anything so wondrous, like I was staring at the deepest mystery in the world, laid bare even as it was rendered useless and irrelevant. Maybe it wasn't the ability to speak that made these people so different and more powerful than us, and that gave them the ability or the right to lock us up. Perhaps it was because they had this ability to bleed and suffer, and to make others suffer in such exquisite and horrible ways. Even though I had just heard the men saying such terrible, evil things, I could feel no joy or satisfaction at what I saw.

The man with the gun and his friend ran away from Will in different directions, the former towards the woods where we were, the latter towards the truck. Will fired again and the man running toward the truck fell, the blood spreading out beneath his motionless body. The gunman pulled the bald girl up by her shoulder and dragged her into the trees and bushes right by me. Will fired at him but missed.

I didn't think. I'm sure if I had, I wouldn't have done anything but stand and watch. I suppose I just reacted. I lunged at the man, seizing his left arm. He was startled at first, and let go of the girl. She scrambled off to my right as he and I struggled. He was much quicker than me, and I thought for sure I was going to die. He brought his gun up, and I grabbed at it before he could fire. The man clutched my neck, but I had both my hands on his gun hand, so I was able to hold on to it, even though he seemed stronger than I was.

From out of the corner of my eye, I saw Lucy move up slowly and deliberately on my left. She was still so graceful, gliding into view as she raised her tiny hand above her head. The man saw her and released his hold on my neck to pull away from me, but I was still holding his arm.

Lucy hit him in the head with a large rock, one a little bigger than my fist. He dropped his gun and staggered to the side as I let go of him. Lucy stepped in front of me without a sound and hit him again. He turned, fell on his face, and she immediately dropped onto his back and kept bringing the rock down, flinging blood onto the bushes next to her with each upstroke. She continued until the rock came up with dirt on it, as well as blood, and the man's head was an unrecognizable pile.

The girl watched us from a few feet away. She looked more surprised than scared, but she also looked ready to run if Lucy or I made the slightest movement towards her.

Will came through the trees and bushes. He backed slightly away from Lucy and got between her and the girl. "It's okay now," he said. "It's okay, Zoey."

The girl stood up. "They killed him. But then they just stopped and stared at me. What's wrong with them, Will?"

"Some of them are smarter than others," he said. "These two are especially smart, and they don't want to eat people."

Lucy cast aside the bloody rock. She reached into the remains of the dead man's skull and came out with a long, wet mass that she raised and stretched till it snapped off in her hands. She seemed nearly oblivious to the rest of us now.

"Well, not so much, at least," Will said. "She's much more coordinated than other zombies, but I guess she still likes to eat some of the time. He doesn't eat at all and he can even read. They understand you when you talk. I think they understood what these guys were going to do and they wanted to stop them. And, well, now she's a little distracted with eating him. I mean, it's not like they're perfect."

Lucy had her face in her hands, chewing at the wet, spongy mass.

The girl watched her for a moment, frowning. "Not perfect? Will, she's eating a guy's brain right in front of me."

"Yeah, but he deserved it."

The girl paused, then nodded. "All right. You have a point."

I bent down and picked up the dead man's gun. I was afraid of it because I didn't have Lucy's dexterity, so I scooped it into my palm, the barrel pointing off to the right. I stepped around Lucy, who had reached in for more to eat, and very carefully presented the gun to the girl. She watched me intently the whole time I was moving.

"Thank you," she said as she took it from me. "Thank you for saving me, too. You could've been killed. Well, you could've been shot, at least. That was very brave of you."

I nodded. It felt good to be called brave, even if I didn't think I deserved it. I wondered if I'd ever been called that before, when I was a professor. I doubted it.

"You two stay here," Will said to me. "I'll come back for you." To the girl, he said, "I'd appreciate it if you didn't tell the others about these two. I don't know if people would like having them out of their holding area."

"Sure," she replied as they walked back out to help the others. She kept watching me as they left.

They got the other girl off the ground, then went and untied the woman. I could see them getting stuff out of the back of the truck. Then they all walked to the front of the house, where I could hear their conversation, and see that they had retrieved a lot of guns from the vehicle.

"It was total chance I found you guys," Will was explaining. "I was out past the fence and saw the tire tracks and I didn't think it was right, so I followed them here." They paused to survey the carnage. "Awful." He looked over at the big truck. "What's that flag?"

The woman looked over at the truck too. "I don't know. They weren't much for conversation about themselves, just talking about what they were going to do to us, the sick bastards. Maybe it's the flag of their group or tribe or whatever the hell these animals were a part of." She nudged a body with her foot.

"Yeah. Well, you didn't see what they did to the fence. Not just a hole to drive their truck through, but they deliberately tore up a huge section of it. You all should go to the next farm and send for a crew to fix the fence as quickly as possible, or we won't know how many zombies have gotten in and this whole area will be dangerous. I'll burn the bodies and then I'll double back to the hole in the fence and try to round up any zombies that have wandered through. Zoey, could you take this for me? I want to travel light and I don't want to lose this out there." Will handed the girl the little pack with the books we'd gathered from my college. It all seemed so long ago and unimportant now.

"It's a good enough plan, Will," the woman agreed. "What a mess. Come on, girls."

She led the girls away. The older one, who had seen us, looked back toward me. I thought she looked like a very kind, and most of all, very intelligent person. I was again in awe of Will and his friends, that they could all be such fine and virtuous people. But the dead men had also been able to talk—and bleed—and they seemed the absolute opposite of fine or virtuous. There was something more to their differences that I still couldn't figure out. I don't know if I ever will.

I touched Lucy on the shoulder and she finally looked up from her monstrous feast. Her mouth and chin were covered with blood. Stringy bits were stuck between her teeth. I helped her stand up, then bent down to tear off some of the dead man's clothes; I cleaned off her chin with the pieces of cloth. The blood was still hot and wet, so it came off pretty well. I couldn't do it perfectly, but it definitely looked better. I supposed Lucy hadn't been able to help herself, and it was a little enough of a weakness; as Will had said, we were no more perfect than the other people. It had been fortunate indeed that Lucy had acted so decisively against the man, as I don't think I would've been able to do much against him by myself. But I was glad she was done feeding and back to normal. I could never understand why living—any kind of living, even the most regular and necessary of tasks, like eating— had to be so ugly.

Will dragged the bodies into a pile in front of the house. The woman and the girls had walked out of sight, so I dragged the gunman's body out to the pile as well. As soon as Lucy saw what I was doing, she lent a hand.

I looked down at the dead bodies as Will splashed fuel all over them. Now they didn't seem so wondrous or revealing, just embarrassing, like they should be put out of sight as quickly as possible; all their mystery was gone and replaced with disappointment and meaninglessness and ugliness.

Will had us step back, knowing our fear of fire. I watched impassively as the flames reached into the bright, sunny sky and smeared it with a greasy, foul smoke, an offering of something worthless to something inscrutable and unknown.

Chapter 17

After we left Will and his zombie friends—if that's the right word for them—the three of us walked down the road to the nearest farm. It was a couple miles, so they might have heard the shots, but they might have thought we were shooting some animal—a coyote or fox that was attacking our livestock, or a deer for food. Guns were so much a part of our lives it wouldn't necessarily have set off any alarms. We walked for a while in silence, but eventually we needed to talk.

Fran looked down at me. She knew I was always thinking about something, and at a time like this more than ever. "You okay?" she asked. "They didn't hit you too much. You either, Vera."

"No, they didn't hit me too much," I said. Vera agreed. I looked up at Fran. Both her eyes were blackened. Some blood had dried at the corners of her mouth and under her nose. She walked kind of slow, like something hurt inside—probably a bruised or broken rib. It probably wasn't worse than that—if the rib had punctured something, she wouldn't be walking at all. "They hurt you a lot worse."

She shrugged. "Not too bad."

"I think he didn't want to hit me in the face too much before he... you know. Before he did what he was going to do." I could use the word "rape" when I thought it to myself, but saying it out loud wasn't possible yet, especially in front of Vera.

Fran looked at me again. "That might have been what he was thinking, yes. Sometimes there's no telling what people like that are thinking, or if they think. Most days I've hoped that we were rid of all that. I'm sorry you had to see it at all. You kids see so much violence and death already. That kind of shit should just be over and in the past. You shouldn't have to live with that, on top of everything else."

"It was lucky Will showed up when he did," I said. It was what we were really thinking—not what had happened, but what could have happened.

"Sure was." Fran could be more laconic than my dad.

"And what if he hadn't?"

We walked for several steps without an answer. "I remember the first time I saw you, Zoey. Me and Jack and Jonah—we got there in time to save you. But later, we didn't get there in time to save your dad. I don't know why. I remember when I was little, my mom told me everything happened for a reason. And I try to still believe that. But I don't know what that reason could be when I think of things like what happened to your dad, or what almost happened to us."

"I guess all you can do is be grateful when the person does show up in time."

"Yeah, I guess. Will's always been a brave kid. It helps when someone knows what it's like to suffer; it makes them more compassionate, I think. Those pieces of shit back there didn't know what it's like to suffer. Or maybe they did, and it just made them meaner, made them want to hurt people more. I don't know. I don't give a shit. Some people aren't worth it. I would've made them suffer worse than a bullet through the head if I could've."

We walked on. It was an eminently practical solution—to just not care, to accept things as they had happened, or even to rejoice at the suffering of the wicked. I felt fairly sure, however, that I would never have the kind of stoic outlook that would make the first reaction available for me, and I just didn't have the visceral emotion that would make the second one possible. There was too much wonder and terror in the world for either response. The pull of those two qualities—wonder and terror—in such seemingly opposite directions made any other response seem extremely difficult or dishonest.

We got to the nearest farm, and the people there washed our wounds and gave us food and water. One of the adults left on a bicycle to tell the people in the city what had happened, so workers could be sent to repair the fence and to search for intruders, living or dead. By sunset, I could hear vehicles pulling up outside the cabin. I went outside, and my mom and dad took me in their arms, as Vera's parents hugged her. Mom cried a little and fussed over my new black eye—the earlier one from Ms. Dresden was barely noticeable—but when they saw I was okay, they calmed down.

My dad and the other adults discussed what to do at that point. Fran described the men and their vehicle, but couldn't give any information on where they came from or whether there might be more. She did say they seemed afraid of more people showing up, and were planning on leaving as soon as possible, so it seemed they were alone and not part of some larger group. (Fran left out what they had planned to do with us before leaving, to spare our parents as much as us, I'm sure, even if everyone could fill in the details on their own.) The flag did make everyone wonder, though, if they had come from some sort of "community." She said the men hadn't used a radio to communicate with anyone else, at least not since they broke into our house. She also told my dad that Will had gone back to the breach in the fence to see what was happening there, and no more gunshots had been heard.

After some discussion, it was generally agreed that we weren't under an invasion from some other, large, organized group of humans, and if we could seal the fence back up and clear the area of any zombies that had gotten through, we'd be safe again. My dad, along with Vera's dad and some other people, would keep watch over the breach tonight and make sure no one else got through. When the construction equipment arrived in the morning, they would start the repairs. My mom pulled me away to take me back to the city, along with Vera and her mom.

I knew I'd have to ask my mom while my dad was still around, because I knew what their answers would be. "Can't I stay with Dad? I'm not hurt. I don't want to go home."

They looked at each other. You realize when you get older that divide-and-conquer is how you got most everything you asked your parents for when you were younger, though at the time it was just a natural, reflexive way to approach any request. "No," my mom began, "you can't be out there at night, not with the fence torn open. No."

Negotiation and compromise was another important element in adolescent maneuvers. "No, I didn't mean going out there at night. I'll stay here tonight, with Fran. Then we'll go out to the fence when they go out with the construction equipment in the morning."

"Why in the world do you want to do that? You can't help with the construction. You should just come home."

Logic and practicality were the final, deciding elements you brought in for these kinds of conversations, even if they were, in fact, the furthest things from your reasons. "They'll need someone to keep watch with a rifle, right, Dad?"

He looked between me and my mom. He knew what I was doing, I was sure even then. But he knew I wanted to be with Fran. Vera was young enough that she'd want to be with her mom as soon as a crisis was over. I was just old enough to want to be with the other people who'd survived the crisis. And as I said, he always pushed me to do more dangerous things, to take responsibility, rather than just be kept safe; and there was something in me that always responded to this.

"Well," he began tentatively, watching for my mom's reaction. I knew he'd give in to her if she were really adamant about it, but with the conclusion that we were not under a general siege, I suspected she might not be completely dead set against my staying out here. Danger was all around anyway, as Mr. Enders and Ms. Dresden's baby had shown. "She's as good with a rifle as anyone I know," Dad said. "We could use her and Fran looking out for anything sneaking up on us. If you think you'll be up to it tomorrow morning, Fran."

"Sure," Fran replied. "I just need some sleep tonight. I'll keep an eye on her. We'll just sit there with our binoculars tomorrow."

I looked back to my mom. She finally agreed. She hugged me. "You poor, little thing," she whispered, "always trying to be so big and responsible. You come back and just stay with me after this and not do anything with guns and dead people for a while."

I hugged her back. "I will, Mom," I whispered. "I want that too."

I slept in the farmhouse with Fran and the other people that night. I was on the floor. Fran was on the bed closest to me, since her injuries were worse and would cause her more pain. Before we fell asleep, she leaned over and rubbed my head.

"Thanks for sticking up for me, Fran," I said quietly. "I wanted to stay out here with you and Dad."

She smiled a little. Like Ms. Wright, it wasn't a frequent expression with her. "I know, Zoey. But your mom is right too. You took your vows and everyone knows what you can do. I saw you in the cabin, so I definitely know. But you don't always have to be hard and strong and in control. You can be a kid sometimes."

"I know. I want to be. But later. Not right now."

The next morning I was awakened by the sound of big, diesel engines.

The other people in the cabin were already making breakfast outside. I joined them as the trucks pulled up, hauling the construction equipment and supplies.

Ms. Dresden got down from the cab of the one truck. Unlike Fran or Ms. Wright, she smiled more frequently, even after all she'd been through. Her smile was pretty, too, like the rest of her. Her eyes sparkled and she seemed radiant that day. "Oh, I'm glad to see you," she said as she hugged me. "I was so mean to you, and then to have this happen. I just wanted to see you as soon as I could."

Someone passed me a plate of fried eggs, and I shared them with Ms. Dresden. They were hot, with runny yolks, and we both giggled a little as it ran down our chins and we tried to wipe it up.

It felt good to laugh with her. As Fran had said, sometimes suffering made you feel closer to other people.

"Come on, ride in the truck with me," Ms. Dresden said as we finished eating. We walked over to a big flatbed truck. On the bed of the truck was a backhoe that had been fitted with a post hole digger. Ms. Dresden climbed into the cab next to the driver and pulled me up next to her.

We drove to the fence and I saw the damage Will had described. It was senseless and excessive and useless. Maybe they were trying to let in more zombies so we'd be less able to defend ourselves. Or who knew? I remembered the etymology of the word "vandalism" and that's what it reminded me of—barbarians destroying something civilized and peaceful, not even for tactical reasons, but just because of what it represented.

Ms. Dresden drove the backhoe off the flatbed. Other people moved about, unrolling fencing, mixing cement. Fran walked over from one of the other trucks and handed me an M16. No scope, but for picking off things at a distance the M16 with iron sights was a perfect choice. It felt good to hold it—solid, reliable, powerful. Fran had the same kind of weapon. My dad came up to us a minute later. He smiled and squeezed my shoulder. "You okay, kiddo?"

"Yes, Dad. I'm fine."

One big panel truck used to bring supplies was parked on a slight hill away from the others. My dad pointed to it. "I figure that's a good spot for you two."

"Sure is," Fran agreed. "Where's Will?"

"He was here when we got here last night, but then he went off to scout around farther out. You know how he is. There's no telling him to do anything, other than what he thinks he should do. And I don't worry much about him, the way he handles himself.

"Anyway, I got to check on the supplies," my dad concluded. "The hole's a lot bigger than we thought. Give a holler if you see anything."

Fran and I walked up the hill to the truck. With the driver's door open, she pulled herself onto the roof of the cab. I handed the rifles to her, then she helped me up. We had to stretch to pull the door closed, but once we did, there was no easy way for someone to climb up after us, which was always the first thing you looked for in a spot you wanted to occupy all day out here. We climbed to the top of the cargo part of the truck, eleven feet or so from the ground. Fran spread a blanket, so we wouldn't get burned as the sun heated the metal roof. We sat cross-legged, facing opposite ways, leaning against each other's back. It was a funny position, but it felt nice—sturdy, restful, and intimate. Our rifles lay across our laps and Fran handed me binoculars as she got out a pair for herself. We scanned all around as the people began their work beneath us. Beyond the workers, out in the fields and hills for hundreds of yards around, we saw the occasional rabbit, deer, or bird, but no humans, either living or dead.

"You sleep good?" Fran said to make small talk.

"Yes, really peaceful," I replied. "You?"

"Great. I remember I used to have trouble sleeping, years ago. But not since we've been living in our little group. I always sleep so well now. Straight through the night, and I either have no dreams, or nice ones about my parents or friends I knew when I was little. I bet people would think we'd have nightmares now, living the way we do. Isn't that funny?"

"Sleep is the cousin of death." I remembered reading that somewhere.

Her back moved a little against mine, like she was sitting up straighter and partly turning toward me. "What?"

"Sleep is the cousin of death. They're related, similar. They're almost the same. So maybe we got so used to death being around all the time that sleep comes to us more naturally, more easily." I really had never thought of it before, but it just kind of came together that way in my head.

Her back shook a little bit from a chuckle, and her muscles rippled and slid against me as she turned back the other way. "Zoey, you say the damndest things sometimes. You really do."

"I know. Sorry."

"Don't be sorry. I like it."

"Thanks, Fran. Thanks for not thinking I'm weird." I wasn't sure where this came from, either, but it also just occurred to me.

She reached over her own shoulder to squeeze mine. "I'd never think that, Zoey. You should know that."

"Yeah. I guess I do. I'm glad you're my friend."

"I'm glad too."

We sat up there and kept watching, talking on and off about unimportant things. It couldn't be as carefree as things had been before, but it was still peaceful and calm, as the thump and rumble of the workers steadily edged up and past us, and we watched over them like friendly gargoyles perched there with our glass eyes, our weapons of black steel, and our softly spoken questions, jokes, and secrets.

Chapter 18

When the flames had died down enough that Will wasn't afraid of it spreading, he led us away from the pyre and took us toward the dead men's truck. It had been such a strange and overwhelming day, first at the college with all its revelations, and then with the terrible violence wrought by those men against Will's friends, and the deadly response of Will and Lucy. I remembered the very kind and intelligent-looking girl, and I looked over at Lucy, wondering again how such beautiful and graceful creatures were always surrounded with pain and ugliness. It never seemed right.

As we walked over to the truck, Will looked to Lucy. "Are you okay? I didn't mean to get you into all this. But I'm glad you were there to help with Zoey—that's the name of the girl you met. But, well, I don't want to be mean or ungrateful, but I have to ask: are you still having that feeling where you need to eat people? I mean, that was a little hard for someone like me to watch and not get nervous."

Lucy looked embarrassed and shook her head. I knew what Will meant, but I also knew that he and the other men had been the ones who had started the killing, not poor Lucy. She just had been a little overwhelmed and had lost control.

"All right. You know I trust you. And I need your help."

Will inspected the contents of the men's dump truck. The back was full of miscellaneous practical things—tools, chains, ropes, rolls of tape, tarpaulins, extra cans of fuel. Near the back of the truck bed, Will gathered the ropes and chains and some of the rolls of thick, grey tape. "I'm not exactly sure how this is going to work," he said to us, "but we should have some plan before we get there. The truck will act like a zombie magnet. Things that make mechanical sounds always do. I'll lead them away from the hole in the fence and we'll try to restrain them. Depending on how many there are, I might need you to help. Are you up to it? I won't hurt them if I can help it. You know that."

We agreed immediately.

By the time we got near the huge gap in the fence, several of the people who can't talk had walked through and were now wandering into the fields. As Will had predicted, the people heard the truck and tottered towards us. Will drove through the gap in the fence and stopped the truck next to the base of a huge, metal tower, the kind that holds the wires that used to carry electricity.

Will climbed out of the truck as we got down from the back. "All right. Let's move," Will said. "If more show up and we get in trouble, I can always climb up the electrical tower, but for now you guys go to the back of the truck."

Lucy and I shuffled toward the rear of the vehicle as Will climbed up into the bed of the dump truck. He made his way over the various things there till he was near the back, where we were. The other people were approaching, moaning with increasing volume and what seemed like excitement. Will handed some of the ropes and chains down to us, then tossed more of them, along with the rolls of tape, farther away from the truck.

"They'll head for me. It'll be hard for them to climb up, so you should be able to yank them off pretty easily. I don't think they'll understand you as a threat or know how to respond to someone who's the same as they are, pulling on them. Drag them away from the truck and either tie them up, or at least tie them to the base of the tower. Work together. I only count six of them, so it shouldn't be too hard."

The first man had approached us and began clawing the side of the truck. He didn't seem as emaciated as most of us. His jeans were a faded blue and his shirt was reduced to tatters. His shoes were completely gone. He seemed almost unaware of me and Lucy, even as Lucy slipped a chain around his waist. She passed it over his shoulder and back down, then she and I pulled on it. Rather than turn and attack us or try to untangle himself, he kept trying to pull towards the truck; he couldn't get much traction in the grass, so it was fairly easy for us to move him. We got him to the base of the electrical tower and secured the chain to it with a padlock that was hanging on the chain.

A man, a woman, and a child were now grabbing and groping at the side of the truck. The child would be the easiest to deal with, but the woman seemed more dexterous and she had already climbed partway up the side, standing on the left rear tire. I tied a thick rope around her ankle and pulled her foot out from under her. Will was struggling with her as well, and finally her other foot slipped and she fell to the ground. I held her down and Lucy tied her up.

The man was less coordinated than the woman had been, but definitely more aggressive and stronger. He shook me off several times as I tried to get a rope around him, then finally he turned his attention from the truck and threw me down. With a snarl, Lucy grabbed his right arm. It never ceased to amaze me, how savage she could be. I scrambled to my feet and got a hold of his left arm. It was a struggle, but together Lucy and I wrestled him over and got his hands behind him so she could tie him to the tower. The grey tape worked better for this than the ropes or chains, I noticed.

By now the last two people had arrived at the truck. One was another child, and the other was a man who, like the woman, had climbed up on top of the truck's tire. Will punched him with his gauntleted fist, but couldn't quite get him to fall. Finally Will stepped back, picked up a shovel, and hit him in the face with it. He could easily have killed the man, but he just smacked him in the face with the flat of the shovel—not gently, but definitely not hard enough to kill. The man fell back and Lucy and I dragged him away much more easily than the previous one. The two children were small enough that we could each carry one over to the tower and secure them.

When we finished, Will climbed down from the truck. I hadn't liked doing any of it, especially with the children. It just didn't seem right to fight with them when they couldn't understand that what they were doing was wrong, or understand we were only trying to keep them from hurting others. But seeing how desperately they all struggled in their attempts to get at Will, I didn't see any other way. I remembered the day Milton explained to me why we should be locked up; he had made it seem so much more just, as well as easier for me to accept. Since I couldn't give such an explanation to these people, I could only feel glad that it was over with as quickly as it was, and that at least it had gone better than the grotesque violence back at the house with the men. These people, even though we couldn't communicate with them, didn't seem as bad as that; the other men, even though they could communicate and reason, had been much more intent on hurting others more cruelly, with lingering pain and humiliation.

One woman we had bound, closer to the truck, never stopped looking at Will and moving her mouth, growling and snarling with a low, simmering ferocity. And the more savage she was, the more I had to fight back an urge to kick her in the face, just to make her stop behaving so bestially. Both her behavior and my reaction were embarrassing, and I just wanted it to end. I was again confused about what we were, or what exactly we were meant to do here.

Will watched the woman too, and I think he sensed my confusion. "It's okay, Truman. We didn't cause this. We didn't make things the way they are. Well, I mean, maybe we did, like the whole human race is responsible, but not just you and me, and not her. We try to stop people from hurting each other. And we try not to hurt people. But sometimes people still get hurt. I can tell you don't like that. And, well, that's a good thing, when doing something even a little bit wrong still bothers you. But not everyone feels bothered by it. Not these people here, and not those guys back there at the cabin. That's just the way it is. I guess it's the way it will always be. Now come over here and help me."

I calmed somewhat and nodded to Will. He and I picked up the woman and put her with the others, then Will sat on the ground in the shadow of the truck, hiding from the people so they would calm down a little. He looked out over the fields, watching for the approach of anyone else. Lucy and I sat a little back, facing the other way, so we could keep an eye on the ones we had tied up, and also look for more in that direction. None appeared.

It was getting late. I didn't know about Lucy and Will, but I felt exhausted. I just wanted to sit and rest, but I sensed there would be more to do, what with the new threat to Will's community.

As the sun went down, Will looked to us. "You two go over into those trees there, farther away from the fence. The other people from our city should be here soon. I'll tell them what happened, and I'll join you as soon as I can. Be careful. Don't go too far." It was always nice, how he expressed concern for us. Lucy and I walked off and sat among some scrubby little trees, maybe a hundred feet from where Will and the truck were.

After it had just gotten dark, headlights approached. The moon was up and bright enough that I could see a little of what was going on. There were a lot of people and several vehicles. One tall man and another man spoke with Will before he left them and trotted through the grass to where we were. It took him a second to find us, but then the three of us started walking through the trees, away from the people.

When we had gone a little ways, Will said, "Those people will keep an eye on the fence until they can fix it in the morning. They'll take the zombies to one of the holding areas then too. I told them I'd scout around out here, see where those guys came from. I need to keep moving, so can you guys stay with me?"

We nodded.

"All right. It's not really safe for me out here at night, and I can't really follow the tracks anyway. So let's get back on the road. I saw a billboard there when we came out here earlier. I'll climb that and we can all have a rest."

The billboard—or what was left of it—stood a little ways away from the fence. The pole and the frame that had held the sign were still there. The sign itself was long gone, of course. Lucy and I sat at the base of the sign.

"Thanks, you two," Will said. "I don't know if I could've saved Zoey if you weren't there. And I want you to know that it's true what I said to her: I think it's okay you killed that guy. Not just okay, in fact, it was a good thing, a brave thing."

Will took a step away from us and lit one of his cigarettes. I could see the end glow against the night. He exhaled and talked more quietly. "The eating part isn't so easy to get over, but I still think you're a good person and you should be treated with respect. I mean, I know all of us are taught to respect you, but now that I've met you two, I don't know if locking you up is always the right way. If you're still members of our community, you should do things to help out, like you did today. I'm sorry you had to see all that. It was ugly, and you two are nice and shouldn't have to see things like that. I wish more people were nice like you."

He finished his cigarette and crushed it out on the ground. "Now I'm going to go up there, tie myself down, and try to get a little sleep. I hope you two can rest a little too. I guess you don't sleep or get tired exactly like we do, but you look tired and you did a lot today."

Lucy and I both made our little affirmative wheezing sound. Will leaped and caught the bottom of a ladder that led up to a narrow platform under where the billboard used to be. He pulled himself up and in a second he was above us, lying down and going to sleep.

Lucy and I leaned against each other, quiet and calm for the first time that day. The moon had risen higher, casting a lovely, softening glow on the fields. As with speaking or even bleeding, I envied Will's ability to sleep. For as soothing and beautiful as the moonlight on those fields was, I would have much preferred to just stop remembering and thinking about all the terrible things I'd seen that day, to have just a few hours of release. Considering all the things—many of them beautiful and good, I'm sure—that I had somehow been forced to forget, it hardly seemed fair that a whole new set of horrors had been shoved into my memory and could not be forced out or even softened.

The moon set, the stars wheeled, and finally the horizon lightened to purple, then red, then orange. The sun warmed me and I felt slightly better after the previous day's events and the night's cold and damp. I did not know that equally important and terrible events would take place that day, even if it began as another beautiful, summer morning.

Chapter 19

Sometime late in the morning, my dad came up to the truck Fran and I were sitting on as we kept watch. "Hey, you two," he said in his kind and jovial tone. It made me relax to hear him back to his more normal tone, without the concern and fear of the night before. "They did a lot more damage to the fence than we expected. We don't have all the supplies we need. I don't think we even have enough back in the city. We weren't expecting this kind of damage this time of year, and right after the usual damage that the spring storms do to the fence."

He held up a tattered, multi-colored sheet of folded paper and gestured with it to my right. "I checked the map. Just past the fence over that way, there's the edge of where we've scouted in any detail, and I've got one spot marked as still having building supplies. Milton's been through there several times, so it should be quiet. Jonah and I are going to take a truck and try to find the stuff we need. Mostly posts and fencing. We got the concrete and the equipment and we can add the barbed wire later. You want to come with us, Zoey?"

Fran and I stood up and stretched. "Sure, Dad. Do I need the rifle?"

"Yeah, bring it with you."

Fran gave me one of her slight smiles. "You be careful, kid," she said as she rubbed my head. "Get us some stuff so we can finish this up and get on home to your mom. I don't like sitting out here getting sunburned because some animals messed up everything we've worked for."

"I will," I said. I climbed down, and Fran resumed her watch.

As my dad and I walked to the other panel truck, he smiled at me and reached around to look at my black eye. "Bad day, kiddo." He'd be strong and optimistic in front of Mom, but he knew I knew how he really felt, if that makes any sense. "Sorry you had to get up close and personal with some bad guys, princess. It happens. I'm glad you were strong. Fran and Vera were lucky you were there. But if you need to go home or anything, just say so. You don't have to be all tough in front of your dad."

I nodded. "I know, Dad." I understood that I had fought as best I could, but I also knew that Will and his friendly zombies were a big part of why we were all still alive. If it were a source of fear that you didn't know where the threats and dangers would come from every day, it was an odd kind of wonder that you also never knew where help might come from—unasked for, unexpected, unpredictable.

We got to the other truck, where Mr. Caine was waiting for us. Dad and I got up in the cab with him. Mr. Caine was driving and my dad sat between us. As Dad had said, it was a short drive to the remnants of civilization—ruined buildings and a denser concentration of wrecked and abandoned cars. There was a big city out here beyond the fence, and these were the outskirts of it. When we had first built the fence, the city was full of zombies. Even now, with so many hiding places, we couldn't be sure that Milton had found them all, and the city was considered the most dangerous area beyond the fence. We would never venture farther into it than these outskirts.

The older people had tried to describe how cities used to be set up. This was hard for younger people to understand, because our own little city was set up in such a haphazard, irregular way—

some parts alive and occupied, while others fell into disrepair and disuse—you could no longer tell what they had once been used for. The way people described it, the center of a really big city had extremely tall buildings—dozens, sometimes as much as a hundred stories tall, as impossible as that seemed now. These huge structures were filled mostly with offices—which were a tough concept in themselves, as explaining what people did in "offices" quickly involved more arcane subjects having to do with money or government or even something called "insurance," for which people could find no adequate analogy or rationalization in our present world.

Farther away from the city center would be the houses and industry. Then even farther out would be more housing, and most of the stores, especially the big ones that sold large items—things like construction supplies or equipment, appliances, car dealerships, those kinds of things. There were some complications in these discussions with older people, of course, because some claimed that a really long time ago, back before most of the older people were born, there were stores in the central downtown, and only later did those move to the outskirts or suburbs. This was then further complicated because in some cities the stores had actually moved back downtown in the years just prior to the outbreak, in a process called "urban renewal," and some rundown buildings in the downtown had been transformed into very expensive housing, a process called "gentrification."

It was at this point that the description and my questions began to break down into complicated, circuitous tangents, because I would ask why they had ever moved out, if only to move back again. As often happened, the details confused and confounded my ability to envision or understand how people used to live. But that day as the truck slowed to a crawl through the increasing number of buildings and vehicles and debris, I could tell we were entering the suburbs of a once large city, now just ruins, wreckage, and supplies to be scavenged for survival.

"There," my dad said, pointing to the remnants of a shopping center on the right side of the road. One of the stores had obviously sold building supplies.

The grass in the parking lot grew between the cars, up to the tops of their wheels. Many of the vehicles were blackened, obviously having exploded and burned twelve years ago. The people's bodies had either walked away or had become food, or had just crumbled into nothingness when I was still a baby.

In parts the cars were packed so tightly it didn't look like we could get the truck close enough to retrieve the supplies from the store, but with some judicious ramming—the truck had an extra bumper welded to the front for just such a maneuver—we got right up to the building.

We got out and Dad gave us flashlights. Rechargeable batteries were at a premium, but we'd need to use them today. Dad surveyed the building. Past a ruined fence there was a big door into the main building. It had been glass and was smashed open. "All right. Zoey, I can't have you going in dark places like this. This is past the fence. There are real monsters here. Stay put. I mean it." His tone dropped enough to express the necessary sternness and seriousness. "We'll get the stuff and you can help load it on the truck."

Dad and Mr. Caine disappeared into the store. Some holes in the roof let in a little light, so it wasn't completely dark, and I could watch their flashlights move through the shadowy space, sometimes scanning up and around, trying to catch sight of what we needed. They stopped, and there was some clanging and banging. Then the flashlights moved back towards the door, until I could see the two of them pushing a big, flat cart piled with metal poles and rolls of fencing. "It's lucky, the stuff we need isn't far inside," my dad explained. He looked between us and the truck. He seemed to think for a minute before he decided it was safe. "We'll go back and get some more. It'll only take us a couple minutes for each cart load. You wheel it over to the truck and start loading it on, Zoey."

I walked over to the truck as they went back into the building. I raised the truck's back door, and set the M16 and the flashlight on the edge of the truck's rear loading area. My 9mm was in its holster on my belt.

There were no cars or other hiding places between the cart and the truck, so I relaxed a little. I pushed the cart slowly to the back of the truck. The rolls of fencing were too heavy for me to lift. The poles I'd be able to get on the back of the truck with some difficulty, but it made more sense to wait for help. I decided I could at least get the poles and the fencing off the cart, so Dad and Mr. Caine could use it on the next trip. I moved the stuff down onto the cracked pavement and rolled the cart back to the door, almost at the same time as my dad and Mr. Caine emerged with another load of supplies.

They took the empty cart while I wheeled the full one over to the truck. We repeated this process several times, then all three of us got the stuff into the back of the truck. The loading made a lot more noise, and I could see Dad looking around, worried that we'd attract attention. The parking lot still looked deserted, and all we heard when we were done clanging around was the buzz of insects and the faint rustling of wind.

We were all a little tired after working in the hot, midday sun. My dad wiped the sweat from his brow and looked around the parking lot and shopping center, always on the lookout either for danger, or for something useful. The neighboring store had a sign that read "Argento's Formal Wear." I didn't understand the phrase. I mean, I knew what the words meant individually, but I didn't understand what kinds of clothes could be described that way. "What's that?" I asked.

Both the men looked. "Formal wear?" My dad thought for a second how to explain it. "You know—fancy clothes, for special occasions."

I tried to put it in a category I understood. "Like the grey clothes we wear for vows? Or the plain white ones people wear for weddings?"

"Well, yes, sort of. I mean, yes, you used to get formal wear for weddings. But no, it wasn't like ours. And those weren't the only occasions you'd go and get formal wear. Not just rituals."

Mr. Caine chuckled a little, as he pushed the stuff farther into the truck compartment and jumped down. "Those are ceremonies, Jack, not rituals. You only do them once, so they're ceremonies."

Dad rolled his eyes. "Okay. But other things, too. Dances. Parties. Things like that."

"We just wear regular clothes to our dances and parties now," I objected. I know I was being a bit of a brat, but I also really wanted to understand these things and not just ignore them, or dismiss them as oddities. As I said, memory is important, way more important than people think.

"Well, yes," my dad said, faltering for the right explanation. Like any kid, I loved to make adults flustered with questions. If it weren't for the seriousness and dangerousness of the previous day, I would've been nearly cackling and dancing by this point, and Roger definitely would've joined me, if he were there. "But back then there'd be this really big dance the last year you were in high school. It was called the prom and you'd get really fancy clothes that you wore just for it. Gals would get big, beautiful dresses, and guys would get tuxedoes."

I scowled. "There were whole stores that sold clothes you'd only wear once?"

"Well, yes. Or you'd just rent them."

"You mean, you'd pay money—this thing, money, that older people always complain about, even now—just to borrow clothes? For one day?"

"Yes. They were pretty expensive, too."

"What on earth for?" I didn't even mean it as sarcasm or criticism at this point. I just couldn't imagine this strange, other world the older people longed for and missed so much, with all its excesses and waste and nonsense. The huge building supply store made sense to me, because I could understand how it would be good and useful to have so many supplies and tools to do work. I'd seen the ruins of food stores and gas stations before, and those made sense, too. The food stores even made me a little curious, with the descriptions I'd heard of things like chocolate and candy and spices—strange, unknown things I'd never eaten. Even playgrounds and carnival rides made sense, and we had a few small examples of similar things in our struggling little city. But what they were describing now was incomprehensible. I would've thought they were making it up, to kid me, but Dad's consternation at trying to explain it seemed real.

Mr. Caine kept chuckling as he patted me on the back—affectionately, not condescendingly. "Jack, the kids don't understand what we're talking about when we get hammered at a picnic and start talking about the good old days and singing Bruce Springsteen, and they don't understand things like this. Let's just go over there and see if there's anything left. Maybe that'd help explain it. We got the building stuff quickly enough. They won't have finished with what they were working on before we get back."

Dad looked around. "Yeah, that's a good idea." He rubbed my head playfully. "Darn kids think they know everything. Let's show her." He picked up the M16 and stowed it in the truck's cab while I picked up my flashlight, and then we walked towards the wreck of the store.

The door and window were gone, as was much of the roof near the front of the building. We made our way in, Dad in front, with me in between him and Mr. Caine. Without the shelter of the roof, the clothes we first found had been reduced to piles of rags on the floor or tatters still hanging from hangers. Mice and rats scurried across the floor and among the rags, and some birds fluttered up through the roof when our shoes crunched the broken glass that covered the floor.

I tried to imagine the place and its contents. It had obviously been a large store, so my difficulty with picturing this many unnecessary, impractical clothes for sale—many of them for one-time use—still persisted, or was even compounded. Whatever clothes or pieces of clothing that were lying around had been weathered down to an even, lifeless grey, like fading smoke or useless, dead ash. I was still fascinated by the place; at once it exuded the hopelessness of a cemetery and the promise of a lost, ruined paradise.

"What colors were these clothes?" I asked softly. The place seemed to call for a certain reverence, not like the loud clanging and crashing we had just been making in the building supply store. "Were there certain colors people wore to this 'prom' thing?"

We were shining our flashlights into the few remaining corners of darkness, surprising a few more rodents, but nothing more threatening.

"They could be any color, especially the girls' dresses," Mr. Caine ventured. "But the boys' tuxedoes were almost always black, and most of the girls' dresses were white."

I kept moving the beam of my flashlight around, examining the wreckage for anything recognizable. "Why would boys and girls wear opposite colors?" Again, in all my reading, I had come across plenty of descriptions of men and women wearing quite different clothing to the same event, but it was still jarringly different from most of our practices, where clothes were functional and mostly unisex.

We moved slowly and cautiously into the store, but still found nothing other than grey rags and rodent droppings. "White always means innocence and purity, I suppose," Mr. Caine speculated. "And prom always took place in the spring, so there were probably some resonances with springtime festivals of rebirth and courtship."

"But then why black for the boys? It sounds like mourning or something bad." I knew I was nitpicking, but it really was making so little sense to me I had to pursue it.

"Opposites attract," my dad offered. "I don't think that's changed too much."

"I guess not." It was a piece of folk wisdom I had heard before, but at that point it was still part of the mystery of boys. Having just seen the ugly, brutal version of masculinity the day before, I didn't want to consider their oppositeness too much, so I filed it away for future reference.

We had made it far enough into the store that we were now under the remnants of the roof, and the clothes there had been protected from at least some of the elements. Here they were recognizable as black pants and jackets, with white shirts, though they were utterly ruined by bugs and other small animals making their homes in them. "Who'd you go to prom with, Jonah?" my dad asked as we inched forward.

"Carrie Talbot," Mr. Caine answered.

I was a little surprised he hadn't paused at all to remember something that had happened so long ago. My dad snickered. "Wow, must've made an impression on you. You didn't have to think one second to remember her name."

"I certainly didn't, because I think of her often, though I doubt the thoughts are reciprocated at this point." His sense of humor was always a little weird, bordering and frequently stepping over into the absurd, irreverent, and macabre, but once you got used to it, it made the oddness and frustrations of life a little more tolerable.

Dad laughed a little louder. "Well, maybe back before she was a zombie it was mutual."

"I doubt it, but you never know. It never hurts to hope."

"Was she pretty?" I asked.

"I liked her, so I thought she was very pretty, Zoey. That's what you think of someone when you like them."

He'd phrased it oddly, I thought at the time, though now it seems quite obvious to me, as an adult. "You thought she was pretty because you liked her?"

"Of course. That's how it works." This was a novel and interesting interpretation to me and I filed it away as well.

Our flashlights glinted off something glass in front of us. We stepped closer and saw that at the end of one long rack against the right hand wall, an area had been separated by a glass wall. This glass wall appeared intact. Behind it was a compartment, like a big closet that we could see into. I got up close to it and looked at the contents. The flashlight beams fingered across white dresses behind the glass. Locked in their big, glass box, the dresses were undamaged, the purest white, and not only were they the color of snow, but most of them even sparkled like it.

I let out a low exclamation of amazement as I realized what some of the fuss had been about. "Wow. They are beautiful. How do they sparkle like that?"

"Sequins," Mr. Caine explained. "There are tiny plastic disks sewn onto the fabric and they catch the light. It looks even better on a woman, as she moves and they twinkle."

"I bet." I studied the dresses. Even as breathtaking as they were, there was something tragic about them, trapped in there for so long, never fulfilling their purpose, always waiting, like cocoons that never opened. Stillborn, I thought bitterly—the whole world stillborn. How many buildings and closets were there like this, packed with the frozen hopes of an entire world? I understood a little bit better what the older people felt as I gazed into that little glass sepulcher.

My dad found the glass door to the compartment and opened it. "Come on," he said. "Let's take some. It'll be fun." Dad's thoughts on the dresses didn't seem as morose as mine, but I could see where he had a point, and it would be fun to retrieve something beautiful from this decaying wreck. He and I stepped into the glass closet and started going through them. There wasn't room in there for three people, so Mr. Caine stayed out in the main part of the store. Out of the corner of my eye I could see his flashlight scanning the walls and racks, and it moved a little away, as he took a couple steps. Nearer the back of the store, there were more holes in the roof, and he moved towards the swaths of sunlight let in by those.

As Dad and I started taking down the dresses, there was a very loud tearing, crashing sound out where Mr. Caine was. The beam of his flashlight was gone.

My dad shoved me to the side as he ran out of the glass compartment. "Jonah!" he shouted.

I got out of the glass compartment and drew my 9mm.

I stepped towards where Mr. Caine had been. I couldn't see my dad now, either. I had been holding the flashlight under my arm when we were looking at the dresses; with my free hand, I racked the gun's slide, then took the flashlight in my right hand to see better. There was a large, jagged hole in the floor. It must've collapsed and Mr. Caine had fallen through. A huge cloud of dust had shot up and filled the upper room now, making me cough. In the beam of my flashlight, the tiny particles swirled up and around in a graceful dance.

I stepped closer to the hole and shined my flashlight into it. Both men were down there. I don't know if Dad had slipped into the hole by accident, or if he had just immediately jumped in to help Mr. Caine. They were both covered in dust and up to their knees in debris. Both were trying to get up and get a firmer footing.

My back and neck went cold and prickly when the moaning started.

Chapter 20

As the sun rose, Will climbed down from the billboard and we followed the tire tracks again. After walking for some ways, I noticed there were more buildings and more empty vehicles on the road. It seemed we were moving into the ruins of a city. Eventually it became impossible for Will to detect the tire tracks, since the roads were not as overgrown here. The men who had attacked Will's friends must've come from somewhere in this city, but now we couldn't be sure where. We sat on the bumper of an old car and Will thought about what to do.

"This is about as far as I've ever been," he said as he looked around. "I know Milton tried to clear the city even farther, but no one besides him has been out here, since there are still a lot of you people around. And he hasn't been over this way lately. I know there's a big river if you keep going east, so let's head that way. Maybe we'll see something."

We made our way through the city. It was terribly eerie being among so many empty buildings, with almost no sounds and absolutely no one around. There must've been so many people here before, and now they were all gone. I suppose most of them were dead, while a very few were in Will's community, some of them were in the prisons where Milton had led them, and some were just standing around, as I had been doing before Milton found me. So now all of these buildings and things just sat here—dead, decaying, disappearing.

I wondered at all the things that must be inside the buildings—the remnants of people's lives, dying slightly slower deaths than their owners, lingering longer and even more pitifully. It was much worse than when Will had led us through the town near our home and I had seen some of the collapsed buildings there. In this city there were thousands of them, and even more vehicles lying around, broken and useless. There was a slight whistling sound as the wind cut through the streets and around the buildings, almost like breathing, though this was irregular, labored, and spasmodic.

The only really tall buildings were in a cluster off to our left; we were moving through a neighborhood of smaller buildings. Will extended his arm to make us stop walking, and he crouched behind the cab of a cement mixer. Lucy and I followed him. "There's one of those flags up ahead," he whispered. "In front of a building."

I peeked around the side of the cement mixer. The flag was identical to the one on the men's truck—two wavy blue lines, a red handprint, and a red sun. This time it was on a flagpole. The wrecked vehicles in the street prevented me from seeing what else there was around there.

I looked to Will and saw that he was obviously considering what to do next. He looked up at the truck we were hiding behind, then climbed up on the running board to look inside. He opened the door and I watched him as he rummaged around inside the truck. He climbed down and was holding two hard hats, the kind construction workers wear. "It's not much, but maybe it'll give you some protection," he said as he put one on my head, one on Lucy's. "I shouldn't have brought you along, but I didn't want to detour back to your place. I wanted to catch up with these guys so badly after what they did. I'm sorry to put you all in danger."

I looked over at Lucy. We both appeared ridiculous, of course, wearing the battered, old hard hats. Her look was more sinister, however, her chin still stained and streaked with pink.

Even if the hat precariously bobbed above her small, delicate face, there was still the hint of savagery and violence about her. It always frightened me. But her eye was as serene as ever, and I took heart. We both nodded at Will.

"All right," he said. "I don't know exactly what's going to happen. I'm going to get closer to the building. There are plenty of vehicles in the street for me to hide behind. You two stay here. If I don't come back, then please, just go back along this street. Follow it out of the city. Don't go near anyone or they'll probably try to kill you. And try not to get hit in the head, okay? I'd feel so bad if you two got hurt."

As usual, I thought he was being so nice to us. We really owed all our freedom to him, so why would we blame him for anything? We could've been killed many times before he even found us, and at least he'd given us a chance to learn who we were, and also a chance to make ourselves useful and help people. It would be absurdly ungrateful for us to feel ill-used or mistreated by him at this point.

I watched Will make his way quickly between the vehicles till he was out of sight. Then I just stood by the cement mixer with Lucy and waited. Although I wasn't mad at Will for what had happened, or what was happening now, I did find myself longing for the safety of my little cubicle with Lucy, to hear her violin and read my books and just rest beside her. I was thinking how at least we seemed safe for the moment, when, without warning, a man came around the side of the cement mixer. He must have been treading quietly, or perhaps my hearing was not well-attuned, or maybe I had been too distracted with my apprehensive thoughts, because I never heard his steps until he was right on top of us.

The man was dressed much like Will was, his jacket and pants made of a patchwork of fabric and reinforced with bits of metal. He carried a rifle. Actually, I don't know anything about guns—it might have been a shotgun. What I mean is that it wasn't a hand-gun, but a gun with a long barrel that you carry with both hands.

He looked as shocked as I felt when he first saw us. He immediately raised the barrel of the gun towards Lucy's face. I was between them, and much as I had the day before, I didn't think, I just reacted. I grabbed the barrel and pushed it away. He fired, and the bullet hit the pavement beside Lucy.

Still holding the gun with my right hand, I clawed at his face with my left. He gave a cry of pain and staggered back, letting go of the gun. He tripped over some debris and fell backwards. I found myself holding this ugly, unfamiliar thing in my right hand. I flipped the gun around, so I was holding it by the stock instead of the barrel. The wooden stock felt somewhat better, more natural than the smooth, metal barrel, but to me it still felt like some venomous, malignant thing.

Lucy had taken a step forward. I thought she meant to attack the man as she had done in the woods, for I saw she had snatched up a metal bar from the ground. This time, I was afraid and didn't want her to; I didn't think it was right in this case—we had no idea, really, if this man had done anything wrong, even though Will clearly thought these people in the city were allied with the men who had attacked the women the day before. So I extended my right arm, still holding the gun, to block Lucy's progress. She looked over at me and growled, but stayed where she was. Her mouth always looked so hideous and inhuman at these moments; it was only her eye that gave me any confidence or hope.

The man on the ground was moving away from us, backwards, on his back, like a crab. He looked astonished at how Lucy and I were behaving. I suppose he expected us to fall on him, tearing and biting, the way people so often expect us to do, but we just stood there for a moment.

I heard several shots off in the direction Will had gone. This seemed to make the man on the ground decide on more violence, so he reached for a pistol that was in a holster on his belt. Lucy and I were not quick enough to dodge or run for cover, so again I didn't think, I just reacted. I pointed the gun and pulled the trigger.

I had no idea if I was aiming it the right way, but I was very close to the man, so I thought I might hit something. The sound of the gun was terribly loud. Of all the things that had happened to me, that deafening blast pushing back on my face was the only thing that I remember distinctly as pain—and as guilt, sharp and penetrating as the retort or the bullet.

Above the elbow, the man's arm exploded into bloody flesh and fabric, and he let out a howl. He clutched at the wound with his other hand, which was instantly covered with blood that oozed between his fingers. He fell back on the pavement.

He had already gotten the gun out of the holster with his right hand, but he couldn't seem to raise it with his wounded arm. I walked over to him. Lucy was at my side, and I again barred her with my right arm, holding the gun. I think the sight of the blood stirred up her unholy appetites, and I didn't want to see that again. She turned slightly away from me and growled, but she seemed to master herself, or at least tolerate my restraint. I took another step and pressed my foot onto the man's wounded arm. He writhed and howled again, and finally dropped the pistol. I kicked the handgun under the cement mixer. Then I stepped back with Lucy.

I didn't know what had happened to Will, and I didn't know if we should leave as he had instructed, or try to help him somehow. I feared the worst, but unlike when it happened in the heat of battle, making such tactical decisions was beyond me, once there was the possibility for consideration; I became totally paralyzed.

The wounded man watched us. You could see how scared he was, but even through his obvious pain, the main thing I detected was shock and wonder at how Lucy and I were acting. He was breathing hard, and seemed to be in disbelief at how we just stood there.

Fortunately, after a few moments of this standoff, Will came running back. He also looked surprised at what he saw, looking from the wounded man, to the gun, to me, to Lucy, and back to the man. Unlike me, he paused only for a minute. His gun was already out and aimed at the other man. I grabbed Will's arm. He looked at me and I shook my head.

He looked back to the man. "All right, let's go." He pushed Lucy and me down the street, back in the direction we had come.

Will kept looking over his shoulder, and we deliberately cut over one street, rather than continue on the street we had been on. In a few minutes, we were entering the less densely built-up part of the city, and there was still no sign of pursuit or attack. Will pulled us under a tattered awning, into a doorway, and let us rest for a minute.

"What happened, Truman?" he asked. He immediately realized the futility of asking this way. "That guy must've been a guard on patrol. He found you, somehow you got his gun, and you shot him. Is that what happened?"

I nodded, realizing I still carried the gun in my right hand. I was still revolted by it but now also fascinated. I held it by the stock, pointing down, and offered it to Will. He took it from me slowly, carefully.

"It's all right, Truman. You were only defending yourself. You did the right thing. I found their little headquarters or base or whatever it was. They had another truck out in front of it. This one was a Humvee, more military-looking and well-kept. I punctured the tires on the one side, but then the guards there heard your shots, and they spotted me too. We both started shooting. I think I hit two of them. But they probably think they're being attacked by more than just the three of us, and they're not coming out. That's good. We should be able to get back to the fence and warn everyone that those guys who attacked Fran and the kids came from some base out here and we need to get ready for more attacks and fighting."

I nodded. I was just glad to be away from that dead and frightening city.

"But what am I going to do with you two?" Will wondered out loud. "I don't want to take you back to the storage place, even if I had time to make that detour. If there are other people out here, especially if we're at war with them, then I don't know what they'd do if they found a bunch of zombies just fenced in and defenseless. They'd probably burn the whole place down and kill you all. You'll have to come with me and I'll explain it as best I can. Zoey can tell them how you helped save her. They've got to understand."

We kept moving along the street into an area where the buildings and vehicles were much more sparse. Soon we'd be back where at least Will was relatively safe, and I hoped Lucy and I would be too.

Then I heard a loud roar ahead of us. It went on uninterrupted for several seconds. Unlike the previous day, I knew immediately that it was gunfire. And this time there were many more than just three shots.

Will quickened his pace, and I wondered if these strange, powerful people ever stopped shooting at each other, ever stopped bleeding and cursing and dying.

Chapter 21

The sound was loud and sudden, like something angry being awakened. There were several pitches and tones, and it seemed to come from all over, down in the hole Dad and Mr. Caine had fallen into. I raised the 9mm and the flashlight until the beam found my dad. Grey, ghostly hands were grabbing at him.

"Daddy!" Nothing in the cabin had given me such uncontrollable, unrestrained panic and terror. It was the only time I got close to losing it, and I've often thought since then how it was way too close for all of us. I shouldn't have done that, but there was no way not to, I think.

You always hear how in those situations, it's as though things happen in slow motion. I don't really remember it that way, but it's possible, I guess. As I've said, memory is funny. I mostly remember, after my initial shriek, that things appeared so clear and precise, even though the room was still full of swirling dust that was making my eyes and throat burn. My dad and Mr. Caine were trying to stand up amidst the wreckage. Both were also trying to draw their weapons. But there were two hands on Dad's right arm, and because of his uneven footing in the debris, he was having trouble drawing his gun, or breaking away from the groping hands.

I moved my beam slightly to the right and found the head that was guiding the two hands. Hairless, sexless, faded—it looked more like a ghost than a zombie. But there are no ghosts. There are only our monsters, and they're human, in their own way. They're not wisps that come through walls—they're completely solid and human. And when you shine a light in the eyes of someone who's been in a basement for twelve years, they have to falter for a second. No fear in those lifeless eyes, but for a moment, surprise and blindness.

I squeezed the trigger. More grey, faded matter shot out the back of its head and it fell away from my dad. I felt none of the visceral, savage satisfaction I had gotten the previous day when I saw those evil men killed, but only the most intense relief.

My dad and Mr. Caine freed both their weapons from their holsters. I swept my flashlight around to the right, where I'd shot the one zombie, and there didn't seem to be any more on that side. Dad and Mr. Caine pointed their flashlights to the left and opened fire. It was one long roar for several seconds. Then it stopped. No more moaning, just the small, animal pant of the living. Then a slight scraping sound, and a rasping.

"You missed one," my dad said to Mr. Caine. He held up his gun. "I'm out."

Mr. Caine trained his flashlight on a hand that was moving slightly, then slid the beam up and over to the head. There was one more shot, and everything was silent again.

My dad slid another magazine into his gun. "You okay?" he asked Mr. Caine.

"Yeah," Mr. Caine said, also reloading.

"Haven't done that in a long time. Kind of lets you know you're alive, having to shoot the place up."

Mr. Caine holstered his reloaded weapon. "Yeah, I know what you mean. But I think I could tolerate a more boring, less invigorating life, if it meant not having to go through that."

Dad nodded. "Yeah." He looked up at me. "You okay?"

I kept my own weapon out, pointed down. I could feel myself losing it again. "I don't know. Just get out of there."

"Sure thing, kiddo," Dad said as he reached up. I holstered my gun so I could take his hand and help him out of the hole. He then helped Mr. Caine climb out.

I threw my arms around my dad, letting myself lose control for just a second. "I thought for sure you were going to die," I sobbed into his chest. "I couldn't stand it."

He ran his big, calloused hand over my head, and made those shushing noises people do when someone else is crying. I had made them the other night with Ms. Dresden. They seemed universal, and while not wholly adequate to the situation, they were usually enough to nudge the person back to normalcy and calm. "It's okay," he said between shushing.

It only took me a second to regain control. Something inside me eased, the tension and pain fell below some threshold, and I knew I had cried the right amount and should stop now. I stepped back from my dad and shined my flashlight into the hole, running it across the tangle of limbs, then up the walls to where their brains were now glistening, lumpy stains. I brought it back down and let it settle on the one I had shot. It had been a man, and the impact had sent him crumpling to his side, almost in a fetal position.

"They sat down there for twelve years," I said very softly. "How could anyone do that, just sit there? In the dark. I'd go crazy."

"Anyone would," Mr. Caine offered, as both he and my dad rubbed my back and shoulders. "Maybe they did, too. We don't know."

"To sit there, for twelve years, and then to just have your head blown off." I was biting my lower lip. It was an old nervous habit I'd mostly gotten rid of. "It doesn't make any sense. If they were just going to die anyway, why have them sit there, why not have them just die back when it first started?"

My feelings were vague and hard to put into words, but I think my dad and Mr. Caine felt the unfairness and absurdity just as much as I did. Indeed, Mr. Caine was the main person who had taught me to have such a keen eye for those qualities in the world. "I know, Zoey," Mr. Caine said very quietly, almost in a whisper. "It was their special torment—their fate, I guess people would say.

We don't know why. I'm fairly sure they didn't know why, either. Maybe it was better that they didn't know."

"But there was a reason?"

I wished I could see his eyes and his smile, but it was too dark and dusty in there. Mr. Caine's expression always made me feel more confident when he posed these questions in class, the way I was posing them that day. "I hope so, Zoey. No one can decide that for you. But I've always thought you knew much more about these things than other people do. And I don't know the reason for that, either. I just know it when I look at you."

I nodded. I remembered what Milton had said on the night of my vows, how maybe it would be possible for me to have faith. I also remembered how before my vows, I had felt I was in the presence of something just as mysterious and powerful as it was familiar and trustworthy. I didn't feel that way now, but the memory gave me some confidence and comfort. I took my flashlight off the dead man. "I feel so sorry for them. But I had to save you."

My dad hugged me again. "I know, honey. You did what you had to." It was funny, always doing what you have to. I wondered if people ever got to do just what they wanted to do.

We started to move back out of the store. My dad steered me toward the glass compartment again. "I know it's not as nice now, but maybe we should get some of the stuff anyway," he said meekly. He was right—he had incredibly bad timing, but he was as practical and right as he always was. Rescuing something beautiful from this slaughterhouse and tomb was even more important and significant than it had been before. Not that we thought pretty dresses could make up for or offset the ugliness, but just that they might keep the brutality from overwhelming us completely.

Oddly, I remembered a song my mom had sung to me when I was a baby: it said something about how you should "accentuate the positive," except some of the syllables were stretched out to fit the tune and it made them sound funny.

Each of us took as many dresses as we could carry and loaded them in the back of the truck. They looked funny, draped over the dull metal poles and fencing. As Dad pulled down the truck door, a voice called out to us from the parking lot. "You three, lay down your weapons!"

My dad instantly shoved me and Mr. Caine around to the right side of the truck, which was facing the building. Shots exploded around us, ricocheting off the pavement and tearing into the side of the truck.

Mr. Caine drew his gun and stood by the back right wheel, while my dad pushed me to a crouch behind the front wheel, behind the protection of the engine block. If the shooters were using rifles, the thin metal skin of the rest of the truck wouldn't offer any real cover.

My dad pressed against my shoulders as he leaned down and looked me in the eyes. "This is bad," he said quickly, evenly. He was scared, the way I had been for him back in the store. "People with guns are much worse than zombies. I love you, Zoey. You do whatever it takes to stay alive, you hear me?"

I nodded. He let go of me and I drew my 9mm again. It was hard to tell if we were in worse danger now than we had been in the store, but since my dad was right next to me and not in a hole full of dead people, it certainly didn't seem as bad.

My dad opened the door to the cab of the truck and leaned inside. I heard more shots as the windshield and the driver's side window exploded, but my dad emerged with the M16. It had a long, forty-round magazine in it, and another one taped to the first magazine. My dad closed the truck door and nodded slightly at me. There were no more shots for a few seconds.

"Hey," my dad shouted, "didn't you have enough yesterday? Why do you want to mess with us again? And this time it's not just a woman and two girls. So why don't you all just back up and let us go about our business?"

There was a long pause. Then a man shouted, "What are you talking about? We were attacked a couple days ago, and we just heard that we were attacked again this morning. You people need to throw your weapons out. We should've just shot you, but we saw the little girl."

"We'll be keeping our weapons," my dad shouted back, "so it looks like we have a problem."

Another pause, though not as long as the first. "We don't know who you are. And we've been attacked twice, with people hurt and killed. So I say you need to throw down your weapons."

"Well, we were attacked yesterday, and I don't know who you are, so I'm damn sure not giving up my weapon," Dad replied. "And I will cut down any of you who tries to come closer. We can wait, and more of our people will come looking for us, and then you'll have a real war on."

"No one wants that," came the reply. "Can one of you come out to talk? The others can stay behind the truck, with their weapons."

My dad looked over to Mr. Caine, then down at me. "That's probably as good an offer as we're going to get," he said to me quietly. He tilted his head back and shouted, "All right. I'll come out and talk."

My dad handed me the M16, bent down and kissed my head. "Don't do anything crazy to try and protect me," he said. "Just stay put. But anyone comes around this truck but me, shoot them in the face."

He walked to the back of the truck and handed his Beretta to Mr. Caine. They spoke in low tones, but I could hear them. "It's like déjà vu from eleven years ago, fighting to keep this kid alive and get her home," my dad said. He glanced back at me. "Always good to have something worth fighting for. I know you'll do whatever you have to, Jonah, just like you did then. I'm sorry I got you and her in this mess."

"Not your fault, Jack," Mr. Caine responded. "Just talk some sense into them if you can. Maybe they're not the ones who attacked Fran and the kids. There's no point anybody dying here today."

I watched my dad walk around the side of the truck, then I just listened. It sounded like Dad was talking to a man close by.

"Who are you people?" the other man asked.

"We're from a nearby city. We've been barricaded in there since the outbreak. We haven't seen other people from outside our community for years, until yesterday, when some men broke through our fence and attacked us. We killed them, then we came here, looking for more supplies to repair the fence. Then you started shooting at us."

"These men who attacked you, did they have a vehicle?"

"Yes, a dump truck. There were six of them. They had a flag, with wavy lines, a handprint, and a sun."

"Those sound like the men who attacked one of our outposts. A child escaped from that massacre and described them. That's our flag that you described. They took it as a trophy when they attacked our people."

"And who, exactly, are you people?"

"We are from the River Nation. We've lived on islands up and down the river since the day the dead rose. Gradually, the people got more organized, came together as a group to defend ourselves and find more supplies. And recently, we've been able to move about a little on the mainland. There seem to be less of the dead in this area lately, and we thought it was safe to establish villages here, until we were attacked."

"Yes, there are fewer dead around because we've been rounding them up, to make the area safer."

"You round the dead up? So you can dispose of them?"

"Well, no, we've found places to lock them up, keep them contained so they can't attack us."

There was a longer pause in the conversation at that point. "You keep the living dead around? You don't destroy them?"

"Not if we can help it."

Another pause. "That's very strange. We're not sure—the report just came in and it was very confused—but someone said that in the attack today, the man who shot at our people was seen with two zombies. The zombies attacked one of our men, but they didn't attack the stranger. They ran off with him. That's who we were looking for when we found you. Is this some plan of yours, to train and lead zombies to attack other people?"

"No, of course not. We didn't know there were other people until yesterday. And we don't train zombies. We just put them somewhere and lock them up, so we don't have to kill them. Those assholes in the dump truck attacked you people, then they attacked us, and we killed them."

"And what about today's attack?"

"That I know nothing about," my dad answered truthfully. "I think we just need to calm down and stop pointing guns."

Knowing of Will and his zombie friends, I had to say something. "Dad?" I called out over the hood of the truck, but without coming out from cover.

"Not now," he shot back.

"No, I think it's important. I think we can put our guns down. I think I know part of what's going on."

"Don't come out from behind that truck, Zoey." There was a pause. "Jonah, go listen to what Zoey has to say, then tell me what we should do."

Mr. Caine walked over to me, and I quickly told him of how Will and two zombies had helped save me the previous day. I told him how, according to Will, these zombies were more intelligent than others, and were mostly cured of their appetite for human flesh, though I had seen the one eat a man right in front of me.

As I was describing this to Mr. Caine, I heard my dad continuing to negotiate with the man. "She's my daughter. And the other guy, he's just a school teacher. I'm sort of in charge. You can just let them go, whatever it is that's happened."

Mr. Caine looked very surprised and worried at my story. I knew Will had always been a free spirit at best, and a little out of control at worst, and I'm sure Mr. Caine felt partly responsible if something bad had happened as a result of his adoptive son's behavior.

"Jack," he called out when I was done, "I think we should come out and discuss this. I don't think these people are to blame for what's happened, or their response to it."

There was another pause before my dad agreed, and Mr. Caine and I came out from behind the safety of the truck. The man who had been talking to my dad was dressed in the kind of clothes that Will usually wore when he was out in the wild—heavy canvas with metal pieces sewn onto the fabric to protect him from bites. He was probably my dad's age, not as tall—kind of short, in fact—but he had the same air of practicality and efficiency.

Unlike our clothes, his seemed to have some insignia, like a military rank, and they appeared somewhat better made than most of ours.

I tightened my hold on the grip of the M16 and scanned the cars around us, but couldn't see where the other people were.

My dad put his hand on my shoulder. "Easy," he said quietly. "It's not time for heroics. Just tell me what's going on."

I repeated the story of Will and the intelligent zombies. When I was done, my dad turned back to the military-looking man. "We knew nothing about this. If this is true what Will has done, we will deal with it. But this is not our fault. You should let us go back to our city."

"I believe you," the man agreed. "I don't think you knew about this. But we can't let you just drive away with some vague assurance that you will 'deal with' this madman and his zombies. If you leave here now, you might just protect him. And then we will go to war. We've done it before, against smaller groups who thought they could attack us or raid our supplies."

Dad's grip tightened on my shoulder. "Who said anything about 'smaller group' there, fella? And how did this city get to be 'your supplies' when you're only here because we cleared out all the zombies? I got a whole building full of weapons we've never used before, just waiting for another guy stupid enough to threaten us."

Mr. Caine finally intervened. "Enough of the posturing and threats, both of you. We understand that the River Nation wants justice, and we're sorry for the people who were hurt and killed in these attacks. I take it you are someone in authority?" He was being a lot more obsequious than I'd ever seen him, but he'd judged the situation rightly, I think.

"Yes," the man said in a less threatening tone. "I am a commander of the military forces, Colonel Reiniger."

Mr. Caine saw that he had gained some leverage. "So if you were to come with us and oversee the investigation we make of Will, you'd consider that fair, and you could report back to your people whether or not we had done what was necessary to prevent war?"

The colonel considered, and finally agreed to Mr. Caine's terms. Disaster was averted for the time being, though I wasn't sure we'd be able to punish Will to this man's satisfaction, so I thought the problem had just been postponed.

Five men armed with rifles emerged from among the cars in the parking lot. They were dressed similarly to the colonel, though each one wore a different insignia. The colonel told two of his men to report back to their people in the city. He then turned to us. "You may drive the truck back with the supplies. We didn't think anyone could've survived out here, without the water as a barrier, so we understand if you need to build back up your protection from the dead. We'll follow you in our vehicle."

The colonel and his three remaining men walked out among the cars as we climbed into the truck. Mr. Caine started the engine. "Nice going back there," Dad said. "I let things get a little too heated."

Mr. Caine nodded. "It happens. The 'just a schoolteacher' comment was a little uncalled for."

My dad snickered grimly. "I was just trying to talk you two out of it. Your way worked better."

We saw some cars shudder and jerk slightly, and then the vehicle that had been pushing them out of the way came into view. It was a Humvee, with the same sort of extra bumper for pushing cars that our truck had. With some maneuvering, they turned around, and we pulled out with them behind us.

To leave the parking lot, we had to go under an overpass. I looked into the passenger's side mirror at the Humvee, and I thought I saw something drop down onto the vehicle. The vehicle jerked one way, then the other, and crashed into a concrete barrier.

Chapter 22

After we heard the long burst of gunfire, we made off in the direction from which it came. It sounded fairly close, and Will periodically stopped to look around with binoculars. After moving and searching like this for some time, he spotted something. "There," he said, pointing to the left. "There's a vehicle moving among the cars in that parking lot. We'll be able to see better from up on that overpass."

We clambered up the embankment and over the guard rail, and with his binoculars Will looked out over the parking lot of a ruined shopping center. Several people moved among the cars in front of us, and three emerged from a store, carrying big, white bundles to a nearby truck. I heard a voice, though I couldn't make out the words, then more gunfire; the three people from the store ran behind the truck.

The gunfire stopped, and there was more shouting. One person came out from behind the truck and joined one of the people who had been hiding among the cars. Their voices were low enough that I couldn't hear them, but I took it they were talking again. Then the other two people emerged from behind the truck.

Finally, all the men among the cars came out from hiding. Two of them went off on foot, while the others went back to their vehicle, and the three people who had had the white bundles got into the truck. The other vehicle maneuvered till it was behind the truck, then they both started moving slowly, sometimes bumping into cars and pushing them out of their way.

Will lowered his binoculars and looked around the overpass, which was littered with vehicles and various other things. I could tell he was formulating some plan, and part of me wanted to help, but I also wasn't really up to all this. Out of the back of a pickup, which was smashed into some other cars, Will got out two cinder blocks. He set them on top of the guard rail at the side of the overpass. "The people in the truck are my friends," he said. "The one man is the man who raised me, and then there's Zoey and her dad. I don't know what the other men are doing, but they just shot at them, so it can't be good. It looks like they're leading them somewhere. They're going to drive out this way. You two crouch down here, and after the truck goes past, try to push the blocks over so they fall on the Humvee. I'll go down and try to stop them when they get out."

As too often with Will and the other people, I felt sure that words like "stop" meant "kill." For people who could talk, they certainly did way too much communicating in violent, non-verbal ways.

"Can you two do this?" Will asked.

I doubted very much that I could. I most certainly did not want to, but if the intelligent and kind-looking girl was in danger, I felt I had to help.

"Can you do this?" Will repeated.

Lucy and I nodded.

"Okay. But please, stay up here. This is all too dangerous, and I don't know what's going to happen."

He ran to the end of the overpass. Across his back, he carried the gun I had taken from the man I had shot, and he had his own handgun out and ready to use.

The two vehicles slowly made their way through the parking lot, as it was hard for them to find spaces that weren't crowded with abandoned vehicles. The cars thinned somewhat closer to the overpass, and the two vehicles moved faster, though still fairly slow.

The truck passed under us, and as the other vehicle approached, Lucy and I shoved the two cinder blocks off. I could hear glass shattering, then the sounds of brakes, then more smashing glass and a heavier crunch of metal.

I heard car doors opening, and men cursing. Lucy took my hand and led me to the other end of the overpass. I was frightened, but I couldn't let her go by herself. Besides, hiding hadn't done us any good the other two times these people had decided on violence. We worked our way between the wrecked cars and climbed down the embankment on the side facing away from the shopping center.

As we scrambled down, I heard various shouts.

"No, Will! Don't!"

"What is this, a trap?"

Lucy and I must've made some noise, because suddenly I was staring down the barrel of a rifle. I was surprised to see the intelligent-looking girl holding it. These people even had their children use guns, which I found quite monstrous and reprehensible.

I gripped Lucy's hand tighter, and raised it, along with my other hand, hoping this would be enough of a sign that we meant no harm. The girl slightly lowered the hideous, black rifle and called out, "Dad, they're here. The two I saw before."

She was near the front of the truck, closest to Lucy and me. The tall man and another man were on the other side, closer to the vehicle Lucy and I had dropped the cinder blocks on. Three men were out on both sides of that vehicle. Will was beyond those men, closer to the shopping center. Everyone was holding guns, pointed at each other.

The tall man near the truck looked over his shoulder at Lucy and me. He didn't turn all the way around, but kept his gun pointed at the other men. He looked us over. "These are the ones you told us about, Zoey?"

"Yes, Dad."

He turned away from us to keep his eye on the men from the other vehicle. "Either one of them so much as twitches, blow their smart zombie brains out. Let's see if they understand that."

The intelligent-looking girl kept her gun slightly lowered. "But, Dad," she said.

"I need that order acknowledged, Zoey. Now."

The girl raised the terrible rifle again. She squared her shoulders and her muscles tensed as she lined up the sights, the barrel pointed right at my face. "Yes, Dad," she said more quietly than her father had spoken. There was a little of his edge in her voice, and though her pretty brown eyes still looked extremely intelligent, she narrowed them and they did not look nearly as kind. I was glad she was the one pointing a gun at us, though—mostly because I felt more confident she wouldn't shoot us for no reason. I was glad the gun was pointed at me rather than Lucy. But even more than that, I had a strange sense that if such an intelligent, innocent person were to judge us a deadly, implacable threat, maybe we needed to be put down.

"Jack! No!" Will shouted from the other side of the people and the vehicles. "It's not their fault!"

"No," the tall man, Jack, responded, "it's not their fault, Will, it's yours!"

"You can't, Dad," the girl said, though the barrel of her rifle didn't waver at all. "They saved my life."

"We *can't* shoot zombies? Will went around shooting people, for God's sake! Without letting any of us know, or checking out what was going on. That's what caused this, and now we have to figure out a way to stop it. Shooting zombies is something I definitely *can* do if it helps straighten things out."

"But they attacked us!" Will shouted.

Fortunately, the conversation had not been punctuated with gunfire, but at this point it degenerated into incoherent shouting, in which I could make out variously, "No we didn't! … No they didn't! … Yes they did! … No, you did!" I suddenly felt very cold and empty—almost pained, even though I wasn't sure I could feel pain exactly. Lucy and I were going to die simply because these people seemed to end all their conversations with shooting.

I tightened my grip on Lucy's hand and thought at least I'd die with her, instead of alone. That was something. Maybe I could even shield her if I could move fast enough once these strange, monstrous people started their inevitable slaughter.

The girl lowered her rifle and took a step towards us. She put her right hand out in front of herself, with the palm towards us, as if to show she meant us no harm. For some reason it occurred to me that, from the way she was holding her gun, she must be left-handed, and I thought how ironic that was, since there was an old superstition that left-handedness was evil, and she was the only one behaving kindly, or even rationally. But that was only superstition, and I didn't think people believed in that anymore.

I nodded and took a step back, pulling Lucy with me.

The girl turned towards the men and shrieked, "Stop it! Just stop it!"

The two men closer to her glanced back at her, and they all stopped shouting.

In a lower but very firm and decisive tone, the girl said, "Mr. Caine, tell Will what happened."

"Will," the man beside Jack began, "the men who attacked Fran and the girls had attacked these people the day before. When they attacked them they took the flag of this city. That's why it was on their truck. When you shot at them this morning, you hurt innocent people. You have to stop now, please." He sounded very plaintive and sad, but like the girl, intelligent and reasonable.

Will had said his father was one of the two men, and I sensed such a bond between Will and this man, Mr. Caine.

I was now ashamed at the part I had played in all this, but I also knew I couldn't have let Lucy get hurt, back in the city. So I felt shame, but not guilt. I could see Will was distraught at what had happened, too.

"Will," the tall man said, "you need to stand down and come with us."

"What?" one of the men by the other vehicle objected. "We're taking him prisoner!"

"You know you have no right," Jack said with exceptional evenness, clarity, and coldness.

Besides the girl's rifle, every other gun was still pointed at someone's head. I again got that empty, icy feeling that I was going to die next to Lucy.

"You have no… no… jurisdiction," Jack said. "That's the word."

The other man gave a snorting laugh. "Jurisdiction? What are you talking about? There's no jurisdiction or law anymore!"

"Suit yourself," Jack said. "But if there's no law, then there's just guns, and we both got 'em, and that's how we'll settle it. But he is definitely coming home with us now, and we'll decide what happens to him."

There was a pause that seemed endless to me. Mr. Caine spoke. "Colonel Reiniger, this doesn't have to change our agreement. You come with us, we decide what happens to Will, and you report back to your people. If our decision is unacceptable, then there's war, but not now."

"He attacked us again!" the other man said.

"All right, that's true," Will's father said wearily. "But so long as your driver isn't too badly hurt, then I guess what we're asking you to do is to overlook this last incident, to forgive that mistake, so we can decide on what to do and not have more killing."

"We were ambushed. You might try it again if we come with you. I never should've trusted you," Colonel Reiniger said.

Mr. Caine sighed. "All right," he said as he put his hands up and walked over to the truck. "I'm putting down my gun." He set it on the hood of the truck. "I'll stay here with your men. Will is my son. It's fair I stay here in his place. You go on ahead. Is that fair enough?"

I was amazed all over again; these people were ready to kill for no reason one minute, then ready to sacrifice themselves for each other the next. I felt it was some kind of mystery that I might never understand.

"Jonah, you don't have to," Jack said. "You shouldn't."

"Or what, Jack?" He sounded exasperated as well as weary. "You said it yourself—the other choice is we start shooting. Maybe, if they're lucky, then Zoey and those two," he tilted his chin towards us, "would be left standing, since they have a better position behind us and the truck. I know the meek are supposed to inherit the earth, but shit, Jack, I don't feel like shooting any-more today. And I want someone to get home."

"No, don't," Will protested. "I'll stay."

"No, Will," his father said, "Jack's right—we can't let these people decide your fate. It's not their place. You're our responsibility. You're my responsibility." He turned back towards the men by the other vehicle. "Now, Colonel, is that fair, so at least they can get home?"

The colonel stepped back and looked inside his vehicle, like he was checking someone there. "His head's banged up and bleeding, but I think he'll be all right," he said. "He'll stay here with you and one of my other men, and they'll take you back to our base. I'll take one man and go on after the truck. That is a reasonable solution."

I wasn't sure if "reasonable" was the right word for it, or if these kinds of decisions were supposed to be governed by reason, but at least it seemed to be a non-violent solution.

"What about them?" the girl asked, gesturing towards Lucy and me. It seemed to be yet another problem of being mute—people tended to ignore and forget about you when they were talking and making plans. Though in the preceding conversation, I had been glad they'd left us out of most of it.

Will had joined Jack and Zoey, while Will's father had gone over to join the men by the other vehicle. "They'll be shot if we leave them here," Jack said.

"We should take them with us," Will suggested. "Later you can take them back to the storage place where Milton put them."

Jack considered us. He pulled open the door at the back of the truck. "All right, there you go."

Lucy and I climbed in. They all looked at us for a moment.

"I heard about what you did for Zoey," Jack added. He sounded a little contrite. "I'm sorry about the thing I said to Zoey—you know, to shoot you. You all kind of showed up at a bad time in the conversation, but saving someone's life deserves a lot better than how I treated you. I'm sorry. We'll protect you now, and we're grateful for what you did for Zoey."

I nodded. Lucy seemed a bit more sullen, but at least she didn't growl at them. I would've felt embarrassed if she had, for I knew they were doing the best they could, given their shortcomings and violent urges. The tall man closed the door, and we were left in the dark. I put my arm around Lucy and held her as the truck lurched forward and we bounced along to whatever these people were going to decide was our fate.

Chapter 23

I was so sorry to leave Mr. Caine with the people from the River Nation, but he had been right—there was no other way for us to leave without more people being killed. We couldn't just hand Will over to strangers, and we couldn't expect them to trust us without some sacrifice on our part. We drove in silence back to the hole in the fence. In the time we had been gone, Rachel and the other workers had put in many new posts, anchoring them in newly dug holes with concrete; the fencing had been unrolled and secured to them. Now they were just expecting us to deliver supplies, so they could finish and go home. They must've been surprised and curious to see another vehicle following us—the first new people anyone in our community had seen in years.

We got out, and the workers gathered around us and the two newcomers. Milton had also arrived while we had been gone. He was invaluable for keeping the undead away from the people as they worked on the fence, of course, but now I thought he would help resolve this situation with Will, though I was completely at a loss as to how.

If the people were amazed at the sight of two newcomers who were not from our city, they were shocked and audibly gasped when Dad opened the back of the truck and they saw two zombies sitting there—zombies who didn't try to attack, but who sat meekly watching us. Well, the man zombie was meek; the lady zombie looked much more dangerous—though Will and I were the only ones who knew firsthand how savage she could be. She didn't make any outward signs of aggression now.

My dad explained everything—who the attackers had been, what the River Nation was, how Will had attacked the wrong people that morning, how there were now smarter zombies among the dead, and how our community was now threatened with war against another group of living humans. Everyone paid rapt attention to the story, with occasional ripples of excitement and whispers through the crowd. Everyone except Fran, who was still keeping watch from atop the truck; I was sure she was ready to shoot the newcomers, either living or dead, if she deemed it necessary, or if my dad gave the command.

Milton shook his head slowly and sadly. "There is no precedent for this. It has been years since Jack and I assumed any kind of governing or judicial role over our people. And we have never considered the implications of having to deal with a group of people outside our community, whose customs and values might be different than ours. This is serious and confounding. Perhaps if we considered in what ways Will has broken our own laws, and then try to justify them to these new people. First, I suppose we should determine what damage has been done. Colonel, do we know what happened to your citizens whom Will and these two dead people attacked this morning?"

"The last report I received, three men had been shot. This man from your community shot two of them. Both were wounded quite severely; one of them may not walk again. The one shot by these two *creatures* was less severely wounded and should recover fully."

Milton sighed. "Let us be thankful the damage was not worse. Nonetheless, Will, there seems no way to take your actions as protecting the living. There was no self-defense, except perhaps by these dead people, if they were confronted suddenly with a guard who tried to shoot them—*after* they'd been put in that situation by *you*, Will. Most alarming is the carelessness with which you pursued and shot at people, without knowing their exact identity or guilt. We can be thankful you did not kill anyone, but if you had done this to members of our community, there would be grave punishment. And we cannot count the lives of others—whom we were lucky enough to finally find today, when we thought ourselves the only living people left—as any less worthy of our concern. I cannot see any other way to interpret this."

There was a low and reluctant murmur of agreement from the crowd.

"But I am also very curious about what you thought you were doing by letting the dead out of their holding area. This was a huge risk to yourself, but more importantly, to others, more so in our community than elsewhere, since the holding areas are just outside the fence. What led you to do such a thing?"

I could see Will was struggling with his own guilt and regret. But on the topic of the zombies, he seemed to pick up, as though this were something he had thought about much more, and something he thought defensible—even if to the rest of us, it seemed the most bizarre part of his behavior. "I didn't mean to put anyone at risk. These two..." he gestured to the zombies, who were standing nearby, under guard. "They were different. You saw for yourself, Milton, how different he is."

"I did, Will. That's why I explained to him why he needed to be confined and kept away from the living. I'm not in the habit of explaining myself to dead people, but I thought it appropriate in his case."

"Yes, and I think he appreciated that. But I spoke to him more, and I could tell he knew more, and he needed more from us. I found out his name. It's Truman. I don't think I've ever known the name of one of the dead people we round up. I knew he wasn't dangerous."

"But he was, Will. He shot a man. And the woman killed a man and... ate him."

"They did, but both times were to defend someone. The woman saved Zoey. I couldn't have gotten to her in time. And I found Truman after he'd shot the man. He had only wounded him, and the man was defenseless, on the ground, but they didn't do anything more to hurt him. I've never seen people more restrained. Well, except the eating part. But I knew it was wrong to keep them locked up. I know you've done a lot for us, Milton, and you showed us how it's wrong to kill the dead, but sometimes you treat them like dolls or statues—these sacred, fragile things that you need to shut up and look at once in awhile at funerals, like things in a museum, or like they used to do with animals in the zoo. I think they're just people. At least, I know these two are. I'm sorry I hurt those men, but I'm not sorry I let Truman and Blue Eye out."

Milton nodded slowly. I looked over at the two zombies. They obviously understood what had been said about them, mute as they were. Unlike when I imagined a dead person looking sad or angry, you could tell they were embarrassed to be the center of attention, just like a "real" person would, and they looked remorseful for their part in the unnecessary bloodshed and the problems it now caused us. I could see Will's reckless attack on the River Nation had been the result of impatience, anger, and thoughtlessness, but his relationship with these two *people* had been very well considered, thoughtful, and careful.

Milton seemed to agree. "Will, your actions with these two dead people are not culpable, I don't think. But like your actions this morning, they do show a terrible unwillingness to consult or explain yourself to others. So much pain could've been avoided if you had just spoken to someone else. This is all the more sad, since by what you just said, you can explain yourself to others quite eloquently."

When Milton turned toward me, I suddenly felt very small and cold, even as the blood rushed to my cheeks and burned me with shame. "And you, Zoey—how could you keep this information from others? You were as aloof and secretive as Will. Perhaps if you had told your father, we could have stopped Will before he attacked other people. We cannot let our friendships endanger our community, or they are no real friendships. I trust your father will find some appropriate punishment that will teach you not to keep to yourself so dangerously and with no concern for others."

I had instinctively pulled closer to Dad when accused, and he squeezed my shoulders. "Yes, Milton, I was thinking about that on the way back here, that someone needs a lesson about trusting and confiding in others." I knew Dad would be fair, but I still shivered to hear of some undefined punishment.

Milton paused and turned back to Will. "I think under normal circumstances, your fellow community members would decide on some punishment for you, but now we run into the difficulty that the victims of your crimes are members of a different community, with different laws. Colonel, what punishments do you have in your community for a crime like this?"

"The punishment for most crimes is death. Sometimes we cut off a hand or tongue for lesser crimes. Really minor infractions, like those committed by children, are punished with public beatings." I'd read of such law codes, of course, from the past; even the ones in the Bible weren't that different. But how he could so matter-of-factly describe such barbaric punishments in our day, without any visible embarrassment, shocked me.

My dad was standing next to me. "Figures," he muttered. "Bunch of savages."

Milton did a better job of hiding his incredulity, but he still couldn't respond for a few seconds. "And your community... has survived? With such laws?"

The colonel shrugged. "We had to have harsh laws to survive."

Milton cleared his throat. "Well, I'm sure you did what you thought best. But if such are your laws, then I don't think we can do anything here today that would satisfy you or your people. We have no such punishments. We never have. The most we have ever considered is banishment, and under the circumstances, with no one having been killed, I don't think we would even impose that. It makes no sense to us. But neither does war with other living people.

"Perhaps someone explained to you, Colonel, we do not wage war even against the dead. So the options we are discussing here—extreme punishment or outright war—both of these seem to us senseless, barbaric, and cruel. All we can do now is forgive and protect Will, and leave the reaction and retaliation up to you and your people. But I'm sure Jack has made it clear to you that we are quite capable of defending ourselves."

"I think I made that crystal clear, Milton," my dad growled. It was ugly, this side of him—ugly and inevitable.

Will had returned to being anxious, moving restlessly from one foot to the other. He finally spoke up. "You can't do that, Milton. You can't protect me and have people fight and die over it. That's really senseless. I guess it's not barbaric, it's kind of the opposite of barbaric, but it's definitely senseless. Individuals have to sacrifice for the community all the time. We're taught that."

"But the community can't force people to sacrifice themselves," Milton answered. "That's what creatures like ants do. And the community can't be forced to commit violence, just to avoid the threat of more violence. That's blackmail." He turned back to the colonel at this comment. The colonel only shrugged again.

"I understand," Will said. "But I can leave the community. There is no rule that a person has to stay in our community. We're all free to leave at any time."

Milton nodded and sighed again. "That is a brave suggestion, Will. As you say, we have no means to stop you. But if your sacrifice wouldn't even accomplish what it was meant to, what would be the point? So I would have to ask the colonel—if Will leaves our community and goes off into the wilderness, would this satisfy you and your people that we meant you no harm or offense, and we had adequately punished the person who had harmed you?"

The colonel frowned. "I think it would seem absurdly lenient to any of my people, but perhaps, since you people are so different and have grown accustomed to such strange, impractical ways of life, perhaps we could overlook this lack of wisdom, this harmful mildness that you embrace. I would take this report back to my people, that the culprit has been caught and he will be exiled. I would play down the fact that he chooses this willingly, if I were you. But with that punishment, I think we would probably refrain from further bloodshed and try to live with you more peacefully."

"What about them?" Will asked, pointing at the two zombies, who still patiently and shamefacedly awaited the decision of us, the living, though I wondered if they thought we really had any jurisdiction or right to rule over them. I wondered it myself, when I saw how calm and harmless they looked against the blustering and threats of the colonel—and even, I thought, of my dad. "What are you going to do to them?"

"I was going to put them back with the others," Milton answered.

The colonel waved dismissively. "You yourself said that your people treat them like animals in a zoo. When a dog bites someone in our community, we don't beat the dog. That just makes the dog more violent. We demand that the owner keep the dog restrained, and we whip the owner for his carelessness. So as bizarre as your treatment of the zombies is, I have nothing against you keeping dead people locked up. As you said, if they get out, they're more likely to come and attack your city."

Will stepped over by the two dead people. "I'm glad they're not talking about punishing you two," he said to them. I was just close enough to hear him. "That would be really unfair. You'll be safe back at your place. But I think you'll have to stay there now. I don't think anyone will take you out again. But you have lots of books, and I'll tell Milton where the college is, to get you more. I don't think they'd object to that."

"Of course not," Milton agreed.

If Will's voice had sounded sad, the look on the two dead people's face was heartbreaking. If Will's mom and dad had been there, they couldn't have looked any more distraught at the prospect of leaving him. Truman looked at Blue Eye, and she shook her head.

"I'm sorry, Blue Eye," Will said. "I don't think there's a choice."

Blue Eye poked her finger at her own chest, then at Truman's chest, and then she pointed at Will's.

"You want to come with me?" Will asked.

They both nodded.

"No, you'd be safer back at your place. Besides, I don't know if they'd let you."

Milton shrugged. It didn't have the same distasteful air as when the colonel did it. "Will, you'll be beyond our borders,"

Milton said. "They would be no threat to us. We would be as safe as if they were locked in some enclosure just beyond our fence."

The colonel again waved dismissively. Everything related to the zombies, and not directly related to punishing Will, seemed of no interest to him. "Kid, shooting at people is one thing. It has to be punished, sure. But I mean, shit, it happens all the time. But wanting to be alone with a couple *monsters* instead of with people—that's just bat-shit insane. But really—there are billions of those *things* out there. What the hell difference would two more make? When they eat you and come wandering back towards our city, we'll just shoot them in the head like we've always done. Until then, knock yourself out."

I could see Will hesitate, but oddly, I didn't think it was because he was concerned for himself or our community—this was the concern both Milton and the colonel had addressed—but because he was concerned for the safety of the two dead people. "Are you two sure?" he asked them.

They both nodded. And for them, there was no hesitation that I could see.

"All right, then."

There was movement in the crowd. I was surprised to see Rachel move to the front. She paused there—embarrassed, blushing—then stepped over towards Will. They stood close, talking, but their voices were too quiet for me to make out what they were saying.

Chapter 24

The fate that the people decided on, after much more discussion and recriminations, was that Will was to be banished. Though I was so sad to hear that he would have to leave his family and his community, I was relieved that we would be going with him, and that Lucy had even been the first to suggest it.

After Will had agreed to this, I was surprised to see a red-haired young woman walk up to him. She didn't look as unusually intelligent as Zoey, the younger girl we had seen, but she seemed somehow reliable and confident, like someone you could trust. Although she had an exceptionally pretty face, her body was not delicate, but muscular and thick, like she was used to labor and being outdoors. She glanced at Lucy and me, then spoke to Will in a low voice that I thought only Lucy and I were close enough to hear.

"Will," she began, "I'm sorry you're leaving. I wanted to see you more."

I thought Will looked surprised and a little sheepish around her. He reminded me of how I felt around Lucy. I felt glad and sorry for him at the same time, that he could lose his composure and strength and confidence, but do so with a person so beautiful and so obviously caring and trustworthy.

"I didn't think you did, Rachel," he said quietly.

She smiled, a display of joy and regret, desire and coyness, both revealing and concealing the way a woman's beauty always is. Perhaps all beauty does this, but in a woman it is the most noticeable and mesmerizing. I could see immediately that, like Lucy's enchanting eye, this woman's smile would be completely disarming to a man she cared for, to a man she gave that special look to. Will visibly slackened at the sight of it.

She stopped smiling and looked serious for a moment. "I only said I wasn't sure you were the father. Only you thought that meant I didn't want to see you."

"And now you can't. Now it's too late." He sounded more petulant than angry—weak, hurt, unsure, insecure.

She slipped her hand under his and brought it up slightly. Now was when she would show more of her true feelings, I thought, when she would show whether she, too, could be vulnerable. "Will," she dropped her voice a little more, till I could barely hear her, "don't make me beg or apologize for who I am. I've been wild, I know. But God Almighty, there's so much misery in this world, would you really begrudge me some fun, some little pleasure, to make me forget all the pain and ugliness once in a while?"

He didn't take his hand away. "No. I don't. I just thought it meant you didn't want to be with me."

"Will, we weren't married. You never talked like you wanted something more." The muscles in her arm flexed as she tightened her grip on his hand. "But all right, I'll tell you what I regret. I'll tell you what I'm sorry for. It's not for having sex with lots of people. You knew I did that, and you have no right to judge me for it." She bent her head down and forward, to catch his glance, since he was looking down. "The only thing I regret is not realizing that of the men I slept with, you were the only one who gave a shit about me. That was wrong and stupid and immature of me not to see, and that's how I hurt you, and why you misunderstood me. For that I'm sorry, Will. I'm very sorry."

He nodded and kept trying not to catch her gaze, I think because he knew as soon as he did look in her eyes—which sparkled more with tears in them now, thereby increasing their terrible loveliness and strength—all the initiative and power went to her, a prospect I felt sure he longed for as much as he dreaded. "It's all right. You don't have to apologize. Like you said, I didn't tell you what I felt or what I wanted. Milton just said, I don't talk to people enough, and they don't know what I'm up to. It was the same with you, so it wasn't your fault."

"It doesn't matter whose fault it was, Will. All I care about now is that you know I want to be with you."

He lifted his head. "All right. But now you can't. I don't see why you're telling me this."

He was looking in her eyes, and now she smiled again. She was in control. And I think I was as glad of that as Will was, though he didn't know it. "Will, I spend most my life out here, past the fence. Going back to the city is like a little vacation from my real job, from who I really am and what I'm supposed to do. So what's so impossible or unbelievable about me leaving too?" She tilted her head down a little and dropped the fateful and captivating smile. It was a final show of vulnerability and weakness, and an absolutely necessary one if it were to work out how they both wanted it to. "Unless you don't want me to?"

"Of course I do," Will exclaimed a little louder. He looked around at the crowds surrounding them, now very self-conscious. "Let's kind of discuss this later, okay?"

She smiled and blushed and let go of his hand. "Sure, Will."

I did not know what to make of such beautiful, overwhelming devotion, especially following the harsh and legalistic discussion over the fate of Will and ourselves. I could not conceive of how these people lived, constantly going back and forth between such extremes. As impressed as I was with the heights of their virtue and bravery, I really would be relieved to get away from them.

Although I was very glad to be going with Lucy, Will, and his friend, I had at first felt some disappointment that all my books, along with Lucy's violin, were back at the storage facility. I was also afraid that if we were marching into the wilderness, we wouldn't be able to carry such things. So my joy was greatly increased when they granted us a few days to prepare for our journey, and that when we left, it would be on a boat, floating down the big river and away from here forever.

I had the time to pick out the books that most interested me, and most importantly I had the time to finish this journal. I will give it to the very kind and intelligent-looking girl, Zoey, tomorrow when we leave. I think she would be interested in it. And since the story so much involves her and her community, it would be best if they had it. I am sure there will be plenty of other things for me to record, stories of other people and places, assuming the four of us are lucky enough to survive beyond this place. I fear there will be things as horrible as some of the events I've witnessed in the last few days. But I also hope that there will be things as wondrous and good as these strange, fascinating, but unfortunately very violent people whom we will now leave behind.

Epilogue

Will and Rachel drove up to the dock with their two fellow exiles, Truman and Blue Eye. They unloaded their few possessions into it—including, I was surprised to see, what I thought were the cases for a violin and a typewriter. It was only later that I found out what these things were doing there. When they were through, there was a long and very desperate farewell between Will and his parents. Ms. Wright tried hard to control herself, but you could tell her anguish was unbearable, and in the time I've known her since, she often seemed not the same person, but withdrawn and less full inside.

While they were saying goodbye, Rachel and the two zombies were sort of left alone. It was a good moment for me to speak to them. I walked over and hugged Rachel with all my strength. I pressed my face into her beautiful red locks and we both wept softly. "You take care, kid," she said. "You be strong and keep an eye on these people. You're good at that."

I stepped back, nodding and dabbing my eyes. There was nothing I could say to her to take in the enormity of her decisions.

I felt little fear for her. Everything she did, she seemed to do out of love and hope, so what fear or regret could either of us have?

I turned and handed Truman the little pack that Will had given me when he went off in pursuit of the men he thought had attacked us. "Will gave me this to hold on to," I said. "I don't know whose they are, but perhaps you'd like to take them with you."

Truman took it and opened it, and he looked very happy to have it back, though he held back a smile. As with the typewriter and violin, I only found out later what the pack contained.

Truman set down the pack, and Blue Eye helped him get out a sheaf of papers from a bag he was carrying. They handed them to me.

"You wrote this?" I asked. He nodded. "You don't want it?"

He shook his head. He slowly put his finger on my chest and pressed.

"You want me to have it?"

He nodded.

All I could do that day was thank him for it. Later I would find out what he had written and all they had been through.

They then got on board the boat. It was a good sized sailboat, which the people of the River Nation, despite all their bellicose bluster, had helped us equip. Mr. Caine and my dad helped with the lines, and the boat pulled away, slowly at first, till the current nearer the middle of the river picked them up and they started moving faster. They left us behind, drifting serenely down the huge waters of the river—Rachel and Will, together with Truman and Blue Eye, who I later learned was called Lucy, though I suppose she herself would never know that name.

After that day, I spent the rest of the summer with the people who train our city's guard dogs. Sometimes I even had to wear the big, padded suit while the dogs learned to bite, hold, and take down an assailant. With my intense fear of canines, it was a punishment both more and less traumatic than I could've imagined. When I first heard of it, I could barely breathe, I was so terrified. And for the first several weeks that I worked with the animals, I'd come home and sob uncontrollably till I fell asleep. I almost succeeded in driving a wedge between Mom and Dad, and nearly got her to relent. But she had been so aghast that my silence had endangered me that she resisted my crying till it abated. Those weeks left me with a vivid memory of pain and fear to remind me never to ignore or keep secrets from others. But once I was past the first few weeks, working with the dogs was just another part of my life in our community, a necessary job, one that most of the time was more enjoyable than some others. I never got to like dogs, but I respected and valued them after that.

Since that summer, I have often imagined all the adventures they must be having. I only imagine good ones—the lost cities they rediscover, the other people they meet, even other smart zombies who befriend them. It's wishful thinking, of course, and they may well all be long dead by now. But it is a hope, and as Milton said, of all other virtues or feelings, hope—together with love—is the one we rely on the most in our world. I think those four people had a purpose—first, to leave us a record of what they went through and learned that summer, and then to leave us with such a hope that their learning and growth were not for nothing, that it enabled them to accomplish more.

In my imaginings, they never stop or settle down, but just keep going. They find a bigger boat and cross the ocean and they take the paintings off the walls of the Louvre before they rot away completely; they hang them on the bridge of their ship so they can enjoy looking at them, and also so they can show them to others. Everywhere they go, people think what a strange and wondrous group they are—two living, two dead—and they send them on their way with more stories and good wishes—like an Odysseus, Dante, Ishmael, or Gulliver. They are always wandering, because, of course, they never quite fit anywhere they go, as they couldn't quite fit here among us. In that way, they're more like another wanderer, Cain, but I always feel that their road is quite different from his.

If they were marked by us for exile, I like to think they were also given a protective mark by something higher, more permanent, and wiser than we are. It was just that our rules, our categories, couldn't understand or accommodate people who were uncomfortable in society, or people who felt more comfortable with those of the other group than they did with those of their own. Will had been right—we do tend to treat the dead as either precious idols, or deadly demons. That they were still just people is too hard for us to comprehend; dealing with the few living people is complicated and confusing enough.

In my head, they don't just wander, of course. They each find their own happiness in their little ark. Lucy plays her violin to crowds all over the world, and people remember what beauty is and they want more of it. Truman keeps reading and learning, till eventually he writes new books and they drop these off at new ports for people to learn from. And Will and Rachel have a brood of children who grow up knowing this strange new world and only the good possibilities of it. For them, death and life coexist without fear or ignorance, and only killing is a terrible mystery they fear and shun. And for them, freedom is more a reality and necessity than we can ever know in our community.

Our life here in the city after they left has been much less adventuresome or dramatic than any of my fantasies. The people of the River Nation lived quite differently than we did. They had retained some government, strangely loose and harsh, and at times more restrictive and burdensome than we could tolerate or understand. And although everything was still traded by barter among them, because their villages had been spread out along the river, they also had a more complex, varied economy than ours.

When I later read Truman's journal, I smiled at Will's cornsilk cigarettes; tobacco became widely available once we began to trade with the River Nation, since their colonies extended down to southern areas where they could get the deadly but comforting little weed. Little by little, our lives have become intertwined and melded with those of this other "nation"—one nation combined with one non-nation, forming something for which we still have no name or word.

As we adapted to their economy, so they took up our ways of dealing with the dead. They realized that much of their growth and safety had been due to Milton clearing the dead out of nearby areas, and they were grateful to us, and also eager to give up their own practices of cruelly executing the deceased. Eventually, Milton got too old to constantly be out in the wilderness, rounding up the dead, but by then there were enough people that it could be done without him. The dead were also getting slower, tired, more fragile, and increasingly posed less and less of a threat.

Of course, my own individual life bears little resemblance to my fantasy of the four people who left us that day, except in the one detail of begetting children. I grew up and married, one of the first brides of our time to wear a real dress, one we had salvaged from the dead city; even though it was meant for the prom, it was beautiful, its sequins catching the sunlight just right. I sit here writing this now, my belly huge with my first child. I suppose that's part of what made me want to put everything down on paper—so the story of Truman, Lucy, Will, and Rachel wouldn't be lost for my children, but they would always know of the sacrifice, difficulties, wisdom, and mistakes of those four from years ago. It is my tribute to them, because I know I'm here only because of them, and as I learned that summer, gratitude and reverence are as important as hope, and as potent as love.

Acknowledgments

Critiques of this story were offered on a chapter-by-chapter basis by Robert Kennedy and Marylu Hill. Both brought their particular gifts of insight to the narrative and improved it. Specific points related to the handling and use of firearms were provided by the ever-efficient Scott Field, the indefatigable Christopher Iwane, and Douglas Wojtowicz.

I again thank my editors at Permuted Press, Jacob Kier and Dave Snell. They are a rare and true pleasure to work with—for their efficiency, love of the genre, and encouraging and positive personalities.

Of my new friends in the horror community, I would like to extend special acknowledgement and thanks to Aaron Bennett, Joe Branson, William Carl, Ron Dickie, Bob Freeman, Fran Friel, Lynne Hansen, Kelli Jones, Tracy Jones, Brian Keene, Karen Koehler, Steve Lukac, Jonathan Maberry, Nick Mamatas, Joe McKinney, David G. Montoya, Christine Morgan, Paul Puglisi, Mary San Giovanni, Nikki Threat, Victor Voyles, Doug Warrick, Dave Wellington, Zoe Whitten, and Drew Williams. All went out of their way to welcome me into their community and help me with my writing. Many helped with quick answers to technical questions by posting on the greatest horror-related message board, The Other Dark Place. I may well have given up on my dream of being a novelist were it not for the help of such kind and talented people during the last year.

And as I have promised often in the last few months—I've tried to incorporate the comments of reviewers, most of which I thought offered very constructive and perceptive criticism. I hope you enjoy the story of Zoey and Truman, and that it casts some light on your own life.

Finally, I have dedicated this book to five of my teachers from middle and high school—Marion Finch, Louise Holladay, Ruth Meeker, Lois Sharp, and Marylou Williams. My twenty year high school reunion put me in mind of them, and how much I owe to their patience, sternness, intellect, and dedication. Though only Mrs. Holladay and Mrs. Sharp taught English, all five worked long and hard to discipline my immature mind, and whatever successes I have achieved at analyzing literature or producing my own are due in large part to them.

Kim Paffenroth
Cornwall on Hudson, NY
April 2008

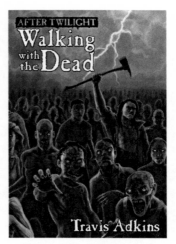

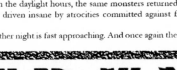
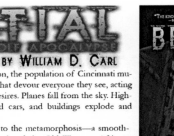

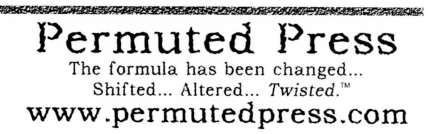

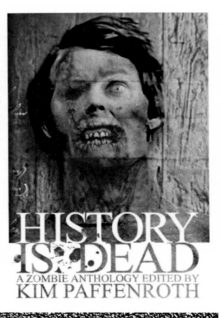

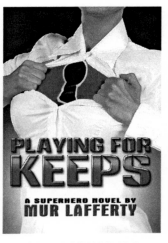

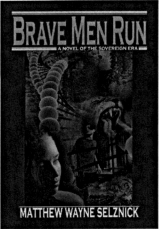